Passion too good to forget... Temptation too strong to resist...

As heiress to a media empire Alessandra Sinclair was raised to put family obligations first. But everything changes the night her first love walks back into her life and turns her whole world upside down. Haunted by the memories of a secret romance with a boy from the wrong side of the tracks, she can't seem to get Hudson Chase out of her mind. Once again torn between two worlds, Allie must decide how much she's willing to risk to have the love she's always longed for.

Ten years is a long time to wait, but billionaire Hudson Chase didn't become CEO of one of the country's fastest growing companies by giving up on what he wants. Now that he's got Allie in his sights again, he's determined to make her regret breaking his heart. And this time, he's going to make damn sure he's not so easy to forget.

"Walker and Rogers strike the perfect balance between blistering physical desire and heartfelt connections . . ."

   ~ *RT Book Reviews* Magazine on *Remind Me* ★★★★ 1/2

"Seriously sexy and sinfully steamy."

   ~ Tara Sue Me, *New York Times* Bestselling Author

D1523771

PRAISE FOR REMIND ME

"One of the best series that I have read in a long time."

~ *Underneath The Covers*

"This is one steamy page turner you don't want to miss . . . the chemistry between Allie and Hudson is off the charts."

~ *BFF Book Blog*

"The hotness came straight in from the Sahara . . . you may want to read this in a room with AC."

~ *Wicked Reads*

"This one needs to be on your reading radar."

~ *Bookish Temptations*

"Grab your fans ladies because Hudson Chase is HOT and you will need something to cool yourself down. Words cannot express how much I loved this book. I was hooked in the first chapter."

~ *Martini Times Book Blog*

"I have a new book boyfriend. His name is Hudson Chase."

~ *Reading Between The Wines*

"If you like them wealthy, possessive & with a side of dirty talk then . . . meet #HudsonChase."

- Dirty Girl Romance

"Secrets and romance combine to make *Remind Me* a sultry, sexy and passion-filled read. "

- The Sassy Bookster

"An excellent read, I was hooked by 10%!"

- About That Story

ALSO BY THE AUTHORS

By Ann Marie Walker & Amy K. Rogers

Chasing Fire Series
REMIND ME
RELEASE ME
RECLAIM ME
EMBRACE ME

By Ann Marie Walker

Wild Wedding Series
BLACK TIE OPTIONAL
ICING ON THE CAKE

REMIND ME

ANN MARIE WALKER
AMY K. ROGERS

After —
So great meeting
you at #WWS
A McWalk

Remind Me

Copyright © 2015 Ann Marie Walker & Amy K. Rogers

Excerpt from *Release Me* copyright © 2015 Ann Marie Walker & Amy K. Rogers

All rights reserved. No part of this publications may be reproduced, stored in a retrieval system, or transmitted, in any form or by any means, electronic, mechanical, photocopying, recording, or otherwise, without the prior written permission of the publishers, Ann Marie Walker & Amy K. Rogers.

All characters appearing in this work are fictitious. Any resemblance to real persons, living, or dead, is purely coincidental.

Trade Paperback ISBN: 978-1-797-66622-8

InterMix/Penguin eBook ISBN: 978-0-698-19476-2 (out of print)

Cover design by Simone Renou/In My Dreams Design

First Edition

For David Gandy, a face to launch a thousand . . . books.

Thank you for inspiring this one.

There were few things in life Hudson Chase couldn't control. He'd conquered Wall Street, dominated the business world, and had a net worth that made him a regular on the pages of *Forbes*. But rushing a woman when she was getting ready for a black tie affair was a power even he didn't possess.

"Cut the overhead by twenty percent." With the cell phone tucked under his chin, Hudson's free hand pushed up his sleeve. He stole a glance at the platinum watch peeking out from under his French cuff before turning his attention back to the hired suit billing by the hour on the other end of line. The bastard had the balls to feed him an endless stream of excuses.

"The 'how' isn't my problem." Hudson's tone was razor sharp. "That's why I pay your law firm a ridiculous amount of money." He crooked a finger, tugging at his black bow tie. How long does it take to put on lipstick and a pair of shoes, anyway?

Just when he'd reached his limit, the limo door swung open to reveal a red dress and a set of legs splitting open a convenient slit to heaven. Goddamn if he didn't plan to have his head in the clouds.

Sophia slid onto the bench seat beside him and adjusted her

gown, optimizing his view as she languidly crossed her legs. The dress clung to her, accentuating voluptuous curves maintained by the top trainers in Chicago. Hudson's gaze swept over every inch then settled on the Harry Winston nestled between her breasts.

The limo pulled away from the curb and he immediately hit the button to raise the privacy screen.

"Liquidate the assets we discussed," he said, cutting off the suit from enjoying the sound of his own voice. His hand came to rest on Sophia's knee. "This isn't personal, it's business. Start letting people go on Monday."

As the limo picked up speed down Michigan Avenue, so did Hudson's hand. He smoothed his palm up Sophia's leg while listening to his lawyer fast talk his way back into good graces. Just picturing the sweat forming on the guy's brow caused Hudson's mouth to curve into a satisfied smirk.

"No, tomorrow. I'm attending an event tonight." And hell if it was by choice. Hudson would have preferred to simply cut a check to the charity and spare himself the glad-handing. He'd been flying under the radar since his arrival in Chicago, but with his name going up on a building, his PR department decided it was time for him to make the rounds. Their persistence was the only reason he was sitting in a godforsaken limo being strangled by a motherfucking bow tie.

Hudson glanced at Sophia as she purposefully uncrossed her legs. His eyes flared slightly at the panties she wasn't wearing. "Keep me posted," he said, abruptly ending the call.

The limo rolled to a stop just as his hand slid between Sophia's thighs.

Well, fuck.

The Field Museum of Natural History soared above them with stately columns lit from below and banners announcing the latest exhibits flapping in the late September breeze. Hudson climbed out as soon as the valet opened the door, eager to get this shit over with. Make a donation, shake a couple hands, then he was out of there. He buttoned his tuxedo jacket and offered Sophia his hand. She placed her palm into his, strategically exiting the limo without flashing the waiting photographers. He pulled her into to his side and his lips brushed her temple. "We're not staying long."

She ran a finger along his jaw. "I hope not."

Hudson cocked a grin that was more forced than genuine. He knew Sophia wanted to be more than just a leisurely fuck. She wanted to be Mrs. Hudson Chase and there wasn't a chance in hell that was happening. He wasn't interested in walking down the proverbial aisle. With anyone. Ever.

Sophia was nothing more than a current distraction.

They stepped onto the red carpet and cameras lit up like the damn Fourth of July. Sophia leaned into him, offering a seductive smile to each photographer who called their names.

She was in her element. Hudson was on autopilot.

This sort of thing grated on his last nerve. But he'd made the effort to be there, might as well document it. He let them snap some pictures, gave a few brief nods, and then was ready to move on.

With his hand on the small of her back, he guided Sophia up concrete steps littered with guests entering the building checkbook first. Once inside, he scanned the room for the nearest bar. He had expected endless rows of tables for ten where he'd be trapped for hours talking to whoever had been seated next to him for a dinner of rubber chicken under an indistinguishable sauce. But the room before him was far from anything he expected. Swathes of sheer fabric cascaded down walls, vaulted archways glowed with ambient lighting, and plush rugs formed seating areas where coffee tables replaced dinner tables and overstuffed couches replaced straight back chairs. The entire place had a high-end club vibe.

"Mr. Chase."

Hearing his name, Hudson turned. An older gentleman was

beating a path his way. His hand was already extended and judging by the look on his face, he was gearing up for a request.

Sophia touched Hudson's forearm, but her attention was on the room. "I'm heading to the bar," she said, her eyes already scanning the crowd. "Can I get you a scotch?"

For a moment he thought about following her simply to escape a conversation he already knew he didn't want to have. "Blue Label. Make it a double."

"Elliot Shaw," the man said, somewhat out of breath, "executive editor, *Chicago Magazine*. So glad to run into you. I've left several messages with your assistant."

Hudson shook his hand. "What can I do for you, Mr. Shaw?"

"I'd like to feature you in our annual 'Power 100' issue."

"That's handled by my PR department. I suggest you talk to them."

"I have," Shaw politely persisted, "but we want more than a standard press package. We'd like an exclusive interview."

Hudson was about to cut him off when Shaw played his trump.

"In return we're willing to offer you the cover of the issue and rank you number one on the list. Not every day someone moves to town with the clout to knock Oprah off her throne." Shaw chuckled at his own joke then launched into a well-rehearsed spiel. "In the local market our circulation is larger than *People . . .*"

Hudson tuned the man out. He was scanning the crowd for his date, and more importantly his scotch.

And then he saw her.

His heart beat like he'd just finished the Chicago Marathon.

The hem of her black dress sat conservatively above the knee and the neckline was far from revealing, yet she was still the sexiest damn woman in the room. Sophisticated and elegant.

She turned towards a petite redhead, revealing the low cut out in the back of her dress and a whole lot of perfect skin.

Holy shit.

Hudson drew a sharp breath. He couldn't help but wonder what she was wearing underneath. Or how her blonde hair, once released from the pins holding it in place, would tumble in loose curls around her face. Soft waves that would brush like satin across his bare chest . . . his abs . . . his . . .

". . . Of course the social media element can't be minimized." Shaw's voice yanked Hudson right out of his fantasy.

"Do you know that woman?" He inclined his head in the blonde's general direction. "Speaking with the redhead?"

Shaw followed his gaze. "Yes, that's Alessandra Sinclair, the event chair. Her family—"

"Thank you, Mr. Shaw. Excuse me." Hudson strode confidently through the room, reaching Sophia just as she turned away from the bar with two drinks in hand. He caught her by the elbow without ever breaking stride.

"Careful," she warned, "this dress cost a fortune."

Hudson snatched his scotch out of her hand and drained it, skidding the empty glass across a table as he passed. He steered them quickly towards the blonde, his awareness of her heightening with every step. When he was standing behind her, he took a deep breath, steeling himself for her reaction.

"Excuse me. Who should I see about making a rather sizable donation?"

Sizable donation? The words were music to Alessandra's ears. A confident grin spread across her face. Convincing fat cats to part with their cash was her specialty. This guy wouldn't know what hit him.

She turned around, prepared to give Mr. Potential Donor the full benefit of her charm, and froze.

It couldn't be.

Her practiced smile slipped as she gaped at him in disbelief. He was older, obviously, and dressed in an Armani tux instead of faded Levi's. His dark, wavy hair was shorter than it had been and his once wiry frame was replaced with the muscular build of a man well acquainted with the gym. He was taller, his shoulders broader, and even his stance had changed. The boy she'd once known was now a man who exuded an overwhelming sense of masculine power.

So much about him was different and yet his eyes, those gorgeous blue eyes, were exactly the same as she remembered.

"That would be us," a voice to her right offered. She could barely make out the words over the sound of blood rushing through her ears. "I'm Harper Hayes and this is the event's chair, Alessandra Sinclair."

"Alessandra," the man said, a smirk tugging at the corner of his mouth as he offered his hand. "Hudson Chase."

For a moment her gaze lingered on his full, sensual lips. His strong, rugged jaw. The designer stubble he wore now made him look even darker and more mysterious than he had when she'd first met him. She wondered how it would feel beneath her fingertips, against her cheek, between her thighs . . .

Harper's elbow nudged her arm, pulling her from her errant thoughts.

Holy hell, where did that come from?

Alessandra looked up to find Hudson watching her, one brow quirked, and a warm flush crossed her face. She placed her hand in his, hoping he didn't notice the way her fingers trembled.

"So what's this you were saying about a donation?" Harper asked.

Hudson held Alessandra's hand, his eyes locked on hers, as he answered. "Perhaps this is a matter I can discuss with Miss Sinclair over a dance?"

For a moment the atmosphere between them seemed to shift, becoming charged with anticipation as his question hung unanswered in the air. Then the woman on Hudson's arm interrupted with an exaggerated sigh. She feigned disinterest, inspecting her perfect manicure as she shifted her weight from one stiletto to the other. Alessandra studied her. Curvy in all the right places with legs that went on forever. Lush red lips matched her barely there dress and dark, cascading curls framed a face worthy of a magazine cover. Granted, the magazine would likely be *Maxim*. But still, she was stunning.

Alessandra quickly withdrew her hand but Hudson's gaze was steady. "I'm considering writing a large check this evening," he said. "The least you can do is dance with me."

"She'd love to," Harper volunteered.

Alessandra whipped her head around, her narrowed glare meeting Harper's broad grin.

"Work it," Harper mouthed as she nudged her forward.

Hudson waited, his blue eyes fixed on her. She knew she should politely decline. She could turn him down and no one would be the wiser. After all, she was the event chair. Any number of responsibilities or pressing issues could be deemed a plausible excuse. But at that moment, she couldn't think of a single one.

"After you." He waved her toward the parquet dance floor as his date beat a hasty retreat to the bar. The orchestra began to play Frank Sinatra's "Summer Wind." Hudson slid his hand around her waist, pulling her against him with a gentle pressure. "You look lovely as ever," he said, his breath hot against her ear as he spun her slowly into the crowd.

Alessandra felt a shiver run down her spine. She pulled back to meet his piercing stare and a spark passed between them, so potent it was nearly tangible. She swallowed hard to find her voice, and when she did, blurted out the one question that had been on her mind since she'd discovered him standing behind her. "What are you doing in Chicago?"

His brow creased. "Exercising my right as an American citizen to move about this country."

She blinked up at him, his cold reply taking her by surprise.

"My business is here." Hudson stopped dancing and nodded to a photographer poised to snap their photo. "Smile pretty for the camera, Alessandra."

Flashes fired in rapid succession. "Thank you, Mr. Chase," the photographer said before scurrying off the dance floor.

She used the brief interruption to regain her composure. "What type of business are you in?"

"I acquire things." His tone lacked any trace of humor.

So much for making small talk. She stared over his shoulder, watching the other couples sway and turn as they moved around the dance floor. Ms. *Maxim* Cover Girl was standing under the giant T. rex, scowling from behind her flute of champagne. *Jeez, if looks could kill.*

"You're not doing a very good job convincing me to part with my cash, Ms. Sinclair."

She reared back to look at him. "You were serious about that?"

He leveled his stare at her and the intensity was almost too much to bear. "I take a million dollars incredibly serious."

"A million dollars?" Her words came out in a high-pitched squeak. She cleared her throat and lowered her voice. "You want to donate a million dollars?"

"Yes," he answered matter-of-factly.

Confused, Alessandra stared at him blankly. He'd just pledged a million dollars with no more fanfare than if he'd told her he'd bought a bottle of wine from the silent auction. A million dollars was more than a "sizable" donation. It was *four times* the highest amount she'd ever received from a single donor. Surely he was joking. How could he not be?

As if reading her mind, Hudson offered a vague explanation.

"A lot can change in ten years, Alessandra. Though I see you're still using your formal name."

"You're the only one who ever called me Allie," she whispered. Her eyes met his, searching for any sign of the boy she once knew. His gaze softened, and for a moment she felt it, the connection that made her knees go weak even now.

Their dance slowed to nothing more than a gentle sway as so much passed unspoken between them. Allie hadn't even realized she'd stopped breathing until a hand touched her shoulder and she jumped.

2

---

*H*udson bit down hard, his jaw flexing. He was convinced he'd rearrange this guy's face purely for interrupting.

A thick French accent sliced between them. "May I cut in?"

Shock widened Alessandra's hazel eyes. When she regained her composure, what Hudson saw in them resembled guilt. As if she suddenly realized whose hand was gripping her waist. Her spine straightened and he felt the weight of her hand leave his shoulder.

"Of course," she said. "Julian, this is Mr. Hudson Chase. Mr. Chase, this is Julian Laurent."

The pretty boy extended his hand, but not before flipping his hair like he'd just stepped out of a shampoo commercial. "Marquis Julian Laurent," he said, emphasizing a title that was nothing more than a mouthful of elegant bullshit.

Hudson's glare narrowed on this grade-A prick. The guy was sizing him up as if he was wearing Men's Warehouse instead of custom-tailored Armani. There were two options, he decided: mock the smug son of a bitch or serve him up a bunch of "fuck off."

Option two was arguably not a terrible idea.

Instead he slid his hand off Alessandra's waist and extended his arm. "Mr. Laurent."

"Mr. Chase has generously pledged a million dollars to the foundation," Alessandra said.

Abruptly, Julian's eyes locked on Hudson's. His expression was one of pure arrogance. "People donate what they can."

Option two was beginning to look really good. It would take a minute tops, he thought, to flatten this bastard.

Julian's stare drifted from Hudson and he smiled. "Alessandra, some guests want to speak with you."

Hudson's mouth curved, unable to suppress his amusement at being dismissed. Saving his PR department a clusterfuck of spin doctoring, he dipped his head in a polite bow. "Thank you for the dance, Alessandra," he said, carefully enunciating her name.

He turned away and the shift was palpable. One encounter with her and the control he'd so carefully mastered was nearly shredded. Every muscle tensed to fight the urge to go after her, to press her against a wall in the dark recesses of the museum and fuck ten years of unresolved lust out of his system. Instead he searched the dense mass of partygoers for his date. Stalking toward her, he caught her wrist. "We're leaving."

Sophia set her half-empty champagne glass on a table as they hurried toward the door. "We just got here and I was . . ."

Hudson glared over his shoulder, effectively silencing her. He reached inside his jacket, yanked his phone out of his breast pocket, and ordered in a string of clipped, single syllable words, "Pull the car up."

He practically dragged her down the stone steps of the museum, the click-clack of those skyscraper heels, which would look fan-fucking-tastic over his shoulders, echoing behind them. By the time they reached the bottom of the steps, the sleek black car was waiting. Hudson urged Sophia through the open limo door and gave the driver a cursory glance.

"Drive until I say otherwise," he said, unknotting his tie and ducking inside.

———

Allie pushed through the museum doors, welcoming the gust of crisp air. The night had been a huge success. Final numbers wouldn't be tallied until Monday morning, but all indications were they'd met their goal. She took a deep breath and inhaled . . . smoke? She turned to find Julian cupping his hand around a lighter. "No smoking within fifteen feet of the building," she reminded him.

"Damn Americans," he said, talking around a cigarette defying gravity as it dangled from his lips. "Ridiculous laws."

"It's meant to protect people from inhaling secondhand smoke."

Julian threw his arms out wide. "There's no one here, Alessandra."

"I really wish you'd quit," she suggested softly.

A stream of smoke filled the space between them. "I'll quit when I'm dead."

"You didn't have to be so rude." She started down the stairs and Julian followed.

"Fine. I'll put it out." He sounded like a petulant teen.

"I'm not talking about your cigarette. I meant earlier, with that donor."

"What donor?"

"The one who pledged a million dollars." She couldn't bring herself to say his name out loud.

Julian stopped short. "I thought I was very courteous considering he had his hands all over my date."

"We were only dancing."

He gave a harsh laugh before continuing down the concrete steps toward the valet. Allie joined him a few moments later and they waited side by side for their limo. A breeze blew across Lake Michigan, sending a cloud of smoke in Allie's direction. She turned her head and moved closer to the water's edge. The bright lights of the Navy Pier Ferris wheel blinked patterns of red and gold. Her thoughts drifted as she watched it turn. Had it really been ten years? When she closed her eyes, the memories played through her mind as if it were only yesterday.

The wind kicked up again and she shivered.

"Are you cold?" Hudson asked her.

"I'm fine." She smiled. The summer wind wasn't the reason Allie shivered. It was Hudson, sitting so close, that made her tremble.

"Here, let me warm you up." He wrapped his arm around her, pulling Allie tight against him. "I think you can see the whole town from up here."

Allie hadn't noticed. Their car had been perched at the top of the carnival's Ferris wheel for several minutes now as they waited for passengers to load, but she'd barely noticed the view. She couldn't take her eyes off Hudson Chase. With his black T-shirt, faded jeans, and motorcycle boots, Hudson was what her mother would have called a thug. But Allie knew better. And there, high above the town, no other opinion mattered.

She wanted to stay at the top of that Ferris wheel forever.

"You know," he said, a devious smile on his face. "If we're going to be here a while . . ." Allie's heart raced as Hudson leaned closer, his lips hovering just inches from hers. "We might as well make good use of the time."

The ride lurched forward and Hudson cursed under his breath as they were swiftly lowered to the exit platform. Allie tried her best to stifle a giggle.

"Oh, you think that's funny, do you?" Hudson asked. He climbed out of the car and offered her his hand.

"Actually, yes," she said, grinning from ear to ear.

He gave her hand a sharp tug, pulling her body flush against his. Her breath caught in her throat as his blue eyes locked on hers.

"Hudson!" A voice called out.

Hudson dropped his chin. "This just isn't my night," he mumbled.

Allie covered her mouth to hide her smile as Hudson's little brother, Nick, ran up, completely out of breath. "There you are. I've been looking everywhere."

Hudson laced his fingers with hers. "What's up, little man?"

"Can I have a dollar?"

"Why do you need a dollar?" Hudson asked, running his free hand through his unruly brown hair.

Nick bounced on the balls of his feet. "I want to play darts."

"Darts?"

"Yeah. If you break three balloons, you win this awesome remote control race car. Pleeeeeease," he begged, his words coming out in a rush. "It's super cool. It's got flames up the side and these wicked chrome hubcaps. It can spin up on two wheels and make jumps this long." Nick stretched his arms out as far as he could.

Hudson laughed. "Okay, okay. I get the picture." He turned to Allie. "Do you mind?"

"Not at all." Allie couldn't say no to Nick any more than she could resist his charming older brother.

Hudson flashed her a grin before turning back to Nick. "Lead the way."

The first three darts clattered to the ground. Nick's big brown eyes turned glassy but he shook it off. "Probably a piece of crap anyway."

"Hey, watch your mouth, little man."

Nick's face fell. "Sorry."

Hudson reached into his back pocket for the wallet he kept secured with a silver chain. "Here, let me give it a try."

Allie watched as Hudson peeled bill after bill out of his

wallet. Best she could tell he'd gone through a full shift's worth of tips by the time he popped three green balloons in a row.

"What color do you want, Nicky?"

Nick walked over to the glass display case. He chewed on his thumbnail as his eyes roamed from one car to the next. After a few minutes he motioned for Hudson to bend down and whispered something in his ear. Allie couldn't hear all of what he said, but she definitely picked up on the word "girlfriend" said with the kind of exaggeration reserved especially for teasing older siblings. Allie had to bite her lip to keep from laughing at the look on Hudson's face, but a moment later his expression grew serious.

"But what about the 'super cool' race car?" he asked.

Nick looked at Allie as he whispered his reply.

"Are you sure?" Hudson asked.

Nick responded with a huge grin and a nod. The two boys huddled together in front of the glass case. Allie saw Hudson point to something, and when he turned around, he was holding a seashell anklet.

"Nick gave up his prize." Hudson's mouth curved into a shy smile. "Wanted me to pick something for you."

"Aww, thank you, Nick. That was very sweet of you." She leaned down and planted a kiss on Nick's cheek. "I love it."

"Here." Hudson held out a couple bucks. Nick grabbed the cash and took off, his cheeks blazing red.

"Will you do the honors?"

Hudson dropped to one knee. He wrapped the delicate string of shells around Allie's ankle and fastened the clasp. When he finished, his hand lingered. Her skin tingled as he slowly brushed his fingertips up her leg, tracing a pattern as he worked his way to the hem of her yellow-and-white sundress.

"So what about me, Allie?" he asked, looking up at her from beneath long dark lashes. "Do I get a kiss, too?"

"What are you waiting for, Alessandra?" a voice asked from behind her.

Allie startled, brought back to the present day by the sound of her name. She turned to find Julian standing by the open limo door. He waved his hand impatiently, his cigarette glowing as if he were landing an aircraft. "In the car, s'il vous plaît."

Allie ducked into the limo. Julian dropped his cigarette on the sidewalk before sliding in beside her. "Peninsula Hotel," he told the driver.

"If you don't mind, I think I'd just like to go to my place."

He glanced at her before amending his instructions. "Still one stop. North Astor. Fourteen hundred block."

"I'm really very tired, Julian. I'd rather just go to bed. Alone." She met the driver's eyes in the rearview mirror and held up two fingers. "Two stops, please."

Julian blew out a harsh breath. "You've spent the whole evening working the crowd, talking to everyone."

After a beat, he angled his body toward hers and ran his knuckles up and down her arm. His chin lowered so that he looked up at her from beneath the tousle of light brown hair that fell in a sexy mess across one eye. "What about a little time for me?" he whispered, his accent caressing her every bit as much as his touch. Normally that was all it took to reduce her to an agreeable puddle. But not this time.

The air in the limo felt thick and warm and her temples throbbed.

"It's been a long night and I have a terrible headache. I think the stress of this event has finally taken its toll."

Julian's expression hardened. He dropped his hand and straightened in his seat.

Allie sighed. She hadn't meant to hurt his feelings. But it was late and she'd hardly slept the past few days. After a good night's sleep she'd feel more like herself.

"I'm sorry." She reached across the seat and covered his

fingers with hers, giving them a gentle squeeze. When he looked at her, she offered a reassuring smile. "Rain check for tomorrow?"

He pulled his hand free and reached into his breast pocket for a pack of cigarettes. "Fine. Rain check." The lighter flamed to life and Julian took a long drag, cursing under his breath as he exhaled. "C'est des conneries."

Cracking the window, Allie stared out across the dark lake as the lights of the Ferris wheel glowed in the distance.

3

*A*llie could hardly believe what she was hearing. She listened intently, pressing the phone to her ear as she tried to commit every word to memory. A flash of red hair caught her eye as Harper charged through the door. She was in the midst of an exaggerated U-turn when Allie waved her into the office.

"You're very kind, but it really was a team effort," Allie said into the phone.

Harper's pleated miniskirt fanned out across her lap as she collapsed into one of the small upholstered chairs facing Allie's desk. The pattern of bright polka dots was accented perfectly by the multicolored bangles stacked high on her wrist. Although she could never pull it off herself, Allie loved Harper's quirky style, a cross between Phoebe on *Friends* and Jess from *New Girl,* with a dash of Joan from *Mad Men* thrown into the mix.

"I will. And thank you again for thinking of me."

Harper raised a single brow. "What was that all about?" she asked the moment Allie hung up the phone.

Allie rounded her desk and shut her office door. "That was Oliver Harris."

Harper looked confused.

"From the Harris Group."

The lightbulb turned on. "The PR firm?"

Allie nodded. "Apparently Mr. Harris was at the museum Saturday night. He was just calling this morning to tell me how much he enjoyed the event." She shuffled a few papers on her desk, trying to play it cool. "And to offer me a job."

Harper's eyes grew wide. "No way!"

Allie broke into a huge grin. "He asked me to join his nonprofit division and oversee all event planning."

"Shit, that's big time. They're the ones who did that huge fund-raiser in Lincoln Park last summer."

"At the zoo?"

"Yup. And I heard it was amazing. They even had Neon Trees."

"What are neon trees?"

"They're not a *what*, Alessandra, they're a *who*. A band, actually."

Having no clue, Allie shrugged.

The look Harper gave her only reinforced Allie's belief that her friend considered her a total nerd when it came to her choice in music. "Oh, c'mon, you have to know who they are." As if to prove her point, Harper sang a few lines. "Hey, baby won't you look my way; I can be your new addiction."

Allie laughed at Harper's pitchy vocals and bobbing head. "Okay, okay . . . yes, I've heard the song."

Harper stopped her impromptu concert. "So when do you start?"

Allie sank into her chair. "I don't."

"Come again?"

"I thanked Mr. Harris for thinking of me and told him how flattered I was, but that I couldn't possibly leave my position at Better Start." With the first charter school only up and running for a little over a month, and the groundbreaking for the second scheduled to take place in the spring, there was no way she could even consider it.

"Look, no one would miss you around here more than me, but I don't see how you can pass this up. Sounds like your dream come true."

Under normal circumstances that might have been the case, but Alessandra Sinclair's life was anything but normal. As the daughter of Victoria Ingram, she'd been born into a family whose name was mentioned in the same breath as Vanderbilt, Rockefeller, and Hearst. With that life of privilege came certain responsibilities, and at the top of that list was family. Nearly every part of Allie's life was connected to Ingram Media somehow. Always had been. Her grandfather's empire had touched most of the city in one way or another and from a very young age she'd been taught what was expected of his heirs. Being involved in the family business was simply a given.

After college Allie had spent the better part of two years getting to know Ingram's various subsidiaries. But it was the time she spent at her family's charitable foundation that made her feel the most fulfilled, and she'd been working at their newest venture ever since. And not in the way her mother did, squeezing ribbon cuttings and board meetings in between morning tennis and afternoon tea. No, for the past three years Allie had worked long hours at Better Start and she was proud of what they had accomplished.

"I'm happy where I am," she told Harper. And while that was true, recognition from someone as respected as Oliver Harris meant a lot, especially when a small part of her still wondered if she only held her position because of her name. The opportunity to prove herself on her own merits was certainly tempting, but for Allie the phrase "family first" was non-negotiable.

"If you say so." Harper's smile didn't reach her eyes.

"So what had you so fired up on a Monday morning?" Allie

asked, ready to move on to another subject. "You seemed like a woman on a mission when you came through the door just now."

"Oh my gosh, I almost forgot!" Harper pulled a newspaper out from under the stack of proposals she was carrying and laid it on Allie's desk. "Page six."

Allie turned the pages until she came across an image that made her heart skip a beat. It was a photograph taken at the Field Museum.

Of her. In Hudson's arms.

Event chair Alessandra Sinclair with Chicago's newest eligible bachelor, business tycoon Hudson Chase.

Her mouth went dry as her eyes roamed from his satisfied grin to the hand curved possessively around her waist. This was more than just another publicity shot from just another charity event. This was the first photo ever taken of the two of them. She'd been heartbroken when their summer romance had ended so abruptly, and not having so much as a single photograph made the loss that much harder to bear. But now there they were in black and white. She stared at the photo, drinking in every detail until the sound of her ringing phone broke its spell.

"Well, aren't you the popular one this morning," Harper said.

Allie frowned at her as she snapped the phone off its cradle. "Alessandra Sinclair."

"Miss Sinclair, attractive photo in the paper this morning. Very photogenic."

Her breath hitched at the sound of his voice. "Mr. Chase."

Harper's eyebrows shot up. She leaned forward, the bangles clinking down her arm as she propped her elbows on the edge of Allie's desk and rested her chin on her hands.

"I'm glad you called. I never did get the chance to thank you Saturday night."

"For the money or the dance?"

Allie could almost see his smug smile through the phone. She paused, then chose to ignore his question. "Your donation was very generous."

"Which brings me to the purpose of this phone call, along with my lack of trust in the noble United States Postal Service," Hudson said. "I'm sure you're eager to obtain my . . . generosity." His voice had changed with the last line. It was darker, almost seductive.

Harper leaned closer. "What is he saying?" she whispered. Honest to God, she was acting like they were teenagers at a sleepover. Allie half expected her to activate the speakerphone, or worse, run around the desk and press her ear to the receiver.

"It's very kind of you to follow up," Allie said. "I'd be glad to send a courier over to pick up the check."

"No, I insist on delivering the check into familiar hands."

Allie nearly choked on her words. "You want me to pick it up personally?" She knew her voice sounded several octaves too high, but there wasn't a damn thing she could do about it. She panicked, unsure of how to respond to his unusual request. On the one hand, she owed it to her employer to collect the donation. On the other hand, the last thing she wanted was to see Hudson again. Her eyes drifted down to the photo in the newspaper. Well, maybe not the *last* thing.

His deep voice interrupted her internal debate. "Yes or no, Miss Sinclair?"

Harper gaped at Allie, her mouth hanging open. "If you don't go, I will," she offered. *How generous.*

"Fine." She reached for a paper and pen. "Where?"

"My office. This evening."

Allie quickly scribbled down the address, trying to wrap her head around the fact that in a few hours she would once again be in the same room as Hudson Chase.

4

On the south bank of the Chicago River, perched high above the others, Hudson leaned over his desk and slashed his John Hancock on the bottom of a million-dollar check.

The offices of Chase Industries occupied the top six floors of what was previously known as the Leo Burnett building. Made up of granite, glass, and steel, the postmodern structure exuded power and strength and was every bit as masculine as the man who sought it out as his command center.

Hudson set the Montblanc on the mahogany and hit the direct line to his assistant. "I'm expecting Miss Alessandra Sinclair. Show her in as soon as she arrives."

Straightening, he turned to face the floor-to-ceiling windows that displayed one hell of a showstopping view. As the sun settled behind the skyline, turning the urban sprawl into a shimmering vista, he thought about how ten years ago he wouldn't have been able to write a ten-dollar check; the crap apartments that offered nothing but a ground-level view, and the pathetic future he'd been segregated into.

Now he carried a black Amex, drove a luxury sports car

packing a lot of horses under the hood, and lived in a three-story penthouse that had previously been the HQ of the magazine most teenage boys spent hours with locked up in the bathroom.

He infinitely preferred this life, the control it brought him. He'd done the blood and sweat thing to get here and his hard work had paid off. He had everything he'd ever wanted, except the woman who'd drop-kicked his heart and walked away without so much as a good-bye.

Hudson checked the LeCoultre strapped to his wrist; ten minutes had passed. He was so over this shit.

But some things were worth waiting for.

Just as he reached for the check with an impatient hand, there was a knock at the door, then a male voice. "Mr. Chase, Miss Alessandra Sinclair is here."

Hudson looked across the immaculate office at his assistant. The guy was a wrestling match between hipster-geek and an ad for J-fucking-Crew. Dollars to shit piles, those horn-rimmed glasses he wore weren't even prescription. And the bow tie, the motherfucking bow tie. But the guy was a good assistant and didn't pull any crap.

"Thank you, Darren. That will be all for the evening."

His assistant's brow shot up. "Ah, thank you, Mr. Chase. Have a good one." The surprise on Darren's face was obvious, a direct correlation to the numerous hours the guy had been pulling at Hudson's demand. And well compensated for, he might add.

Whoever said being a CEO was a fairy tale had their head up their ass. Sure, you may have the castle in the clouds, climbed the fucking beanstalk to get there, but at the stroke of midnight you were more likely to find yourself wanting a few hours of shut-eye versus waking Sleeping Beauty to go a round with a glass stiletto digging into your ass.

Darren exited the office, grinning like he'd just won the lottery. A second later, Alessandra stepped through the archway.

Damn. She was even more beautiful than he remembered.

"Good evening, Alessandra." He moved around his desk. "Take your coat?"

"I'm fine." He could tell by her tone this wasn't a pleasure call. She was doing her job, nothing more.

"Nice office," she said. "I saw a crew hanging the new sign downstairs. Did you buy the whole building?

"Not the entire building, no." A smug grin curved his lips. "But enough that they let me put my name on it." He leisurely crossed his arms over his chest, watching her with fervent eyes as her gaze slid over the black leather couch, then shifted to the numerous flat screens mounted side by side on the wall. The silence stretched on as she absorbed every detail of her surroundings. The artwork, the view, even his oversize desk. When her stare lingered on the bar showcasing a collection of crystal decanters, he dropped his arms to his sides and shifted his stance. "A drink, perhaps?"

The gold flecks in her eyes shimmered with defiance. "No, thank you."

Hudson let out a short laugh. "You're killing my attempts at being a gentleman, Alessandra."

She reached up to tuck a strand of hair behind her ear. Her blonde curls were down this time, falling in soft waves around her shoulders. As Hudson watched her, he found himself wishing it were his fingers buried in her hair.

"I believe you have a check for me, Mr. Chase?"

"Ah, yes. My generosity." He twisted around and lifted all those zeros off the desk.

"Thank you. This will go a long way toward making the new school a reality." She took the check and stuffed it into her purse, then paused and looked at him. "Why did you insist I come here? You could have easily mailed it."

"As I said on the phone, I lack confidence in the US Postal Service."

Liar. Fucking liar.

"I offered to send a messenger," she shot back.

"I wanted to make sure you got the money, Alessandra." Hudson stared into those amazing eyes of hers. "I know how important it is to you."

A little wrinkle formed between her eyebrows. "What are you talking about?"

"Your preference for men who are taller when standing on their wallets." Screw tiptoeing into the minefield; he was going in at an all-out sprint.

"You know nothing about me or my preferences."

"I know ten years ago you got a good, hard look but went running to that Ivy League fuck as soon as he flashed his trust fund your way." His words were clipped and cold.

Her voice raised a couple octaves. "It wasn't like that."

"How was it, then?" Hudson's gaze was rock-steady as he stared into her flushed face, her gaping mouth. "You sure as hell had no problem telling me no. Leads me to believe you have an affinity for spreading your legs if the price is right."

Alessandra's pupils dilated. For a split second she was stunned silent.

That's when he saw it coming.

Her palm opened and her hand traveled through the air. Hudson's body fully engaged, his weight shifting from one foot to the other, and in a flash of movement he caught her wrist and hauled her against him.

She glared back at him, her chest rising and falling. He knew he should push her away, send her out the door with his check and never bother with her again. But she stayed in his arms, her fiery gaze almost daring him to make the next move.

He slid his mouth over hers, thrusting his tongue between her lips, and a deep, primitive sound vibrated in the back of his throat. He was a selfish bastard for taking her like this, but he couldn't let her leave without having a taste. Her breath was sweet and the scent of her went straight to his thickening cock.

Alessandra shoved against his shoulders but Hudson held her in place, tightening the arm banded around her waist and fisting his hand into her hair. As if a sigh of relief, her resistance dissolved. Her purse dropped to the floor with a thud and her hands found their way around his neck and into his hair, pulling on the dark waves.

He groaned into her mouth. Goddamn, he wanted her to pull harder.

Hudson deepened the kiss, exploring her mouth in lush, firm strokes. His heart pounded and his muscles flexed with restraint. She was delicate and thin against his powerful frame and his body was aware of every soft curve. The contrasts between them extended far beyond the physical. If she was the hottest summer, then he was a stage-five hurricane altering everything in its path.

His hand shifted, splaying his fingers on her ass and urging her against him. God, he wanted her in a way he'd never wanted any other woman, and his cock was pounding, ready to take.

To own.

After all those years of wondering and wanting, he was going to have her, and there wasn't going to be anything slow or gentle about it.

In a surge of power that roared through his body, Hudson lifted her, and with their mouths still fused, laid her out on his couch. Leveraging over her with his knee pressed into the rich leather and his elbow flush with the cushions, his body lowered, stretching over hers. His hand gripped the back of her knee, curling her leg around his waist. The slit of her burgundy dress fell open and he pressed between her thighs, hissing at the contact he'd been craving. The feel of her beneath him was everything it had been ten years ago; hot, passionate, and so fucking good.

He took her mouth again, kissing her deep and long. As her

tongue slid over his, Hudson's hips rolled with fluidity, massaging the thick ridge of his erection against her sex. The rhythm was deliberate and inexorable.

Allie moaned and her hips tilted up to meet his, responding to his every touch.

"Christ . . . you're killing me." He dragged his open mouth down Alessandra's throat to the deep V of her wrap dress, his lips relentless in their pursuit of her skin. Irritation burned through him at the clothes between them. Lacking the patience to fully undress her, he wrenched open the fabric, exposing perfect breasts covered in black lace.

His breath caught. "Fucking hell. You're beautiful." He traced the edges of her bra with his fingertips before palming her breast. The weight was heavy and full in his hand. Lowering his head, he brushed his lips across the rough lace, then tugged her straining nipple between his teeth. A soft gasp escaped her lips.

Her hands raked over his back, pulling him closer as he continued his barrage against her senses. He yanked the lacy cup down and sucked the taut peak into his mouth. Shit, she tasted fantastic. And he bet even better once his tongue was thrusting inside her until she fell apart against his lips.

The sound of a phone ringing ripped through their heavy breathing like a lightning strike.

Alessandra tensed beneath him.

"Ignore it." He captured her mouth again in slow, teasing licks and she parted her lips, inviting him back in. He had her. She was right there with him.

Ring two.

For the love of fucking God.

"Stop." Her head arched back. She was breathless, her lips swollen from his merciless kisses.

"Are you going to make me beg for it now like you did back then? Because I will." Pride be damned. He needed this woman out of his head once and for all. He shifted to her other breast, promptly pulling her nipple between his teeth.

"I can't do this." She shoved hard against his chest and pried herself out from under him.

Hudson stood and rearranged himself with a curse.

"I have to go." Alessandra worked on retying her dress as she rounded the couch and snatched up her purse, the phone still wailing inside it.

He dragged both hands through his hair, waiting for his hard-on to take a number. "Tell me this isn't about that pretentious fucktwit with the bullshit title?"

Her hazel eyes met his as she yanked open the door. "That pretentious fucktwit is my fiancé."

All the air sucked out of the room as if he were trapped in a vacuum.

Hudson watched her take off as though she couldn't get out of there fast enough. For long moments he stood staring blankly at the door, pretty damn sure shock had just taken over.

He should let her go.

He had to let her go.

But he already knew he wasn't going to.

5

---

*A*llie couldn't help but wonder why her father had suggested they meet for dinner at his North Shore country club on a Wednesday night. Richard had scarcely said two words to her—or her mother, for that matter. Instead he'd spent the entire evening huddled with Julian discussing business.

Victoria didn't seem to mind. She was far too busy catching Allie up on the latest gossip to pay much attention to her husband or future son-in-law. Allie had hoped to discuss the allocation of proceeds from the benefit but her mother was in club mode, not to mention on her third glass of wine, which meant any discussions pertaining to the foundation would have to wait until morning.

Allie watched her mother scan the dining room, her green eyes shifting from one linen-covered table to the next. She knew it wouldn't be long until there was another scandal or rumor her mother just *had* to share, although she couldn't imagine what secrets remained. She'd already heard about every tummy tuck and facelift. She knew whose kids were going to Ivy League schools and whose would be in jail if not for a team of high-priced lawyers. She was caught up on every impending divorce and knew who'd been to rehab, even though they called it a "retreat."

The moment the server cleared the dinner dishes, Victoria inclined her head toward Allie. "Such a shame."

"What's a shame, Mother?" Allie despised gossip, but she knew ignoring the comment wouldn't dissuade her mother. It would only make her angry. Sometimes it was just easier to play along.

"What happened to Jennifer."

Allie did a quick run-through of her mother's so-called friends and drew a blank. "Jennifer?"

"Jennifer Larson." Victoria lifted a perfectly sculpted brow. "Our waitress."

"Jenny Larson?" Allie peered around her leather wingback chair and caught sight of a young blonde carrying a tray of dirty dishes to the club's kitchen. "Jenny works here?" she asked after turning back to the table.

"You'd think her mother would have more pride." Victoria made a clucking sound with her tongue. "But with all their assets frozen . . ."

"What?" Allie asked a bit louder than intended. Julian and her father looked up from their conversation. Her father frowned before turning back to whatever had the two of them so engrossed.

"Honestly, Alessandra, do you listen to a word I say?"

"Of course." Well, sometimes. "I just don't remember you saying anything about the Larson's having their assets frozen."

"They have Bernie Maddoff to thank for that," her mother scoffed. "Now it's freeze first, investigate later."

Allie sat back in the oversize chair. Jenny Larson, her high school chem lab partner, was waiting tables at the club. Her table. And she hadn't even noticed.

Victoria reached for her glass of merlot and nodded to a stunning platinum blonde making her way across the dining room.

"I'd bet my Mercedes that necklace is a knockoff," she murmured from behind her wine.

Allie had heard enough. She tuned her mother out, turning her attention to the other side of the table.

Her father was leaning close to Julian. "We're moving up the timetable," he said.

"Do we know who it is?" Julian kept his eyes focused on the stem of his wineglass as he rolled it between two fingers.

"No, it appears to be shell companies." Her father drained the last of his gin and tonic. He usually had one and then switched to wine with dinner. Not tonight, though. Tonight he was on his third cocktail. "We'll need to close the deal sooner than expected."

"That will require the liquidation of additional assets. I can discuss it with my attorneys when I'm in New York on the eighth."

The eighth? They had plans for the eighth. At least she thought they did. Allie was about to ask him when she saw a deep crease form on her father's brow.

"I'm not sure a trip is wise right now, Julian." Richard tugged on the knot of his tie. "This is a critical time."

"Unavoidable," Julian said with a slight shake of his head. "Laurent family business." He lifted his glass, swirling the wine before taking a sip. "Everything is fine, Richard, no reason to panic."

There was a lull in the conversation and Allie took the opportunity to question her fiancé. "You're going to New York?"

"It's only for one night, ma chérie." Julian covered Allie's hand with his.

"I thought we were going to the symphony on the ninth. Tchaikovsky's fourth, remember?"

"It slipped my mind. Forgive me?" He lifted her hand to his lips, pressing a kiss to her knuckles.

Victoria touched Julian's forearm. "Of course she forgives

you, Julian." She beamed at him before turning her attention to Allie. "Better get used to it now, Alessandra. Once Julian takes over the business he'll be traveling and working late hours all the time. Don't you remember how it was when you were young? I think your father spent more nights at that office than in his own bed."

"It's not like *your* father gave me much choice, Victoria. That man was as single-minded as he was ruthless when it came to his company."

"And look where it got him, Richard. Where it got you, for that matter." Allie noted an edge to her mother's voice, but it softened as she spoke to Julian. "I just wish Alessandra's grandfather were alive to see the two of you marry. He'd be so proud knowing his company was being passed down to royalty."

Allie corrected her even though she knew it would fall on deaf ears. "He's not royalty, Mother." Far from it, in fact. While Julian's title was still passed down through his family, it was an honor in name only. The French no longer recognized any class of nobility.

"Close enough. He's practically a prince." Victoria laughed. "Although I dare say, your ring puts Kate Middleton's to shame. Let me see it again, Alessandra."

Allie extended her left hand, allowing her mother the opportunity to admire her engagement ring. Normally she was happy to show off Julian's family heirloom, but when Jenny returned to serve the desserts, Allie suddenly felt self-conscious. She tried to pull her hand away but her mother's grip tightened.

"This was your mother's ring, Julian?" Victoria asked as Jenny set a chilled dish of lemon sorbet in front of her.

"Oui." Julian smiled, clearly enjoying the attention. "The diamond has been passed down for many generations, given to the first Marquis Laurent by Louis XIV."

Victoria's eyes widened. "Louis XIV? Now there's a man who knew how to live."

Allie gaped at her mother. Clearly she'd forgotten the fate of the French monarchy.

"I toured Versailles the last time I was in France." Victoria sighed and placed her hand over her chest. "The sheer opulence of it! Did you know I used the Hall of Mirrors as my inspiration when decorating our dining room?"

"Ah, yes," Julian purred. "But everything about Mayflower Place is exquisite in its own right. Just like the women of the house."

If there was one thing Allie's mother enjoyed discussing even more than Julian's lineage, it was the ongoing renovations at their Lake Forest home. With over thirty rooms to choose from, Victoria was never at a loss for a project. And she was always happy to describe them. At length.

Allie took advantage of her mother's temporary distraction, withdrawing her hand and placing it discreetly in her lap. She smiled up at Jenny as her former classmate set a chocolate sacher torte on the table in front of her. "Thank you."

Jenny smiled back and then quickly moved around the table, setting plates in front of Richard and Julian before dashing back to the kitchen.

"When the Schweppes owned the estate they played host to Wallis Simpson and the Duke of Windsor," Victoria boasted. "Were they ever guests of the Laurents?"

Allie knew where this was headed. Whenever the conversation turned to Julian's homeland, Victoria eventually got around to mentioning her desire to return to France. She'd invited herself to Julian's family estate more times than Allie could count and she had no desire to watch her add one more to the list.

"I have some news," Allie said. Her announcement had seemed like the perfect diversion, but as she glanced around the table at three sets of inquiring eyes, she wasn't so sure. She took a deep breath. "I received a call from the Harris Group on Monday."

"Is that so?" Victoria asked. Her voice gave no indication of her reaction.

"Seems one of their partners was at the gala the other night." Allie sat up a little taller. "He was so impressed he offered me a job overseeing their nonprofit events."

Her father paused with a forkful of apple pie in midair. "You have a job, Alessandra, at Better Start."

"Of course. And I told Mr. Harris there was no way I could—"

"And once you're married you'll join your mother and the other ladies on the board, not hire yourself out to other charities."

Join the *ladies* on the board? Where was this coming from? Her father had always been so supportive of her interest in the business side of Ingram Media, encouraged it even. It had actually been his idea for her to spend those two years getting to know the inner workings of each subsidiary. Granted she had no desire to join him in the boardroom, but after the wedding she'd planned to take on a larger role within the overall foundation, not become a figurehead.

"And speaking of the wedding," Victoria began. Allie felt herself deflate as her mother marched on with her own agenda. "We have some wonderful news." She paused, beaming at her husband, "Richard, do you want to tell them?"

Her father placed his silverware on his plate, wiped his mouth with his napkin, and leaned back in his chair. "I was able to pull a few strings—"

Victoria jumped in, unable to contain her excitement. "He was able to book the Drake!"

"The Drake Hotel?" Allie could hardly believe it. "When I called they said they were booked for the next eighteen months. They weren't even adding names to the waiting list."

Richard cut his eyes at his wife. "There was a cancelation. Rather last minute." His tone made Allie uneasy.

"How last minute?" she asked.

"The wedding will be December sixth," he announced.

"*What?*" Allie couldn't hide her shock. Her eyes darted from her father to Julian. Somewhere in the back of her mind it registered that her fiancé didn't seem all that surprised by the new wedding date. "That's just over two months away," she sputtered before blurting out the first thing that came to mind. "People will think I'm pregnant."

Victoria's eyes flicked down to the chocolate decadence waiting on Allie's plate. "All the more reason to skip dessert, I'd say."

Allie blanched but tried her best to ignore her mother's comment. She had bigger issues. Still reeling from the news of her impending wedding date, she turned to Julian. "Are you okay with this?"

He reached for her hand once again, this time brushing his fingers across her wrist. "I'd marry you tonight, Alessandra." She hadn't even realized she had a death grip on the fork until she glanced down at Julian's fingers stroking over hers. When her eyes met his he gave her a comforting smile, but she could have sworn she saw one finger nudge her dessert plate farther away.

The room started to spin, or maybe it was just Allie's head. She'd barely had a chance to adjust to being engaged. Hell, they hadn't even had a chance to plan an engagement party yet and now the wedding was ten weeks away? There were so many details. Menus, dresses, flowers. "How can we pull everything together in time?"

"Don't worry, Alessandra, leave all the planning to me." Her mother reassured her with a pat to her free hand. "The Gold Coast room at the Drake." Victoria's green eyes sparkled with excitement. "We've pictured your wedding there since you were a little girl. I used to take you for Princess Tea on Sundays . . ."

Her mother continued chatting but Allie stopped listening. Their reaction to her job offer, the less than subtle dig on her weight, and now this new wedding date; it was all too much. But as overwhelmed as she felt, Allie knew it was all just the tip of the iceberg.

She'd spent the past forty-eight hours trying to block out what had happened in Hudson's office. But now, just thinking his name made her pulse race a little faster. She knew she'd be in trouble if she allowed her mind to wander any further. She couldn't let herself picture the dark look in his eyes just before he kissed her. She couldn't close her eyes and imagine his hands, his lips, his teeth. She couldn't indulge in the fantasy of his body sliding over hers as . . .

Stop.

She shook her head. It was a mistake, a brief lapse in judgment. Nothing more.

Allie eyed the untouched dessert before pushing it away. Her mother would be pleased. Thanks to the knot in the pit of her stomach, Allie couldn't have eaten her favorite dessert if her life depended on it.

6

*H*udson leaned against a mahogany bar spanning the length of a room that looked to still be in the 1920s. The private club was smothering despite its size, with its dark panels and original wood floors polished to a high shine. Luxurious booths anchored the corners of the room, leather wingback chairs tucked in around tables sat center, and the glow from Tiffany lamps set the mood.

It was the kind of place where men sat around drinking single malt scotch, smoking cigars, and discussing the current state of the market.

As for the culture of the club, things hadn't changed much, though women were now allowed inside. And you didn't have to wade through a thick haze due to the no-smoking laws. But he bet he could still catch an old-timer or two bitching about the good old days.

He'd been invited to join every private club in Chicago, including this one. They were all looking for the next billionaire to boast as a member of their institution. Except Hudson wasn't interested in being institutionalized or taking part in a my-yacht's-bigger-than-yours pissing contest. No, the only thing that interested him was the woman sitting in one of those wingback chairs.

Hudson moved slightly to his left for a better view of Alessandra Sinclair. He watched as she crossed her legs and thought about how good it felt to have them wrapped around him. But those thoughts were soon ruined by an arm intruding on the perfect image.

His stare shifted to the Prada-wearing prick whose fingers were caressing her wrist. Hudson was already in a foul mood, and the more Mr. Touchy got feely, the more he wanted to cut the guy's hand off with a butter knife.

Slowly. Painfully.

Hudson's body warmed and he grounded his weight to keep from hurdling over the tables to do just that. Christ, he was acting like a jealous boyfriend.

As he swirled his glass, he stared at the familiar scene playing out before him. The cubes rattled and beat against the amber liquid that was doing nothing to burn the taste of her out of his mouth. He took another drink, further proving the definition of insanity. What the hell, eventually his tongue would grow numb. But there wasn't anything that could short-circuit the memories that had a merciless grip on him. And they always found a way to the surface. Especially now.

The hours passed slowly and the water taxi he'd been driving all summer couldn't move fast enough. With each ferry run, his excitement grew. His shift was ending soon and she was always waiting for him with a look on her face like she was seeing him for the first time. One smile from her and he was a goner.

He'd "borrowed" this same boat the night before to take Allie on a little sightseeing tour of the island. But all they'd managed to see was a whole lot of each other. His body had been rock hard against the softness of her curves and they were all tongues and hands and breathless lust. She'd locked her arms around his neck and raked her fingers into his hair with a greedy intensity. And when he'd slipped his hands beneath her shirt, unclasped her bra, and cupped her breasts, she'd moaned softly against his lips. He'd pushed her to the limits, begging her to let him inside, but the answer was always no.

Hudson steered the boat up to the dock. He shoved his hand in his pocket and curled his fingers around the seashell anklet, his other hand giving his coworker the finger for thinking he was playing a game of pocket pool. At some point during their tryst her anklet had fallen off, and after a thorough search of the boat, they'd been certain it was gone forever. He'd kissed away her tears and promised to buy her another one. Then this morning when he jumped in the boat, ready to fire it up for the day, the sun caught the little metal clasp. He couldn't wait to secure it around her ankle again. As people loaded and unloaded for the last run of the night, he was sure he had a huge, shit-eating grin on his face.

But when the last passenger boarded, his face fell. It was her. She stepped into the boat with her parents and some boy who looked like he was dressed for a game of cricket. She walked right past him without so much as a glimmer of recognition. No smile, no little nod. Nothing. Zip. Zero. Zilch. The message came through loud and clear. He was the help and she was the one percent. Hudson released the anklet, gripped the wheel, and throttled the boat out across the lake.

He closed his eyes against the recollections, but when he opened them he was met with more of the same: Alessandra sitting with her self-serving parents sporting prideful grins directed at him, the dandy dipshit. And Hudson was right where he'd always been. Nothing had changed. He was still the guy on the outside looking in.

But goddamn it, *he* had changed and so had the rules of the game.

Hudson watched as she excused herself from the table, catching the slight frown playing on her lips. His brow furrowed as he wondered which of the three were responsible for putting it there.

He downed the rest of his drink and dropped a couple bills to cover the 200 percent markup on the scotch, plus a hefty tip. Hudson gave her a head start, then quickly walked the length of the bar, tracking her zigzag movements around the tables. When he reached the lobby he caught the heel of her shoe disappearing around the corner and was tight on her.

She paused for a split second. He halted midstep.

Two biddies wearing the socialite's uniform of Chanel suits were making a beeline for the door marked "Ladies," their heels clacking on the marble floor. Alessandra ducked her head as if she didn't want to be recognized and continued down the hallway.

Hudson moved silently through the paneled corridors, paying no mind to the history depicted in the black-and-white photographs that hung on the walls. His gaze was focused solely on her as his eyes lingered unapologetically on the sway of her hips. As he watched her, he felt himself harden.

When he rounded the second turn into the recesses of the club, she was gone. The place was like a fucking labyrinth with sharks at the center. A door clapped shut. He flattened his palm against it and pushed, walking into a locker room and not giving a shit it was the one reserved for women. He closed the door behind him and flipped the lock in place.

Alessandra spun around, stunned. "What are you doing here?"

"I need to talk to you." He moved across the room in deliberate strides. "And I didn't think you'd appreciate me strolling up to your parents' table."

"So you thought you'd follow me into the locker room?"

Hudson came to a stop in front of her. "Whatever it takes, Alessandra." He inhaled. God, he loved her smell. Clean and fresh with a slight hint of flowers.

She blinked up at him. "For what?"

"For you to admit there's something between us." He hadn't been able to get their kiss out of his mind. Her mouth had been unbelievably sweet, and so soft. Softer than he remembered.

Alessandra opened her mouth to speak, then closed it again. Her eyes narrowed. "How did you even get into the building? This is a private club."

"I'm considering a membership."

"Really? To a North Shore club?"

He smirked. "I heard they have a world-class golf course."

"You golf?" She asked with a nervous laugh.

"Quite well. Smooth grip of the shaft, careful stroke." His voice was deep and resonant. "Perhaps I can show you just how good I am, Alessandra."

She glanced over his shoulder at the door, then back at him. "You need to leave, Hudson."

"You can't ignore what happened. Not this time." He brushed his fingers against her cheek.

"It was a mistake, that's all."

"Your body says otherwise." He stepped closer and heard the catch in her breath.

"This is hardly the time or place to discuss it," she said, her voice wavering.

"Then when?"

"I don't know."

There wasn't a chance in hell he was going to let her blow him off. "If you want me to leave you're going to have to do better than that." His mouth curved into a sensuous grin. "Unless, of course, you want me to stay?"

"Next week," she blurted out.

"No. Try again."

"Fine, tomorrow. Just go."

"Where?"

"Lincoln Park Zoo," she said, exasperated.

Hudson drew back a fraction and looked down at Allie with a whole lot of what-the-fuck on his face. "The zoo?"

"Yes, I'll meet you at noon, just inside the main gate."

"You're afraid to be alone with me, aren't you?" His index finger traced the vein pulsing wildly in her neck.

"Don't be ridiculous." She looked over his shoulder again. "Now will you please go before someone walks in?" Allie's gaze shifted back to him, but her stare didn't match the icy tone of her voice.

Hudson's mouth hovered inches from hers. Allie moistened her lips and as she did, he thought maybe she was right; maybe she shouldn't be alone with him. With the way he was feeling he was liable to take advantage of her slightly parted mouth. He knew she wouldn't stop him if he kissed her. And he wanted to, more than his next breath.

He had to stop.

Boy did he ever.

"Until tomorrow." He brushed the pad of his thumb across Allie's bottom lip before strolling out the door without a backward glance.

Hudson walked halfway down the corridor before he stopped. He ran a hand back over his unruly hair and buttoned his jacket to hide the erection threatening the front of his Tom Ford.

Yeah, he needed to get the hell out of there.

Falling back into stride, he headed for the exit. The powder room door swung open as he passed and out trotted the two women in head-to-toe Chanel. Hudson flashed them both a grin. "Ladies," he said with a slight dip of his head.

His phone vibrated just as he handed the valet his ticket. Reaching into his breast pocket, he yanked his phone out and immediately recognized the number of a shithole on the other side of town. The guy who ran the place probably had him on speed dial.

"Chase," Hudson barked into the phone.

"You better get over here," a man rasped, his voice the product of sucking on cigarettes for thirty or forty years.

Hudson blew out a resigned breath. "I'm on my way." He ended the call with a jab of his thumb and tucked the phone back into his pocket.

The valet pulled up with his car, a gunmetal gray Aston Martin DB9. At top speeds the thing looked like a bullet shot out of a gun. Hudson palmed the kid a tip, unbuttoned his jacket, and slid into the car.

As he pulled out into the Chicago traffic, he wondered what he'd find waiting for him this time.

Thirty minutes later, the DB9 rolled to a stop in front of Anchors. The dive was even shittier than Hudson remembered.

He knew who was waiting for him inside, what condition the "who" would be in, and how this shit was going to play out. The only thing that was ever a variable was the when.

The DB9's cooling system ticked and hissed, cutting through the silence in the car.

Fuck.

This was the last place he wanted to be.

Hudson curled his fingers around the door handle, jerked the lever, and unfolded himself from the luxury craftsmanship. He shoved the key fob into his pocket, not bothering to activate the alarm. This would only take a minute. Besides, anyone who'd try to take his car for a joyride had to have balls of steel. The thing was fashioned with one hell of an antitheft system and GPS. The little blue light flashed "I dare ya."

Hudson walked over to a door that looked like it had once been dark green, and cranked a knob for which he was going to need a tetanus shot .

At the bar the owner pulled his attention away from a long pour of something straight. He didn't need to look to know when to stop; the guy just knew. Skills of someone who'd been slinging drinks as a career.

Setting the bottle back in its trough, the owner took out the cigarette that was pinched between his lips and exhaled. The smoke rocketed out of his nose in two streams before curling upward. Hudson kicked his chin at the guy, then did a fat sweep of the room, spotting Nick hunched over a table. Out cold.

Cursing under his breath he cut through the bar, skidding a couple chairs out of his way as he passed a jukebox bellowing some Johnny Cash tune. As he drew closer he could see the top of Nick's wallet, the leather one he'd given him last Christmas, peeking out of his shirt pocket. At least someone had had enough decency to put it back and not rob the guy completely blind.

A soft snore greeted him. Shit, he was totally wasted.

"Hey, Nick." Hudson's palm clasped Nick's shoulder and he gave him a gentle shake. "Come on, let's go."

Nick lifted his head, his eyes half-closed, and smiled. "Hudson, my favorite brother."

"Your only brother. You've worn out your welcome." He grabbed Nick by the armpit and hauled him out of the chair. "Time to go home."

"One for the road?" Nick slurred as if his tongue was too big for his mouth. He tugged his arm out of Hudson's grip.

"We'll get one on the way." Fucking hell they were.

Hudson's face was drawn with grim lines as he watched his brother take a couple steps, then go tilt-a-whirl. He caught Nick by the bicep, his weight barely registering.

He guided Nick toward the front door, his legs pretty much gone to rubber, and somehow managed to keep him from face-planting. Pulling a Ben Franklin out of his pocket, Hudson slapped it on the bar and slid it toward the bartender. "Thanks, man. That should cover it."

The owner dried his hands off on a rag, then dropped it on the counter and picked up the hundred. "Don't mention it."

Hudson pushed the door open with his hip and dragged Nick over to the DB9. He lowered him into the passenger side, stretched the seat belt across him, and clicked it in place.

Nick opened his eyes. "Shit, you brought the good car."

Ignoring Nick, Hudson didn't waste any time getting behind the wheel. Nothing but the purr of the engine interrupted the silence that stretched out between them as he drove. And as it did, Hudson looked over at his brother; Nick's head jerking up and then falling back again. "I saw her, Nicky," he finally said. Man, it'd been so long since he'd talked about her. Make that never talked about her.

Nick's head jerked up. "No shit?"

His head fell back again. The guy was starting to look like a goddamn bobblehead. "All that pussy you get and you've still got it bad for that one, huh?"

More silence.

"I liked her." Nick's voice was quiet in the darkness of the car. "She was nice to me."

The lights from oncoming cars flared and faded. They passed squatters in alleys. Then tall buildings.

"And you . . ." A teasing laugh burst out of Nick's mouth. "*You* were so whipped for that chick." His head rolled on the padded headrest. "What was her name again?"

Hudson glanced briefly at Nick. "Alessandra Sinclair." He paused, then looked back at the road. "Allie."

Nick clapped his hands, having a eureka moment. "Allie, that's right. All the stupid shit you did to try and impress her."

Hudson's jaw tightened.

"Pussy whipped motherfucker. Tell me you hit that?"

"Shut up, Nick," Hudson growled. "And don't puke in my car. Took me forever to get that smell out last time."

7

*A*llie couldn't remember the last time she'd been to Lincoln Park Zoo. When she was eight or nine, maybe? For the life of her, she couldn't imagine what had made her choose it as a meeting place. Harper had been talking about the fund-raiser there with Neon Trees; maybe that was it. Either way, she'd been so flustered by Mr. Sex-on-Legs that she'd blurted it out and now, against her better judgment, she was standing in front of the main gate.

At least it was a relatively safe place to meet. Despite being nestled in the shadow of the city's skyscrapers, the zoo wasn't exactly the type of place her friends and family frequented. She pulled her sunglasses out of her purse and slipped her cardigan off, tying it in a loose knot around her shoulders. It was the end of September, but unseasonably warm in Chicago.

She took a deep breath and smoothed the wrinkles out of her charcoal-gray pencil skirt. Might as well get this over with.

The zoo was busier than she'd expected. For a moment Allie wondered if she should have been more specific with her instructions, but it didn't take long to find him. In a sea of strollers and school children, it wasn't hard to pick the billionaire CEO out of the crowd. He was standing by the seal pool, his back to her, looking every bit the powerful executive. In his navy-blue pinstripe suit, Hudson towered over the toddlers who stretched on tiptoes for a better view.

Her gaze slid over his muscular frame. She knew exactly what it felt like to have that hard body pressed against hers, and every image evoked a memory. Her fingers winding through his unruly hair. Her hands raking over his broad shoulders. Her heels digging into his firm ass.

Snap out of it, Sinclair.

Hudson turned around as she approached. Damn. The view from the front was even more devastating than the rear.

"Hey," he said, running a hand back through his hair. "Thanks for coming."

As if she'd had much choice. "I couldn't risk you showing up in locker rooms all over Chicago."

"Or just the ones north of a certain street?"

Allie stiffened. How dare he insinuate that she only frequented certain parts of town? She was about to counter his ridiculous claim when one of the gray seals splashed out of the water. Pointing his nose to the clouds, he stretched his mouth open wide and barked at the sky. The sound was deafening as it echoed off the rock formations.

Hudson glanced over his shoulder. "Christ, helluva spot you picked." Firmly cupping Allie's elbow, he led her away from the pool and past a vendor selling popcorn out of what appeared to be a small red fire truck. She watched as Hudson surveyed the area before dragging her under a shady tree near the lion exhibit.

"Why are we here?" she asked, stuffing her sunglasses back in her purse.

Hudson smirked as he leaned his hip against the railing and crossed his arms. "You have a fondness for exotic animals?"

She was not amused. Much. "I mean why were you so hell-bent on seeing me?"

"Because you owe me. I know how you like to cut and run, Alessandra. But not this time."

"What are you talking about?"

"Don't play fucking coy, acting as if nothing happened in my office the other night." His tone turned sensual. "You were right there with me."

Allie's mouth opened on a small gasp. How her traitorous body had responded to his that night was irrelevant. They were in public. Someone could have heard him, for God's sake. She glanced around nervously and was relieved to find only a squirrel within earshot. "Lower your voice, please."

His eyes narrowed. "Right, same with all you debutantes. Taking a walk on the wild side is the perfect rebellion against mommy and daddy, just so long as no one finds out about it." He pushed away from the rail, looming over her at full height. "Does dark and dangerous add to the thrill? Does it turn you on?"

Allie blanched but held her ground. What she'd felt for Hudson all those years ago was real, and her heart had the scars to prove it. She wasn't about to let him reduce it to nothing more than a rebellious fling. "It was never like that and you know it."

"Actions speak louder."

His words were scathing but Allie saw some unknown emotion cross his face. Was it pain? Sorrow? She couldn't say for sure because as quickly as it appeared, it vanished.

"And you sure as hell didn't want your parents to know you'd been slumming it with me, did you? You wouldn't even look me in the eye that last night on the boat, the same boat where you'd been half- naked under me the night before."

His words were like a cold, hard look in the mirror. The reflection staring back at her might have only been seventeen, but it didn't excuse the way she'd acted. Hudson was right; it was shameful the way she'd ignored him that night. It was something she had always regretted.

"Instead you latched on to some pansy-ass bastard." Hudson let out a harsh laugh. "Way to shrivel a guy's balls right up."

Latched on? Allie had no idea what he meant.

High-pitched squeals surrounded them as a field trip of preschoolers was suddenly everywhere. The children pushed and shoved each other out of the way as they vied for a better view of the lions, leaning over the railing and roaring at the top of their lungs.

"Fuck, are we the only people here over three-feet tall?" Hudson stalked away from the exhibit.

"Who are you talking about?" she asked, struggling to catch up to him in her three-inch heels.

Eyes forward, he never broke stride. "The prep in the summer whites. Hell, the guy looked like he was afraid he'd wrinkle. Your parents must have been so proud."

Allie reached for him. "Hudson, stop." His gaze darted to where she'd grabbed his arm and she withdrew her hand. "I wasn't with that boy. He was the son of my dad's friend, not my date." She swallowed, shoring up the courage to offer an apology that was ten years too late. "But yes, I was horrible to you that night. I panicked, and I'm sorry."

He threw it right back in her face. "And in my office, more panicking?"

"No."

Hudson stared at her. Allie knew he was waiting for her to continue, to offer some sort of explanation, but she had no idea what had come over her in his office that night. How the hell was she supposed to explain it to him? Silence stretched between them until Hudson offered up a theory of his own.

"I see. So you make a habit of sliding underneath donors? Sharing is caring and all that. Hell of a motto, Alessandra. No wonder the project is ahead of schedule."

Tears stung her eyes and she bit down on the inside of her cheek.

Don't you dare let him see you cry.

"You're right. A lot has changed in ten years. You've turned into a bitter asshole. Good-bye, Hudson."

She made it all the way to the cab before the first tear fell.

8

----

*A*llie watched as Harper poked at her bowl of field greens. Rosebud had some of the best salads in the Loop, but the sight and smell of the gnocchi, ravioli, and cavatelli being served to the other tables always put Harper in a foul mood. Not to mention the fresh bread. When the man next to them dredged a slice through olive oil and cheese, Allie half expected her to reach over and grab it out of his hand.

"I don't understand," Harper said, turning away from the Italian feast one table over. "I eat rabbit food five days a week and barely lose a pound. Then one margarita and *Bam!* My thighs grow three inches."

Allie fought back a laugh. "It might have more to do with the chips and salsa."

"Mmm, I would kill for a basket of chips with a side of guac right now." She was practically salivating. "Want to hit Blue Agave tonight?"

As much as Allie would have loved a night out at their favorite Mexican restaurant, the list of things she needed to get done was as long as her arm. Her mom was all over her about

57

wedding plans and her projects at work were piling up faster than she could get to them. No matter how hard she tried, she couldn't seem to concentrate on much of anything. For the past few weeks she'd been in a fog, speaking and nodding at appropriate times, but never fully there. Harper had even caught her staring out the window, daydreaming. Twice!

It was all *his* fault. She'd been completely distracted ever since the night Hudson Chase strolled out of her past and into her life, turning the world as she knew it upside down. Until that night everything had been so clear, so black and white. She knew exactly who she was: Alessandra Sinclair, heir to the Ingram Media empire, director of fund-raising at Better Start, and fiancée of Julian Laurent, the man poised to take the reins of her family's company.

But Hudson's return had brought memories so vivid, ten years felt more like ten days. She found herself recalling every detail of the time they'd shared, from the first time he brushed his lips against hers to the moment she knew she was falling in love . But she also remembered the ride back to Chicago that August afternoon and the nights she'd spent crying herself to sleep. Had it really all been over some terrible misunderstanding?

Not that it mattered now. Hudson was Allie's past. Julian was her future. They might not share the same blazing passion she felt when she was with Hudson, but it was safe. It was smart. And there was certainly nothing about being with Hudson Chase that was safe. Or smart. The feelings he'd awoken in her ten years ago had been like a wildfire, hot and all-consuming. But in the end she'd been burned and no high was worth that low. Calm and steady had suited her just fine since then, and that was exactly what she had with Julian. They were compatible, they were content.

Everything was exactly as it should be.

Then why couldn't she get Hudson Chase out of her mind?

She'd hoped his appalling behavior would have gotten him out of her system, but it had been almost two weeks since she'd left him standing in the middle of the zoo, and so far nothing had changed.

"Hel-lo, earth to Alessandra . . ."

Oh God, not again.

"So what do you say, girls' night?"

Allie took her aggravation out on her lunch, stabbing a piece of grilled chicken with her fork. "I can't."

"Why not? Mr. Fancy Pants is out of town, isn't he?"

She shot Harper a look, then nodded. "He left for New York today."

"Then let's go out. We haven't been out for drinks since . . . well, since you got engaged."

"I know, and I promise I'll make it up to you." Allie saw her friend raise a skeptical brow and quickly added the word "soon" to the end of her sentence. "But you wouldn't believe the box my mother dropped off at my condo. Fabric swatches, pictures of floral arrangements, cake designs—"

Harper's head snapped up from her salad. "Oh, count me in on the cake tasting." She tucked a strand of hair behind her ear and Allie noticed for the first time that her earrings didn't match. For a moment Allie wondered if it had been an oversight until she realized they were both the same emerald- green as her ballerina flats. It was an odd combination paired with her navy print dress, but on Harper it worked.

"I'm not sure there will be time for a tasting. The note in the box said she needed my selections 'immediately, if not sooner'."

Harper's phone vibrated on the table. "Shit," she mumbled as she read the incoming text.

"What's wrong?"

"One late package and you'd think the world was ending." She reached for her bag. "And apparently I'm the only one in our office capable of tracking a blasted cardboard box. Must be why I get paid the big bucks." She laughed at her own joke as she dug a twenty out of her wallet. "Sorry to rush off."

"Don't worry about it, I have my Kindle. I'll just read a bit while I finish eating."

"Kindle, eh?" She stood up, slinging her messenger bag over her shoulder. "Must be pretty juicy."

Allie couldn't help but roll her eyes. "No, just convenient."

Palms out, Harper raised her hands in an expression of innocence. "Hey, no judgment here. Nothing wrong with a little smut."

Allie's breath caught. Hudson was suddenly standing behind Harper along with three other men. All four were dressed impeccably in dark, custom-tailored suits, but it was the sight of Hudson, in a light blue tie that perfectly matched his eyes, that made her mouth go dry.

"Ladies," he said with a slight nod of his head. His smooth, deep voice startled Harper and she jumped. Within seconds her face was as red as her hair.

Hudson turned to his colleagues. "Everything sounds good. I'll be in touch," he said, effectively dismissing them before shifting his gaze to Allie. Her nipples hardened under the heat of his stare. *Damn it.* She crossed her arms over her ivory sheath dress, hoping he hadn't noticed. *Yeah, fat chance.*

Harper looked back and forth between the two of them for a second. "Alrighty then, I guess I'll see you back at the office." She took a step behind Hudson and fanned herself in an exaggerated motion. He glanced over his shoulder and she stopped midfan, quickly turning the gesture into a wave and flashing him a broad smile before ducking out the door.

"What do you want, Hudson?" Allie asked the moment they were alone. "Was there some insult you forgot to hurl at me the other day?"

"Actually, Alessandra, I wanted to apologize." He motioned to the empty chair. "May I?"

She nodded, completely caught off guard. An apology was not what she was expecting.

He took a seat, rubbing his hand over the stubble on his jaw. "Discussing the past triggered something." His inner asshole. "Unsettled business, and I was looking to burn off my edge. Not to mention, I have a tendency to be too direct at times."

"Obviously a lot was left unresolved between us ten years ago," she replied stiffly.

"Doesn't excuse my predisposition for behaving badly."

Not giving him so much as an inch, Allie leaned back in her chair, keeping her arms crossed over her chest. "No, it doesn't."

He cleared his throat. "I should have never implied—"

Holding up a hand, she cut him off. Despite the satisfaction she was getting from watching him swallow the lump of pride in his throat, and as much as he deserved to choke on it, deep down Allie knew that Hudson Chase didn't really believe she was a whore. Certainly no more than she thought he was the type of man to call her one. "I think we've both said and done quite a few things we regret."

"I can be a rude son of a bitch." Sincerity burned in his bright blue eyes. "I'm sorry."

"I'm sorry, too, Hudson." There were so many ways she could have finished that sentence. I'm sorry I didn't have the guts to tell my parents about us. I'm sorry we never had the chance to say good-bye. I'm sorry I never told you how much you meant to me. For a moment she just stared at him, willing him to know all she'd never dare say out loud, all that time had made irrelevant. "I'm sorry for the way I behaved on the boat. No one deserves to be treated that way."

He cocked a lopsided grin. "Not even bitter assholes?"

Allie saw a glimpse of the boy she once knew and couldn't help but return his smile. "No, not even bitter assholes."

The waiter approached and reached for Allie's plate. "Are you finished, ma'am?" She nodded and he cleared the remains of her interrupted lunch. "Can I bring you anything else?" The question was addressed to both of them, but she was surprised when Hudson placed an order.

"Coffee. Black," he said. "Would you like anything, Alessandra?"

"I'd love a cappuccino. Decaf please, with skim milk, extra foam. Oh, and hold the nutmeg, but I will take cinnamon if you have it." As the waiter turned to leave she noticed the look on Hudson's face. "What?"

Grinning, he shook his head "You, Alessandra." His gaze lingered for a moment before he straightened, flattening his tie with a sweep of his hand. "Living in the same zip code, we're going to run into each other. Case in point. It would suit us both to maintain a level of civility."

"We're not off to the best start, are we?"

He chuckled. "No. But keep it to yourself, this soft side. It's taken me a long time to cultivate the tough-guy act."

"Is that a sense of humor, Mr. Chase?"

"A man in my position isn't afforded much of one, but it's in there somewhere."

The irony of his statement wasn't lost on her. "Must be the only thing you can't afford. Chase Industries has quite an impressive portfolio."

"How proficient you are with Google, Miss Sinclair." He raised a brow. "Checking up on me?"

Allie flushed, busted for letting her fingers do the walking to satisfy her curiosity. Truth be told, she hadn't been able to garner very much information about Hudson's personal life. About the company? Sure, tons. Chase Industries was quickly becoming one of the most talked about conglomerates in the nation. But when it came to the man himself, there was very little information available. "Just researching the depth of your pockets," she offered as a flimsy excuse. "Always thinking about the next donation."

"You would yield faster results by going directly to the source." His eyes were alight with humor. "They're rather deep."

She somehow doubted they were still discussing pockets and was grateful when the waiter appeared with their coffee. Taking advantage of the brief interruption, she quickly changed the subject. "So what made you move your company to Chicago?"

"I see your predilection for asking a multitude of questions hasn't changed."

Allie gazed at him impassively, waiting for an answer. When he spoke, he was all business. "There are a few companies I'm interested in. Made sense geographically to relocate to a central location."

She rotated the china cup on its saucer, studying the smattering of cinnamon and trying to maintain an air of indifference. "So where are you living these days?"

"The Palmolive building." He lifted his coffee cup and smirked over the rim. "Or Playboy building, as I believe it is commonly referred to among locals."

His adolescent reference aside, Hudson was obviously a shrewd investor when it came to real estate. The Palmolive building was not only considered to be one of the world's finest examples of Art Deco architecture, but it encompassed the three most important considerations when selecting property: location, location, location. The 1920s landmark sat at the north end of the Magnificent Mile, nestled between the Drake Hotel and the John Hancock building, and was one of the few residences where no street address was needed. Simply stating the name of the building would suffice. Allie was impressed.

"What about your little brother?" she asked, lifting her cup. "Is he in Chicago, too?"

Hudson frowned. "Ah . . . yeah, Nick followed me here." He shifted back in his chair and crossed his leg at the ankle. "You've had your turn, Miss Sinclair. It's only fair I get mine. So tell me, what happened to that boy you ditched me for?"

"God, I haven't thought about him in years. And for the record," she corrected, "I did *not* ditch you for him. My dad was working some deal with his father and I was stuck entertaining him."

He gave her a smug grin. "That wasn't so hard to explain, now was it?"

"I can't believe you actually thought I was with him." A giggle escaped her lips as she recalled Hudson's rather accurate description.

"What's so amusing, Alessandra?"

"He really was a pansy-ass."

"And now you're engaged to a . . . what was it he called himself?"

"A French marquis."

"I see." His lips twitched with a hint of a smile. "The title that segregates him from the rest. How did you meet?"

"My father had business with Julian's family. He introduced us this summer."

"How opportune," he said, his tone void of all levity. "When's the big day?"

"December sixth."

Hudson's brow shot up. "You aren't wasting any time."

She felt a sudden unease and her words came out in a rush. "The Drake opened up at the last minute. But yes, throwing a wedding together in less than two months—at least the kind my mother wants—is going to be a challenge. Of course it doesn't help that Julian will be in France most of the month."

"Excuse me." Hudson scowled as he pulled his buzzing phone out of his breast pocket. "What?" he snapped. The crease in his brow relaxed as he listened. "How many? Excellent, keep me posted." Hudson pushed back his French cuff, glancing at his watch, then back to Allie. "Cancel my two o'clock." There was a brief pause. "No, that will be all." He ended the call with the jab of a button before slipping his phone back in his pocket. "Where were we?"

Nowhere I want to revisit.

Allie's reaction confused her. After all, they were just making small talk. Two old friends catching up on the usual subjects: family, friends . . . engagements. And yet she found herself not wanting to discuss Julian or her wedding any further with him. "You were explaining your plans to acquire most of Chicago," she said, trying her best to shift his focus.

"Nice try, Alessandra. Tell me about your foundation. If I'm to consider writing any more checks, I need to be well informed."

Her job? Yes, *that* she could discuss.

Allie told Hudson all about her work at Better Start. She told him about the success of the charter school and how his generous donation meant the second location could break ground in the spring. He listened intently, asking questions and complimenting her on all she had accomplished.

Their conversation flowed easily, the two of them laughing and talking until the manager gently informed them the staff would need to set the table for the dinner seating.

"I believe we're being politely kicked out," Hudson said, standing with authoritative grace and reaching for his wallet. He dropped a few bills on the table as Allie gathered her belongings.

"Hudson?"

His eyes met hers. "Yeah?"

"I'm glad we had the chance to clear the air."

"Me too." His lips quirked up in a half smile and he waved a hand toward the door. "After you."

They stood on the sidewalk, staring at each other for several awkward moments before Allie broke the silence. "Well, I guess . . ." Her voice trailed off as she wondered if this was actually the good-bye they'd missed out on ten years ago. She cleared her throat. "I guess I'll see you around."

"To be honest, I wish I didn't care whether or not we ran into each other again."

For a moment she thought he might say more, but he merely turned and walked away. Stunned by his comment, Allie was still standing there long after he'd disappeared into the crowd.

9

*B*y the time Allie got back to the office it was nearly quitting time. Part of her secretly hoped Harper had already left for the day. No such luck. Her head popped over the wall of her cubicle the minute Allie came through the door, and she was right on her heels as they walked to her office.

Allie heard the door close behind her as she rounded her desk.

"Well?" Harper asked.

"Well, what?" she replied, still holding on to her foolish hope of avoiding the Harper Hayes Inquisition.

Harper's eyes bulged out of her head. "Are you kidding me? What happened with you and Mr. Moneybags after I left?"

"Not much." She kept her tone light as she dropped her purse in the large bottom drawer and kicked it closed with her foot. "We had coffee and talked about the foundation."

Hand on hip, Harper let her have it. "Alessandra Sinclair, I leave you alone with possibly the hottest man I've ever laid eyes on and you expect me to believe you spent three hours discussing alternative learning environments?"

She shrugged. "It's the truth."

"Deny it all you want, but I know there's more you're not telling me. I saw the way the two of you were eye fucking each other at the restaurant."

Allie's gaze shot up from her stack of messages, her mouth gaping open. "We were doing no such thing!"

"Oh please, you looked like you wanted to rip each other's clothes off."

"Might I remind you I am engaged to be married?" Allie held up her left hand as if proving her point. Problem was, she wasn't completely sure which one of them needed the reminder.

"And might I remind *you* that a diamond ring is not the same as a wedding ring."

"I'm marrying Julian," she told her in no uncertain terms. "My relationship with Mr. Chase is purely professional." Allie turned her attention back to the pink slips of paper in her hand. As far as she was concerned, there was nothing more to talk about. Subject closed.

Harper took the hint. "Suit yourself," she said. "But if it were me, I'd drop Prince Pain-in-the-Ass." Her lips curved into a smug grin. "By the way, you do realize you've reshuffled your messages about five times?" Halfway out the door, she glanced back over her shoulder. "Just sayin'."

Allie let out a heavy breath and slumped into her chair. Leave it to Harper to point out everything she'd been trying to ignore. She swiveled around, staring out the window and thinking about all that had transpired over the past few weeks. Her physical reaction to Hudson was one thing—she could almost write that off to an unresolved summer of teenage hormones—but now, talking for hours? And the conversation had been so relaxed, so easy—so unlike any she'd ever had with Julian.

Her fiancé.

A pang of guilt burned in her chest as the image of him on bended knee at Buckingham Fountain played through her mind. She'd stepped out of her brownstone that night to find him waiting in a horse- drawn carriage. Her very own Prince Charming brought to life.

Allie's gaze instinctively fell to the silver frame on the corner of her desk. It was a photo of Julian, proudly holding the flag from the fourth hole at Rich Harvest Farms. Allie wasn't sure what had pleased him more, the birdie he'd shot on a hole known as the "Devil's Elbow," or the mere fact that he'd been invited to play at the exclusive club in the first place. Either way, she'd never seen his smile that wide. They'd had dinner in the clubhouse afterward, recounting the details of every hole they'd played.

Things had been good between them then, but lately she and Julian felt out of sync. Even simple decisions like choosing a restaurant dissolved into tense debates. It had all started to deteriorate shortly after their engagement and had reached a fever pitch just before the gala.

She shook her head. Of course, why hadn't she seen it sooner? Between her long hours at work and the wedding plans that were now taking over her life, no wonder he was distant. Needing to reconnect, Allie spun her chair around and dialed the phone.

"Allô?"

"Julian?"

"Oui. Why are you calling, Alessandra, is something wrong?"

"Oh no, everything's fine." She chewed her lip. Why was this so difficult? "It's just, I never heard from you. I thought I'd check in, make sure you arrived safely."

Someone knocked on his door. "One moment, Alessandra." She heard a muffled voice in the background. "To my liking? If I wanted Cristal, I would have ordered it," he snapped. There was a tense silence followed by a harsh exhale. "Fine. Come in." Glassware rattled as the sound of squeaking wheels drew closer to Julian's phone. "Imbéciles incompétents," he muttered under his breath.

"It's not his fault, Julian. Don't shoot the messenger."

"What does that even mean?" he asked. Without waiting for

an explanation, he continued his rant. "Peu importe. I'm never staying at the Plaza again. A hotel that finds it acceptable to substitute Cristal for Dom Ruinart, c'est ridicule." Allie listened to Julian venting in his native tongue while lamenting the substitution of one four-hundred-dollar bottle of champagne for another. " . . . head so far up their ass, they can't even spell the name correctly on the menu. It's Dom Ruinart," he announced loud enough for the waiter to hear. "Not 'Ruinard'."

"It was probably just a typo," Allie said.

He ignored her comment, his attention focused on the waiter. "Tell your sommelier to correct the name. Fucking insult to the French."

Allie flinched as the sound of a slamming door echoed into the phone. "You didn't have to be so hard on him," she said quietly.

"And just accept the piss they bring me? I'm a French Marquis, Alessandra. I serve only the best France has to offer."

"Are you expecting company?"

"Business associates."

"The meetings must be going well if you're serving champagne."

"But of course, why would they not?"

"You just seem . . ." She paused a moment to consider her word choice. Julian seemed anxious and on edge, but in the end she settled on "tense."

"If I am tense it's because I work hard. There is more to my title than simply tending to various charities, Alessandra. My obligations extend beyond parities."

Allie flinched. "I didn't mean to imply—"

"Was that all you wanted, to check up . . . *in* with me?" A television blared to life in the background.

She sighed. "I missed you, that's all."

"Me too. Miss you," he said, his tone devoid of any emotion.

It occurred to her that perhaps working on wedding plans as

a couple would bring them closer together. It was worth a try. "My mother dropped a box of wedding samples off at the brownstone. I was going to start going through them tonight, but I can wait until you return."

"No, no need to wait."

She tried a different approach. "Okay. I'll sort through them and then we can make the final decisions together."

Her suggestion was met with exasperation. "Pick whatever you want, Alessandra."

"Julian?"

"Hmm?"

She hesitated. Clearly he was distracted, but she had to know. "Do you love me?"

"I'm marrying you, aren't I?"

Not exactly the answer she was looking for.

A lighter clicked near the mouthpiece of his phone. "Is there anything else, Alessandra?"

"No, that's all. Enjoy your evening."

"Yes. . . . you too."

She hung up the phone, Julian's words replaying in her mind. *I'm marrying you, aren't I?* Unbidden, Hudson chimed in. *To be honest, I wish I didn't care.* Her heart raced as their voices grew louder, talking over each other in an attempt to be heard. The room suddenly felt too small, the air too thick. She needed to get out of the office. She needed to get out and think. A run, yes, she needed a long, punishing run along the lake if she had any hope of getting to sleep that night.

Allie grabbed her purse and headed for the door. She suspected she could run halfway to Evanston and still not clear her head, but she was damn well going to try.

10

*H*udson wasn't expecting anyone. He finished buttoning his shirt and shoved the tails into his pants while making his way over to the phone. A muscle in his jaw flexed as he picked up the direct line to the front desk. He hoped like fuck it wasn't another one of those *Architectural Digest* geeks stopping by on the off chance he'd let her take a look at the place.

"Chase," he said, holding the receiver between his shoulder and ear as he zipped his fly.

"Good evening, Mr. Chase. You have a visitor, Miss Alessandra Sinclair."

Surprise flared in his eyes and tension weaved through his shoulders. "Send her up." Hudson set the phone back in its cradle and ran a quick hand through his damp hair.

A subtle ping announced the elevator's arrival as he strode into the main room. When he reached the foyer, the doors slid open and Alessandra was right there, her finger jackhammering the buttons on the panel.

The doors began to glide closed, and lightning quick Hudson stabbed his arm in their way. His eyes darted from her Band-Aid

73

of a sports bra to the tight black running pants, then drifted over every fucking inch of exposed skin, glossy with a sheen of sweat.

Sweet fucking hell.

His hand clenched against the urge to touch her, to see if her skin felt as soft as it looked. "I'm a little surprised to see you standing in my elevator, Alessandra."

Her words tumbled out quickly, "I was running along the lake, and next thing I knew I was at Oak Street Beach and then . . . I don't know, I just ended up in front of your building." She took a deep breath and shook her head. "This is a bad idea. I should go." She reached for the panel, no doubt to get to work on those buttons again.

"After you've gone through all the trouble?" He stepped aside. "Come in."

"I really shouldn't."

"In another five minutes it will be dark. Come in. I'll drive you." Allie hesitated. His palm gripped the edge of the door and he pushed it back as it began to close again. "In or out, Miss Sinclair?"

Reluctantly she stepped off the elevator. Hudson dropped his arm and moved with her, the elevator doors whispering closed behind him. Her soft-soled shoes made no sound on his dark wood floors as she headed toward the sweeping view that any artist would go to his grave attempting to duplicate. One he felt privileged to have, but perhaps took for granted. The entire city of Chicago was revealed below, its glittering lights and the cascading traffic a mesmerizing display.

Hudson leaned his hip against the breakfast bar. He watched Allie as she examined the room, looking for what, he wasn't sure. Insight? As if he could be figured out by the overpriced items selected by an overpaid designer.

She paused in front of a polished steel sculpture, her fingers skimming over the curved edges. The presence of her in his place tightened his skin and an instinctive demand shot down to his groin. His eyes deliberately drifted along the curve of her hips and down her long, athletic legs. He relished the memory of those soft feminine curves underneath him, gasping and leaving him practically begging.

He bit down on a groan. "Are you a fan of Kapoor?"

Jerking her hand away, she looked over at him. "The artist who designed the Bean?"

Hudson nodded.

Confused, Allie looked back at the mirrored sculpture. "I thought he only did public commissions."

He smirked. "Something to drink?"

"I'd love a water," she said, still admiring the piece.

Hudson yanked the Sub-zero open, the cool air wafting from the stainless steel box as he pulled out a bottle of water. When he turned around, Allie's gaze slid up and a perfect blush heated her cheeks. Not from exertion, but because she'd been caught checking him out. A smile tugged at the corner of his mouth as he set the bottle in front of her.

"You look nice. Have a hot date?" Allie cracked open the bottle of water and took a sip.

Hudson leveled his stare. His expression remained impassive. "I do, yes." He lingered on her face, cataloging the delicate details and catching an imperceptible flinch of . . . "You're not jealous, are you, Miss Sinclair?"

Fifteen minutes ago he thought he knew the answer to that question, but that was before she showed up at his penthouse half-naked. He held her stare, willing her to say one simple word. Bastard that he was, he'd drop everything, cancel his date, and spend the remainder of the evening between her thighs.

"Of course not." A brief scowl creased her perfect brow.

His lips twitched. It wasn't the answer he was hoping for but her expression was indeed an admission of the green-eyed monster lurking beneath that beautiful package. "If you say so."

"Same girl I saw you with the other night?"

"Sophia? Yes." His words came clipped and fast.

"Pretty name. Suits her." She avoided his stare and twisted the cap on and off the water bottle. "So, how long have the two of you been together?"

"We're not." He took a deep breath, counting the seconds it would take to get her completely naked. "Ready to go?"

Allie frowned. "Still, you must like her to be in such a rush."

Hudson took a few quick strides toward her. "On the contrary, Alessandra, I'm in a rush because I'm dying to peel you out of that little number you're wearing and fuck you on that barstool until you beg me to stop." His stare burned into her. "And believe me, as hard as I am right now, I'm just crazy enough to do it." She flushed, her chest rising with shallow breathes, and he knew she was picturing every detail. "What's it going to be, Alessandra, barstool or ride home?"

"A ride home would be great." Her voice was slightly breathless and thoroughly lacking conviction.

"I'll get my keys."

Hudson gripped the wheel of his Aston Martin, trying to get a bead on the feeling inside his chest. A low hum vibrated through his body, growing more intense the further he got from Allie's brownstone.

She'd made her feelings on the matter clear, so he'd shoved aside his all-consuming lust. But when he'd said he wanted to fuck her tonight, it was the God's honest truth, and getting away from her wasn't helping or easing his need. No cooling of the jets or simmering on a back burner. Damn it, why in the hell did she just happen to stop by his place? Not knowing wasn't sitting well and heading in the direction he was going seemed like a violation of something pure, something he needed, something meant to be.

The light changed green, and with the reflexes of a race car driver, he hit the gas. The DB9 came awake, roaring across the lanes as Hudson weaved into a turning lane at the next intersection. The light was still green, the arrow a blazing sign telling him what to do. He cranked the wheel with renewed determination and flipped a louie. The DB9 picked up speed, weaving around a soccer-mom special and then a luxury vehicle that was all flash and no dash. Zipping through the intersection and rounding the corner back down Astor, Hudson realized he'd plow down, perhaps kill, anything that got in his way. This time, despite feeling about ten types of stupid for chasing after a woman, he was going to get answers.

---

11

*H*udson's hand clenched tightly into a fist and he pounded on the door. He waited ten seconds, then pounded again. Usually he wasn't into making a scene, but suddenly he didn't give a shit about pretenses and dove headfirst into Idiotsville.

Just when he was about to rip the damn door off the hinges, it swung open. "Took you long enough." Not an ounce of amusement resonated in his voice.

Alessandra stared at him for a beat, her face registering disbelief and bewilderment. "I was in the shower."

Hudson stood framed in the doorway. Right now he wasn't feeling like the billionaire mogul the rest of the world knew, but a man past the limits of control. His eyes raked over her from head to toe and she pulled the lapels of her robe tighter against his searing gaze. "Why did you come to my place?" he demanded.

Her spine straightened. "Shouldn't you be out with a leggy brunette about now?"

"Canceled. Now answer the question."

"I . . ." She hesitated.

"Tell me."

"I don't know." Her grip tightened on the silk robe, wrinkling the fabric.

"Bullshit. You do know. You can't stop thinking about me." He jutted forward, bracing one hand on the doorjamb. "I know this because I can't stop thinking about you."

"Don't—"

"Every time I close my eyes I see you, feel your mouth sliding against mine, and it drives me fucking crazy—"

She held up her hand. "Hudson, please stop."

"Then you show up at my penthouse. And now, knowing you're naked underneath that robe . . ."

"You can't keep saying these things to me."

"You don't mean that. In fact," his eyes flicked down briefly to her nipples straining against the thin fabric, begging for his attention, "I think it turns you on."

"You've got a lot of nerve."

"Do I? I bet if I rip open that robe and feel between your legs, you're soaking wet." His gaze darkened and his voice lowered to an intimate challenge. "Want me to prove it?"

Her jaw dropped. "You need to leave."

When she made a move to close the door, Hudson's palm smacked flat against the wood. "Not until you admit I'm right."

"Is that what this is about, you being right?"

"No, though I am." His voice took on a decisive edge. "The road is paved in hard truths, Alessandra, not denials."

"And you think I'm the one in denial?"

His gaze was rock steady. "I know you are. But fuck if I'll let you push me away again."

"It doesn't matter how I feel." Her voice thinned. "It's too late for us, Hudson."

"The hell it is." His chest expanded and he blew out an exasperated breath. He needed to connect with the girl she used to be, the girl he knew was still there, beneath the layers of socialite status. "Damnit, Allie. Just admit you feel the same."

"Admit what? That I haven't stopped thinking about you since the moment I turned around and saw you at the gala? That I can't stop picturing what could have happened in your office? Or about how part of me was disappointed you didn't fuck me on that barstool? Is that what you want me to admit, Hudson, that no matter how many years have passed, I still want you as much as I did back then?"

"Yes, I need to hear you say it."

"I want you." Her reply was barely audible, but he heard her loud and clear.

His eyes roamed over her face. "Say it again."

"I want you."

A beat of silence passed between them, then his hand fisted in her hair, dragging her mouth to his in a kiss that had Allie moaning her surrender. Her lips were hot, her skin flushed and alive. Her entire body radiated a heat and a need he was more than eager to fulfill.

"I'll have you shouting it by the time I'm through with you." Hudson kicked the door shut behind him and in one swift move had Allie pressed against the nearest wall, every inch of her body aligned perfectly with his. If there was a point of no return, he'd just passed it. He was driven by a desire so raw, so powerful, that it frayed the last thread of his control.

With need grabbing the reins and taking over, Hudson impatiently yanked the sash of her robe free and stripped the satin off her shoulders.

Jesus Christ, she really was fucking naked. Beautifully naked.

It was difficult to think straight with that much flawless skin in front of him. Every base instinct told him to worship every inch of her until they were both sated.

His hands slid down the sides of her bare breasts, pausing to brush his thumbs across her taut nipples before smoothing over her waist and the curve of her hips; the contours of her familiar even after all these years.

"I didn't think I'd make it another five minutes without touching you." He was way past hiding the effect she had on him, or pretending he had any kind of control over the response.

Allie pushed his jacket over his shoulders. He took a half step back and shrugged it the rest of the way off, one arm and then the other, before flinging it to the side. A lamp toppled over on the table beside them and the bulb popped with a flash. As if he gave a shit.

Her greedy fingers clutched handfuls of his shirt as she yanked it out of his pants. One by one she began frantically working the buttons.

"Rip it," he growled.

Allie tipped her chin up to meet his challenging stare. She was breathless and her eyes glowed with unrestrained lust. Gathering the fabric with both hands, she split it open with a sharp tug. Buttons scattered, ricocheting off walls and disappearing across the hardwood floor.

A low groan vibrated in Hudson's chest as he claimed her mouth again, his tongue filling her with deep, searing strokes. His hand dropped between her thighs and he grit his teeth. Christ, she was wet. So fucking wet. The rough pad of his thumb stroked over the top of her sex as his middle finger slid inside. Allie moaned as he eased out then back in with a second finger, her hips circling and rocking against the heel of his hand.

With a shift of his wrist he thrust deeper, all the while imagining how good she would feel sliding over his throbbing cock. He was so hard for her it hurt, the culmination of two weeks of foreplay and ten long years envisioning her just like this. God help him, he had to take her. Right here, right now.

"I need to be inside you," he murmured against her lips. His voice was rough, carnal, and as desperate as the moment between them.

Her hands wasted no time reaching for his fly, jerking his belt loose and yanking his zipper down. She pushed his boxer briefs just low enough to free his aching erection, leaving his pants slung around his hips.

Hudson bent low and lifted her up in a rush, her legs hooked over his arms, his cock laying hot and heavy at the lips of her sex. "Tell me to stop and I will."

"Don't stop." She was breathing hard, panting with need. "Please . . ."

With that he thrust deeply, entering her on a solid stroke, then stilled. If he moved he was going to be royally fucked. She felt so good, too good. Perfect. Like he was made to be inside her.

"Oh, God." She sucked in a sharp breath and shuddered. "You're so deep."

Holding her effortlessly, he pulled out to the tip, then powered into her again. Picture frames rattled on the wall as he took over and over—harder, faster, deeper—fucking her like a man possessed.

Allie's head rolled back against the wall. Her eyes drifted shut and her lips parted on a soft moan as her entire body began to quake.

"That's it, feel it for me." God, he loved seeing her like this. With her back arched, taking all he gave her, his name breathlessly rolling off her tongue.

Her core tightened around him and she cried out, the sounds of her orgasm a symphony as her nails scored his shoulders. The sweet lick of pain that spread across his upper back made him hungrier, greedier.

"Fuck, Allie," he growled, unable to think past the sensations. His head dropped and he started to come, his cock kicking deep inside her as he pitched over the edge into his own release. Once the tremors subsided, he stilled, leaning heavily against Allie and breathing harsh against her neck. His broad palm smoothed down her thigh and carefully lowered one of her legs to the floor.

Her body sagged against his as she struggled to catch her breath. "That was . . ."

"Not my best effort." He lifted his head and brushed her hair away from her face. "But Christ, Allie, you make me lose control like a goddamn teenager."

Hudson cupped her jaw and kissed her softly, feeling his way across her lips. "I think a better demonstration of my skills is in order." And this time he wanted to look into her eyes as she came.

Still buried inside her, he lowered his head and flicked his tongue reverently across her nipple before sucking it into his mouth. As he curled his tongue around the taut peak, he watched her teeth sink into her lower lip. Immediately, he felt himself begin to harden again.

Allie's eyes widened and her breath hitched. "Already?"

"Oh yes." Trailing both of his hands over the curve of her ass, he picked her up. In one fluid movement, he swept the mail off the console table and laid Allie out on top of it. His hand fell to the back of her thigh, lifting her into a deft roll of his hips as he pushed in deeper. "I have ten years of catching up to do."

1 2

*T*he sound of a phone ringing ripped through the silence of Allie's bedroom. Hudson slid his arm out from under her, reaching into the darkness to grab it before it woke the whole damn neighborhood. He was about to silence it when he saw the name on the screen.

"Nick?" He dropped his legs over the side of the bed and scrubbed a hand down his face, forcing himself awake. "What's wrong?"

"It wasn't your fault, ya know?" The words fell lazily out of Nick's mouth.

Hudson looked over his shoulder as Allie began to stir. He lowered his voice. "Fuck, Nick, didn't we just do this?"

"You were only a kid. Crap hand, Hudson, s'all it was. Just a case of wrong place, wrong time."

"Where are you?" Hudson scanned the room trying to figure out where the hell his clothes were.

Allie shot up. Hudson's brow furrowed as she bolted out of the bed and grabbed her robe, wrapping the satin around herself before disappearing into the bathroom.

"And they were wrong about you, anyway." Nick laughed in a short burst. "My brother who turns shit to gold."

"Are you at home?"

"Yeah, and I'm still vertical." Nick laughed as if he was impressed with himself. Hudson heard the furniture skid as two objects did a meet and greet, then Nick cursed when something crashed to the floor. "Sort of. Hey, you wanna get a beer?"

"Christ, it's after four. Go to bed, Nick."

"No? Okay. I'll throw 'em back for the two of us." There was the hiss and crack of a bottle being opened, then a cap clinking onto a counter. The telltale signs of his brother's mission to get rip-roaring. "Cheers, bro." Nick slugged down whatever number beer he was on and swallowed hard. "I just wanted to tell you that I love you, man. You know that, don't you?"

"Yeah, Nick." Hudson's mouth drew into a grim line and his eyes closed. He felt the same aching sadness he did every time his brother started this shit. He needed to get him off the phone.

"You're all I have." Nick's voice was soft.

Hudson heard the sound of splashing water and a moment later Allie appeared in the doorway. He tracked her movements as she darted across the room, gathering his clothes in her arms. When she lifted his pants, a condom fell out of the pocket.

"I have to go, Nicky. Get some sleep. I'll talk to you tomorrow." He ended the call and looked over at Allie with the Trojan pinched between her fingers. The condom was still perfectly rolled up, a testimony to his impatience and a decision that was damn hard to defend. The same panic that flared in her eyes was doing a stranglehold on his chest. God, he was such a bastard for being so reckless with her body. "I'm clean, Allie, I swear. I've always been careful. But so help me, tell me you're on the pill?"

"Yes, of course I am."

His shoulders relaxed. "Good. Now come back to bed," he said, reaching for her.

"You need to go. Here," Allie held out his pants. "Put these on."

Hudson grabbed his pants and tossed them to the side. His mouth curved into a mischievous grin. "A few hours ago you couldn't get me naked fast enough." Pushing to his feet, he reached for Allie again, only to have her slip out of his grasp, his fingers brushing the side of her hip.

"Hudson, I'm serious. The sun will be up soon, and I can't have my neighbors see you." She picked his discarded shirt up off the floor and held it out to him.

"I don't give a shit about your neighbors." He threw the shirt on the bed and tugged on the sash of her robe.

"Please, Hudson." Allie swatted his hands away and retied her robe.

"This isn't about your neighbors, is it?" Hudson grabbed his shirt off the bed and shrugged it on. "What time are you expecting him?"

"I'm not," she said, searching for his shoes and socks. "I just need you to go."

His eyes drifted around the room, looking for any indications of another man. "He doesn't stay here, your fiancé?" With quick jabbing motions, he pulled his boxer briefs up his thighs, followed by his pants. Hudson's hand paused for a moment, waiting for an answer before zipping up his fly.

"He used to, in the beginning." Allie avoided his gaze as she collected his wallet and keys from the nightstand. "He prefers his hotel room."

Hudson closed the distance between them. "Good. I think I'd go half crazed if I could smell him on your sheets." Slipping a finger under her chin, he forced her to meet his stare. "I want them to smell of me. Only me." Hudson took her face between his hands and pressed a tender kiss to her lips. He'd foolishly thought being with her would sate his need, but his hunger had only grown stronger. Even now, just the feel of her lips against his had him wanting more. He felt his cock begin to stir and it took every ounce of self-control not to toss her back on the bed and bury himself inside her till the sun came up. "I need to see you again."

"I'll call you." Allie pushed the rest of his belongings into his hand. "But for now, please, I need you to go." Hudson moved through the house at Allie's insistence. Fuck that. He was being herded.

He stopped in front of the door, shoving his wallet into his pants pocket. "Call or not, Allie, we're not done." He yanked the door open and jogged down the steps of the brownstone with his shoes in hand. Without a glance back, he unlocked the DB9. A grin spread across his face.

Hudson Chase doing the walk of shame.

That was a first.

13

---

*A*llie slid hanger after hanger across the chrome pole. She'd never been one to subscribe to the idea of retail therapy, but she had to get out of her office. It felt like the walls were closing in on her. And since there wasn't time to go for a run during her lunch hour, she'd had to settle for wandering the eight floors of the Macy's on State Street.

She paused when she came across a dark green wrap dress. It was almost identical to her burgundy one, and her thoughts immediately shifted to the last time she wore that dress. It was the night she went to Hudson's office to collect the donation he'd pledged. Her eyes drifted shut and she could feel his hands wrenching open the neckline, his teeth nipping at the black lace of her bra. A throbbing ache spread through her belly. It was the same ache she felt every time she thought about Hudson Chase, which she was ashamed to admit, was far too frequently.

It had been over a week since she'd shuffled him out of her brownstone. Eight days, to be exact. Eight days of resisting the urge to call him. Eight days of hoping the memories of their night together would fade from her mind.

No such luck.

Allie shook her head. She had to stop thinking about Hudson; she was with Julian now. They were planning a life together and she wasn't about to throw it all away on something that amounted to nothing more than residual teenage lust. She'd just needed to get it out of her system that one night, that's all.

Yeah, just keep telling yourself that.

Folding the green dress over her arm, Allie made her way to the next rack, where a black bandage dress caught her eye. It had the style's signature formfitting hourglass shape, but this particular dress had a front panel of thin black strips crisscrossing over sand mesh. *Hmm, definitely a more daring choice.* She held the two dresses up, comparing them side by side.

"The black one is nice."

Allie jumped. She knew that voice . . . intimately. It had whispered roughly in her ear, filling her mind with all manner of naughty images as she was brought to orgasm again and again. Her errant thoughts brought a flush to her face as she turned to find Hudson standing behind her, grinning and looking rather pleased with himself. Where the hell did he come from? It was as if he'd just materialized.

"What are you doing here?" she asked. Lately it seemed as though those were always the first words out of her mouth. At least when it came to Hudson Chase.

"I told you, call or no call, this wasn't over. I gave you a week."

Her heart pounded erratically. She wanted to blame it on the shock of his unexpected appearance, but she knew better. "How did you know where to find me?"

"Your coworker was very forthcoming." His lips curved into an amused smirk. "I suspect she doesn't have a very high opinion of your fiancé."

"No, she just has a high opinion of your checkbook."

He chuckled. "Not even my most impressive attribute."

She fought the urge to roll her eyes. "What do you want, Hudson?"

"I need to see you again." He raked a hand through his hair. "Christ, I can't even concentrate at the office. You're in my head constantly."

Allie glanced around nervously. "You can't keep showing up like this," she said, careful to keep her voice low.

"I can be very focused when it comes to something I want. Relentless, even."

She stared at him blankly before moving to another display. Hudson followed.

"When is he leaving?"

"When is who leaving?"

"Your fiancé. You said he was gone most of the month."

"This is hardly the place to discuss that." She kept her eyes trained on the row of skirts in front of her.

Hudson braced a palm on the rack, halting the incessant skid of hangers. "When is he leaving, Alessandra?"

Her shoulders sagged. Clearly he wasn't going to drop this. "He left this morning."

He stepped so close, she could feel the warmth radiating off his body. "Meet me after work." The dark, sensual edge to his voice sent a shiver through her. With every passing day she was falling deeper under his spell. This had to end.

"I have plans."

"Cancel them."

Her breath caught at his unexpected tone. It was demanding, authoritative, and hot as hell. No, she had to stay strong. "I can't. I promised Harper a girls' night out weeks ago."

Blowing out an irritated breath, Hudson quickly surveyed the store. "This way," he said, taking her by the elbow.

"What are you doing?" she hissed. "People will see us."

He ignored her, taking long strides as he guided her into a dressing room at the rear of the store. "Now if anyone comes in they'll be intruding on our privacy." Turning, he closed the heavy wooden door and flipped the lock.

Allie opened her mouth to protest her abduction but he lunged at her. Both hands framed her face as Hudson pressed her against the three-way mirror and sealed his lips over hers. His tongue pushed into her mouth, taking her in a long, deep kiss. Groaning, he pulled away just long enough to speak. "I'm losing my mind over you, Allie."

With just those few words she was warm and wanting. She hadn't even called him, let alone planned to see him again, but now he was there, touching her, kissing her, and all she could think was how much she wanted him. His lips moved with hers again and Allie's hands found their way into his hair, pulling him closer as the pent-up desire of the past week exploded between them. God, she'd missed this.

Lowering his head, Hudson dragged his tongue up the column of her throat. "I'm aching to be inside you any way I can," he murmured, catching her earlobe between his teeth. He inched her dress up along her thighs, his touch searing against her skin. "Open for me."

She gasped. *In Macy's?* "Is anywhere off-limits?"

"Not when it comes to you. I've had a taste and I want more." His hand moved between her legs and she widened them shamelessly, far too aroused to deny him. A low, sexy sound vibrated in the back of his throat when he found the warm, damp fabric of her panties. Pushing them aside, he slid his fingers over her slick flesh, teasing her slowly, gently. "God, Allie, I want my mouth on you, right here," he eased one finger inside her, "right now."

" Hudson . . ."

"Shh, I need this," he whispered, trailing his nose down her neck. "Give me this."

She pulled his hair, bringing his mouth back to hers. He tugged her bottom lip between his teeth before sliding his tongue over hers in slow, savoring strokes that perfectly matched the movement of his fingers. Allie stifled a moan. There was nothing she wanted more than to feel those same lush, wet strokes between her thighs. But they were in a dressing room at Macy's. Someone could knock on the door at any moment.

A battle waged inside her. She wanted him to stop, but at the same time, keep going. His finger slid in and out as he tortured her in a steady, unhurried rhythm. *Don't stop.* Muffled voices passed in the hall and she tensed. *No, stop.* She was about to push him away when his finger curled forward, massaging a spot she never even knew she had. *Oh, God, don't stop.* Her head fell back against the mirror with a thud and her legs began to tremble. *Whatever you do, don't stop.*

"I could take you here and you'd let me," he growled. "Your body is ready for me." His voice was tight with restraint, his breath harsh in her ear.

She heard the door to the next room close and shook her head. "I can't, not here."

Hudson's teeth grazed her jaw. "But you want to. I can feel you getting closer." His weight pressed against her as he pushed into her with a second finger. Allie whimpered. Her hips moved of their own accord, seeking friction against his hand. "Let me watch you come, give me that much."

"I can't," she said, barely able to push the words out as her body responded to every movement, every skillful sweep of his relentless fingers.

"Yes, you can." Hudson banded an arm around her waist, his erection digging into her hip as he buried his fingers deeper. The heel of his hand massaged her sex and everything inside her tightened. "Let go, Allie, I've got you. Come for me."

The world fell away at his rough command and she shattered into a million pieces. Hudson's mouth slanted over hers, absorbing her cries as she came apart in his hands. Panting, she melted into him, her body going lax as he held her close. He slipped a finger under her chin, taking her mouth in a bruising kiss that betrayed just how close to the edge he was.

His head lifted and he looked down at her with fiery blue eyes. "Tomorrow, then. After work. My penthouse."

Spent and trembling, all she could manage was a nod before Hudson turned and strolled out of the dressing room.

14

*H*arper leaned against the wall as Allie unlocked the door to her brownstone apartment. "Tell me again why I'm being forced to go running before margaritas?"

Allie laughed. "Two words for you my friend: chips and salsa." She tossed her purse and keys on the table by the door and flipped through a stack of mail. Bills, junk mail, Chinese takeout menu. Nothing that couldn't wait.

When she turned around she found Harper sprawled out on the sofa. Clearly she was going to need a nudge if Allie had any hopes of getting a lakeside jog in before indulging in Mexican food. And it wasn't just the impending calories that had her motivated to hit the pavement. After what happened at Macy's, she needed a long, head-clearing run now more than ever. "You can go ahead and change if you want. I'm just going to check my messages real quick."

Harper reached for the duffle bag at her feet and let out an exaggerated sigh as she pushed up from the couch. She paused on her way past the breakfast bar, raising a brow at the small electronic device on the granite countertop. "Expecting a call from the 90s asking for their answering machine back?"

Allie pressed the play button. "I'll have you know I just bought this." Granted it wasn't voice mail, but it was still digital. Jeez, the way Harper reacted you'd have thought the messages were recorded on a little cassette tape. Allie was about to continue the defense of her household appliances when the first message began to play. Loud music and laughter were eventually followed by the sound of Julian's voice.

"Alessandra, c'est Julian." Allie's brow creased. Why had he called her apartment in the middle of the day and not her office or cell phone? "I've arrived in Paris and am checking in, as you like to say." The sound of a woman speaking fluent French could be heard along with Julian's muffled reply. Although she listened intently, trying her best to recall the years she spent in high school French class, the loud music and covered mouthpiece made it impossible to decipher what had been said.

Julian spoke into the phone. "Seems there is more work than anticipated. I'll call when . . ." His message was interrupted again, this time by a loud pop followed by squeals and a chorus of laughter. "Ne renversez pas le champagne tout le putain de tapis," Julian shouted. "Elle vaut plus que ce que vous ferez au cours de votre vie, vous idiots!" He was still ranting about his precious rug when the recording ended, cutting him off with a shrill beep.

"End of messages," the machine announced.

An awkward silence hung in the air for several moments before Harper chimed in with what was obviously an attempt to lighten the mood. "You know what? I vote drinks instead of jogging. In fact, screw the margaritas. I say margarita martinis at Tavern instead."

Allie tried her best to muster a smile. "Sounds like a plan."

Allie sank back against soft red velvet. Tavern on Rush was standing room only but she and Harper had arrived early enough to score one of the couches lining the club's paneled walls. A distinguished-looking gentleman in a dark suit smiled when she glanced his way, but the last thing Allie needed or wanted was a conversation with a man. Any man. Not a French diplomat with a taste for expensive champagne and even more expensive rugs. Not a billionaire industrialist with serious boundary issues. And certainly not a George Clooney look-alike at a Rush Street bar. The only thing on her evening agenda was having a cocktail— make that cocktails, plural—with her best friend.

She gave the gentleman a tight smile and shifted her gaze to the main floor, where a circular mahogany bar sat bathed in gold-and-red lighting. As she scanned the room she realized her admirer wasn't the only silver fox at Tavern. Everywhere she looked she saw gray-haired businessmen in designer suits mingling with young women in black dresses and red-soled pumps. Allie chuckled to herself. Ah yes, the Viagra Triangle. That was how locals referred to the high-priced restaurants that dotted the corners of three intersecting streets. As she took in her surroundings she realized the description was more than just an urban legend and made a mental note to tease Harper about how often she frequented the establishments.

Allie reached for her lemon drop martini, her second of the night, and licked a bit of sugar from the rim. The tangy beverages were going down much too smoothly. If she didn't get some food in her stomach, she'd be paying the price come morning. The last thing she needed was to roll into work with a hangover. "We should order."

Harper took a generous sip of something called a Strawberry Blonde and grabbed a menu off the marble tabletop. She flipped through the small leather binder, bypassing the extensive wine list in favor of colorful drinks with elaborate descriptions. "Oh!" Her eyes grew wide. "How about a Sucker Punch? Vodka, brandy, pomegranate liqueur, fresh orange juice, fresh pineapple juice, and grenadine."

"I meant something more along the lines of dinner, but what the hell."

Harper craned her neck, searching for the waiter she'd been flirting with all night. She startled when he was suddenly at her side.

"Can I bring you ladies another round?" he asked. Allie had to admit he was a bit of a doll. Big brown eyes with lashes that wouldn't quit, dark hair a little longer than most, and a smile to make you forget what you were going to order. At least that was the effect he seemed to be having on Harper.

Allie came to her rescue. "Two Sucker Punches, please." As soon as he was out of earshot she jumped on the chance to tease her tongue-tied friend. "Harper Hayes, speechless. Never thought I'd see the day."

"Oh, shut up," Harper grumbled. Her cheeks were rosy pink as she reached for her glass. "He just caught me off guard, that's all. They should tell him not to sneak up on people like that." She finished off the rest of her cocktail and plucked the strawberry garnish from the edge of the glass. Allie could almost see the wheels turning as Harper regained her composure. "I'm going to give him my number," she announced.

The waiter returned a few minutes later with two oversize hurricane glasses on his tray. The size alone assured Allie the drinks would live up to their name, but when she tried a sip she knew she was in trouble. The fruity concoction was far too delicious considering the pleasant buzz she was already feeling. She stirred the drink with her straw, watching in awe as Harper jotted her number on a napkin and slipped it into the waiter's hand. Allie shook her head. She could never be as daring as Harper. Then again, she'd had a pretty daring afternoon.

Images filtered through her mind. Hudson's body pinning hers against the mirror . . . his warm breath fanning out across her neck . . . his fingers teasing and taunting before sending her spiraling over the edge . . .

"So what's the real scoop with you and Mr. Hottie from the party?" Harper asked as if reading her wayward thoughts.

Allie tried to hide her blush behind her glass, needing a moment to regroup before once again denying any interest in the man who'd brought her to orgasm during her lunch hour. In a dressing room. At Macy's. *Dear lord.* She tipped the glass higher, practically gulping her cocktail.

"He seems like a man who knows his way around a bedroom and would be more than happy to give you a tour."

Allie choked on her drink.

Harper sucked in a sharp breath. "Oh my God, you slept with him." It was a statement, not a question, and one Allie knew there was no point in denying. The proof was all over her face, not to mention spilled half way down her blouse.

She wiped her chin with the back of her hand. "A little louder, Harper. I don't think the valet heard you."

"Sorry. It's just . . . I don't know, you've always been so reserved. You're not exactly the type to get down and dirty with someone you just met."

"We didn't just meet."

Harper paused with her drink in midair. "Come again?"

"We knew each other a long time ago, when we were teenagers."

"I thought he grew up in Michigan?"

Allie raised a brow. Clearly she wasn't the only one who'd done a bit of research on Mr. Chase.

"What?" Harper feigned innocence. "I was curious."

"My parents and a few of their friends rented houses up on Lake Charlevoix the summer before I left for college. I met Hudson on the water taxi the day we arrived."

"Summer romance at the yacht club?"

Already feeling a bit warm and fuzzy, Allie reached for her drink. "Hardly. Hudson worked at the pier. He drove the water taxi."

"And Dick and Vicky were okay with their daughter dating the hired help?"

"They never knew."

"You were able to keep it a secret?"

Allie nodded as she sipped on her straw. "From everyone. We spent the whole summer together and no one ever knew. Well, except for his little brother."

"That is so romantic, like Romeo and Juliet," Harper said.

"You do know they died in the end, don't you?"

Harper frowned. "You know what I mean. So how did it start? Did he slip you a note or something?"

"A note? Seriously?" Allie shook her head. Harper had to stop reading so many Nicholas Sparks novels.

"Whatever. Finish the story."

"I saw him again that night. My friends had heard about a bonfire at one of the mainland beaches and Hudson was there with a few of the other townies. At first I thought he was a cocky little jerk just like the rest of them. They were awful. It started out simple enough, a few whistles, some rude comments from behind beer bottles. But after awhile one of them started to hassle us. He wouldn't take no for an answer, started pawing at me. Hudson knocked him on his ass."

"Holy shit."

"We ended up talking for hours that night, just walking on the beach." She smiled at the memory. "I'd never met anyone like him."

"So what happened?"

"The last time I saw him was on the water taxi. I was stuck playing tour guide to some kid whose dad was doing business with mine. Hudson got the wrong idea, thought I'd chosen the yacht club guy over him."

"Why didn't you just explain the sitch?"

"At the time, I didn't know that's what he'd assumed. But that's only half of it. My parents were on the boat that night, too.

I was so scared they'd find out about us. I thought if I even looked at him, my mother would see right through me." Allie took a deep breath. "I ignored him completely. Acted like I didn't even know him."

"Ouch."

"I wanted to apologize, but I never got the chance. The next day my dad had some crisis at work and we headed back to Chicago a week early." Allie's throat tightened. "I never saw him again."

Harper got a wistful look in her eye. "And now here you are, ten years later, like it was meant to be." Her dreamlike state, no doubt the result of reading far too many romance novels, baffled Allie. This wasn't a Lifetime movie. It was *her* life. A life, she might add, that included wedding invitations that were already in the mail. It was too late to start wondering "what if."

When Harper finally snapped out of her trance, a wicked smile spread across her face. "He was good, wasn't he? Like, multiple orgasm good."

"Harper!"

"Don't bother denying it. I'd bet my next paycheck that man knows "ladies first" isn't just something you say when holding a door open."

Allie's face heated. "No comment."

"He's probably a little kinky, too." Harper leaned forward. "Did he tie you up?"

Allie's mouth dropped open in shock. So much for Nicholas Sparks, she'd gone right to *Fifty Shades*. "We are *so* not having this discussion."

"Oh, c'mon! At least tell me if it was worth the wait. Shit, after ten years of foreplay you two must have been ready to combust."

Allie couldn't help but smile. "Let's just say if I'd known what I was missing back then, I might not have spent so much time saying no."

"I knew it!" Harper grinned. "Although I gotta say, didn't think you had it in you to take on two men at once."

"I'm not . . ." Allie lowered her voice. "I'm not taking on two men. I haven't been with Julian since he got back from New York."

"Really? How'd you managed to keep the Count at arm's length?"

"*Julian*," she said, emphasizing his actual name, "stayed at his hotel all week."

"He seems to be doing that a lot lately."

"I may have given him the impression my period started a few days early," Allie muttered into her glass.

"And let me guess, Prince Prissy Pants has a problem with a little blood?"

Realizing that correcting Harper was a waste of time, she ignored the term of endearment. "He thinks women are too emotional to begin with. Can't deal with all the drama."

"What you see in that man besides his great hair is beyond me."

The waiter appeared at the table, his gazed trained on Harper. "Would you like another Sucker Punch?" he asked. "Or maybe a Screaming Orgasm?"

Oh. My. God. He had to be kidding. Although judging by the way Harper was batting her eyelashes at him, the lame pickup line was actually working. Quite well.

"Just the check, please," Allie said, meeting Harper's scowl as the waiter turned to leave. "Don't look at me like that. We both have work tomorrow."

"So what are you going to do?"

Allie dug through her purse, looking for her wallet. "Pay the bill and put us each in a cab."

"I mean about the Tempting Tycoon."

Honest to God, the nicknames! Allie opened her mouth, intending to change the subject with some pithy reply, but then closed it again. She considered her answer for a long moment, and in the end, simply spoke the truth. "I don't know," she admitted.

And there it was, the doubt she'd been denying since Hudson first kissed her in his office. Apparently two lemon drop martinis and something called a Sucker Punch were all it took to shine a big old spotlight on the truth. She almost laughed in spite of herself. If Hudson only knew. Then again, he did a pretty good job of breaking down her defenses without the help of three lethal cocktails.

Harper was suddenly serious. It was almost unnerving. "Are you going to see him again?

"He wants me to come to his penthouse tomorrow night, but I haven't made up my mind."

"Look, Julian is in France for the next two weeks. It's the perfect opportunity for you to sort this whole mess out. But I've got news for you: you'll never be able to do that until you figure out what's going on between you and Hudson. You need to talk." She raised a brow. "And I don't mean horizontally."

Allie chewed on her bottom lip. "So you think I should go tomorrow?"

"What I think is that this thing with Julian happened really fast. You owe it to yourself to be sure. You're not married yet, Alessandra, and if that message was any indication, the Duke of Bullshit sure as hell knows it.

Allie sipped the last of her cocktail while considering her friend's advice. She hated to admit it, but Harper was right. The only way she was going to be able to move forward was to resolve her feelings for Hudson Chase. Once and for all.

She stared into her empty glass. Her mind buzzed with scattered thoughts and unanswered questions, but one thing was clear: she had to see him again.

15

*H*udson watched Allie move through his living room. His every sense heightened; his hands fisted with a growing, never sated desire. Despite his fear that she would destroy him again, his body ached with a craving that beat out any idea of self-preservation. It was taking everything he had to not drag that beautiful body down to the floor and fuck her with every bit of primal instinct to make her his.

His gaze slid over every inch of her, noting the way her dress clung to his favorite curves, before finally settling on the back of her neck as she arched over the Fazioli piano. She let her fingers skate over the ivories, then looked up, meeting his stare reflected in the window. The predator in him awoke, stretching, unfurling its muscles with graceful fluidity. He wet his lips and locked his eyes to hers as he leisurely stalked toward her. "I thought you'd never get here."

Allie turned to face him, her cheeks flushed, her eyes luminous. "I wasn't sure I was going to come."

He came to a stop in front of her and swept her hair off her shoulder. "Oh, I hope so." He dipped his head and pressed his lips to the curve of her neck. "If you'll let me, I'll show you a hundred ways, if not more." He brushed his nose along her throat to her ear. "I want to learn what pleases you." His lips trailed along her jaw until his mouth hovered over hers. "Will you let me do that?"

Lust pulsed between them. Allie grabbed him by the hair, pulling his head down and crushing his mouth against hers. With a growl that was more animal than man, his hand locked to the base of her neck and his tongue shot between her lips, taking her mouth like he was going to take the rest of her; hard and deep.

There was no denying what he wanted. He'd never stopped wanting her. He couldn't stop. He'd only pushed his feelings for her to the darkest recesses of his mind where they'd rolled around like a grenade with its pin out.

Hudson backed her against the glass wall, the Chicago rush-hour traffic whizzing below them. His hands slid down her arms, lifting them above her head. He cuffed her wrists with one hand, pinning them to the glass as the other moved between her legs. His fingers brushed over her panties before tearing through the lace with deft fingers, shredding them from the place that was his to claim. Only his.

Her head thudded back and her body arched against his chest as his fingers slid through the slickness, spreading the moisture over her sex. "I've barely touched you. See how your body responds to me, Alessandra." Mouth-to-mouth tight, his breath fanned across her lips. "So wet. So ready."

Her hips tilted into his sensuous strokes. "It's not fair what you do to me."

Sinking a finger inside her, he felt her clench helplessly around him. "Who said anything about being fair?" In a deliberate move, he palmed her ass and urged her legs around his waist. A groan vibrated up his throat from the pressure of her making his cock punch to its full length.

Hudson ground his mouth against hers, marking his territory in a possessive kiss, swallowing her moans as their tongues slid over each other. He stepped away from the wall and the heel of her shoe dug into his ass with a satisfying lick of pain. She rocked against his now pounding erection and he hissed.

Faltering, he threw an arm out, catching himself on the piano. His hand gripped Allie's waist as her ass hit the keys in a jarring chord. "I'm dying to be inside you."

"Yes," she said, more breath than voice as he dragged his open mouth down her throat. "Now, Hudson. I want you."

His name sounded perfect rolling off her tongue. He shoved the skirt of her dress around her waist and with dexterous fingers ripped open his button fly. He stretched her leg up and the sight of her, glistening and open for him, had his cock twitching on the edge of an orgasm.

"I want to take my time, but I can't wait." Curling the end of his spine, he thrust into her hard and fast, pushing her back against the piano.

Allie's head fell back on a cry. "Yes."

He pulled out, his body straining as pleasure coursed through him, then pushed into her again, rotating his hips and sinking deeper. "Fuck . . . Allie." His fingers dug into her thigh as he glanced down to where they were joined. He could see himself moving in and out of her, watching the head of his cock make an appearance before pushing deep again.

Allie's body writhed against him with each possessive thrust. Her legs began to tremble and her hands clutched wildly at the keys. Disjointed notes vibrated beneath her, mingling with the sounds of his hunger as the spasms of her orgasm squeezed him in an alternating rhythm. Her knees buckled and Hudson banded an arm around her as she slipped off the piano and into his lap.

"I have more for you," he rasped over her lips. Still buried inside her, he laid Allie out on the wood floor. "You're going to come for me again." With that he arched over her, fusing their mouths together as he pounded into her in relentless, measured drives.

"I want to feel you." She slipped her hands under his T-shirt, running her fingers over the muscles flexing beneath his skin.

Hudson's tempo slowed. Rearing up, he fisted the back of his shirt, yanked it over his head, and tossed it aside. He came back down over Allie, her legs wrapping around him as she shoved her hands under the waistband of his jeans to grip his flexing ass.

"Don't stop," she said, rocking her hips up to meet his thrusts.

"Not a chance in hell." He was a man undone, too impassioned to be gentle. His fingers tightened in her hair, holding her in place as he stroked in and out. Bracing his feet, and with a lithe surge, he leveraged against the floor as his body rolled over hers.

He took her again in a bruising kiss, his tongue filling her mouth. One hand curled around the nape of her neck while the other fell to the back of her thigh. His movements became faster, thrusts more powerful, as they slid together as one across the polished floor.

"Come on, Allie, give it to me," he said, each word punctuated on a breath.

Her thighs tightened around him as her climax plowed through her. A groan vibrated up the back of Hudson's throat, mixing with Allie's cries as his hips powered into her. "Ah, God, Allie." He pressed his forehead against her as he came hard and long.

They lay nose-to-nose as their collective breathing slowed. After a moment, Allie craned her neck and he followed her gaze to find the couch rising like a wall behind her. She looked back at him and started to laugh.

Hudson tossed a lingering stare over his shoulder at the piano, then smirked down at her. "Thoroughly fucked across the room, Miss Sinclair."

"Beautiful piano. How long have you played?"

"I don't."

"Then why do you have one?"

"Because that's what rich people do. Buy things they don't need." He sat up in a fluid movement and cradled Allie between his legs.

She looked up at him incredulously. "So you have a Fazioli grand piano in your home that has never been played?"

"Except by your ass."

Her brow arched. "That's a very expensive piano to have only been played by my ass."

"Worth every fucking cent."

16

*H*udson knew he was in a dream, because for a split second he was happy. Then the gun went off. And all he saw was red. The horror of the nightmare unfolded before him, clear as the first time he'd had it as a child and every time since. He fell to his knees, the threads of his jeans drinking the crimson liquid as it spread around him. He couldn't move, and in his body's paralysis, fear ripped through him. Someone was screaming.

No, crying.

Nick's tearstained face contorted in terror as hands pulled him out of Hudson's reach, his shoes squeaking on the floor as they dragged him away.

Hudson curled his fists and punched them into the mattress as he shot up. His breathing was ragged. Shit, his heart was pounding so hard against his chest. He whipped the sheets away from his naked body; there was nothing red staining his knees. He bent his legs toward his chest, planted his elbows on his knees, and dropped his head into his hands, wishing like hell this panicked, helpless feeling would go away. This attachment to his guilt and the familiar litany of shame sank bone deep.

He pushed his hands back through his hair, wiping the sheen of sweat from his brow. He glanced over at the empty space next to him and began to wonder if Allie, breathless as their bodies slid against each other, was all part of a dream, too.

Fuck, he needed to get a grip.

He dropped his legs over the side of the bed, grabbed a pair of gray cotton pants, and pulled them up his thighs. He tied the drawstring as he padded into the main room and spotted Allie in the kitchen. The sight of her leaning into the fridge wearing nothing but his T-shirt made him exhale a heavy breath. His subconscious was still churning out of control but her presence in his kitchen grounded him with an intimacy just as strong as the one they'd shared in bed.

Allie closed the stainless-steel door to the Sub-zero with her hip. She turned around and a smile to launch a thousand ships spread across her face, then faded. "Are you okay? You're as white as a ghost." She set the carton of eggs on the counter.

Hell if he was going into the unpleasant details of a trip through his subconscious.

"Yeah, I'm good," he said, his voice still groggy from sleep. He inhaled deeply and forced a smile to his face. "Something smells delicious."

"I'm making breakfast." She cracked an egg on the rim of the bowl and let out a slight laugh. "Well, more like lunch."

Hudson's eyes darted to the digital readout on the oven. "I never sleep in. A new occurrence."

Allie cracked the last of the eggs into the bowl and began to whisk the contents. "Well, that's what happens when you fall asleep as the sun is coming up."

"Or fall asleep with you." He slid onto a barstool, still trying to shake the nightmare that was clinging to him. "You cook?"

"A few things. My morning repertoire is limited to eggs, bacon, and toast, though. Don't be expecting me to flip a pancake." Allie began to open one cupboard after another, then glanced over her shoulder at Hudson. "Plates?"

"To your left," he said, waving a hand.

"How about you? Know your way around this fancy kitchen?" She opened the cupboard to her left, pulling out a couple white plates.

"A few things." He frowned. "I learned early how to fend for myself, and someone had to feed Nick."

"What about your mom?" Allie dumped the eggs into a frying pan, then reached over to pop four slices of bread into the toaster.

"She wasn't exactly the Betty Crocker type. Besides, she was usually working." Or drinking herself blind. "Now I have a staff to handle the shopping and cooking, leaving me time to—" he paused, letting his gaze drift leisurely over Allie's body, lingering on her breasts "—do more important things."

Allie's head jerked up from the eggs cooking in the pan. "Staff? Last night when we were—"

"Fucking across the floor like a freight train?" A satisfied grin curved his lips. "Relax. I gave them the weekend off. I assumed you'd prefer it that way."

"Looks like you also assumed I'd stay."

"Hoped."

She opened her mouth to speak, then closed it as a flush spread across her cheeks. "Bacon's almost ready. I seem to have made enough to feed all of Chicago." Allie opened the oven and bent over to flip the bacon. "Hope you're hungry."

Hudson's eyes locked on the exposed skin between her thighs. "Suddenly starved." He pushed to his feet and strolled around the breakfast bar. "No panties. I approve." He so fucking approved. His hands slid under the shirt and over the curves of her naked ass.

"I have you to thank for that, Mr. Chase. I believe my panties are a shredded pile of lace on your living room floor."

Hudson grinned against her neck. "I'll do it again if it gets me what I want." His palms smoothed up the sides of her rib cage and the rough pad of his thumbs brushed over her nipples.

She leaned back against him, her hair soft against his bare chest. He cupped her breasts and his fingers tugged at her nipples.

"Breakfast is never going to be ready if you keep doing that."

Removing his hands from under her shirt, he skidded the pan across the burner and flipped the gas off. "Breakfast can wait," he said, lifting Allie onto the counter and spreading her legs wide. "I can't."

*A*llie rested her head on Hudson's chest, his heart pounding against her cheek as they struggled to catch their breath. "What is it with you and floors?"

A deep laugh vibrated in his chest. "Merely taking advantage of ample square footage."

"I'm going to attempt to make breakfast. Again." She sat up and shot him a look of admonishment before slipping his T-shirt back over her head. "Behave yourself this time."

"I didn't hear any complaints on my most recent behavior."

Her eyes raked over him lying in all his glory on the kitchen floor. *Hmm, definitely no complaints.* Hudson lifted his hips and pulled his pants up, putting an end to her shameless ogling. Just as well if they had any hope of ever eating breakfast. He leaned forward to tie the drawstring and she watched as his washboard abs curled into a perfect six-pack. She fought the urge to reach out and touch him as her appreciative stare roamed the contours of his naked chest. *Must. Cook. Breakfast.* She tore her gaze from his body, focusing instead on his handsome face, and an involuntary giggle escaped her lips.

"What's so funny?" he asked.

"You. Your hair."

Hudson ran a hand through his unruly locks. "Bed head and amorous fingers. Quite the combination." He flashed a broad grin as he stood, grabbing Allie by the hand and hauling her to her feet. "I believe I was promised bacon and eggs?"

"Oh, the bacon!" She spun around and opened the oven door. "Hope you like it extra crispy."

"Perfect. I've worked up quite an appetite."

Out of the corner of her eye she saw Hudson pull a basic, WalMart-issue coffeemaker out of one of the cherry cabinets. "You use that instead of the Jura?" she asked, nodding toward the state-of-the-art espresso maker she knew cost well over three grand.

"It has an on/off switch. Pour water in, black coffee comes out. What more does one need?"

She leaned against the counter, watching as he plugged the Mr. Coffee into the wall and filled the carafe with water. "You don't know how to use the other one, do you?" she asked, trying hard to hide her smile.

He stared at her impassively for a moment. "While it doesn't produce your cappuccino with extra foam, hold the nutmeg," he said, his lips curling into an amused grin. "I prefer to keep it simple."

While the coffee brewed, Hudson poured them each a glass of orange juice. "Anything I can do to help?" he asked.

"Maybe pop in a few more slices of bread?" She nodded to his Dualit toaster. "Unless, of course, you find all kitchen appliances as daunting as an espresso machine."

"Funny, Miss Sinclair."

They worked side by side, Allie scrambling eggs and Hudson making toast. Allie flipping bacon, Hudson setting out silverware. Allie casually eating breakfast, Hudson devouring everything but the plate.

"That was delicious, Allie. Thank you." He swallowed his last bite and wiped his mouth with his napkin. "I have a call to make and . . ." He glanced at the oven clock. "Shit, just enough time to grab a quick shower." He stood in a rush, piling his silverware on his plate. "But take your time, finish eating."

"I'm done." Allie slid off her barstool, taking Hudson's plate and stacking it on top of hers. "Go. I'll clean up."

"I apologize. I shouldn't be long. Help yourself to the shower." He cupped Allie's chin, tilting her head back and planting a soft kiss on her lips. "I'm sorry I won't be able to join you. Rain check?"

"Hudson, I really should go home. I don't have any clothes."

"You look pretty fan-fucking-tastic in my shirt, and I just happen to have a closet full." Hudson spanked her playfully on the ass before sauntering out of the room. "Besides," he called out over his shoulder, "I don't plan on letting you stay dressed for long."

After cleaning the kitchen, Allie made her way to the master bathroom. Dark cherry cabinets ran the length of one wall while two sinks with brushed nickel faucets divided an expanse of black granite. More cabinets sat atop the counter. They flanked either end of the vanity and ran clear to the ceiling, perfectly framing the oversize mirror. A large square tub dominated the far end of the room. It was encased in more black granite and was fed by a waterfall faucet protruding from the wall. While the tub was definitely big enough for two, the shower could easily accommodate five or six. The glass enclosure had two rain showerheads suspended from the ceiling and square body sprays mounted at intervals up and down the wall. Allie had seen her fair share of luxury bathrooms, but nothing quite like this. Everything about Hudson's bathroom was dark, masculine, and larger than life. Just like the man himself.

Tossing Hudson's T-shirt in the hamper, Allie piled her loose curls on top of her head and stepped into the stream of the body

117

sprays. The water was warm and soothing as it pulsed against her aching muscles. Their adventures across the floor, not to mention the three . . . or was it four . . . rounds in the bed left her sore in places she'd never imagined. And now he didn't plan on letting her stay dressed for long? She shuddered as she reached for the bar of soap. Her rational side knew she should go back to her brownstone and try to forget all about Hudson Chase. But all rational thought left her as she ran her lathered hands across her body. Allie's eyes drifted shut as she imagined it was Hudson's hands touching her, exciting her as they slid over her breasts, down her stomach, and between her thighs. Her eyes popped open. This was not helping.

Rinsing quickly, she turned off the water and reached for a towel. She wrapped it tightly around her and wandered over to the vanity, examining herself in the mirror. Not as bad as she expected considering she'd hardly slept the night before. In fact, her cheeks seemed to have a nice glow to them. She pulled the clip from her hair and ran her fingers through her curls. She could survive without makeup or hair products, but she would kill for a toothbrush. She opened the top drawer and eyed Hudson's. Oh, what the hell, after everything else they'd done, what was the harm in sharing a toothbrush?

When she was done she put it back in the drawer, idly taking note of the other items. Toothpaste, floss, a travel-size bottle of mouthwash. Nothing out of the ordinary and nothing to suggest a woman stayed over on a regular basis. Then again, Hudson didn't strike her as the type to have a pink toothbrush lying next to his. No, if anything, he probably had a supply of extra toiletries on hand like the front desk of a five-star hotel. Without thinking she opened the tall cabinet to her left. More of the usual suspects—shaving cream, razor, deodorant—and all of the male variety. No tampons, eye creams, or scented lotions. She shook her head. *Get a grip, Allie.* She needed to stop acting like a jealous girlfriend and find something to wear.

Hudson wasn't exaggerating when he said he had a closet full of shirts for her to choose from. Dozens of crisp dress shirts hung on racks above a row of dark suits that stretched from one end of the closet to the other. She selected a white linen button-down and rolled the sleeves to her elbows. The shirt fit her like a dress, but she wasn't entirely comfortable running around Hudson's apartment without panties despite the pleasurable outcome when making breakfast. She found a pair of his boxer briefs in one of the drawers and slipped them on. Great. Now what?

Allie wandered back into Hudson's bedroom, wondering how much longer he'd be tied up on the phone. She sat on the edge of the bed and her eyes shifted to his nightstand. Harper's voice echoed in her mind. *I bet he's kinky, too.* Unable to help herself, she casually slid the top drawer open, bracing herself for what she might find.

Exhaling, she almost laughed at herself. What was she expecting, a crop and a flogger? Damn Harper and her crazy books. There was, however, a rather large box of condoms. Allie felt an unexpected pang of jealousy before telling herself in no uncertain terms to get over it. The man obviously entertained his fair share of women and he swore he'd always been safe. At least until it came to her. She should have been relieved to see the proof of his precautions stored conveniently at his bedside. So why did the thought of it bother her so much?

Her gaze drifted around the room and a door she hadn't noticed before caught her eye. Curious, she opened it to find a fully stocked wet bar that connected to Hudson's office. Like his bedroom, the office was decorated in dark, oversize furniture. A polished mahogany desk sat facing a marble fireplace and two wingback chairs, while floor-to-ceiling bookcases lined three of the walls.

Hudson sat in a black leather chair facing a breathtaking view of North Michigan Avenue. With his back to her, Allie was afforded a quiet moment to observe the CEO in action. She was certainly no stranger to powerful men, having been around them her entire life, but as she listened to him she realized there was something inherently different about Hudson Chase. It wasn't so much the actual words he spoke—she'd overheard talk of mergers, deadlines, and stop orders more times than she cared to remember—but the way he said them. When Hudson issued a directive there was an indisputable finality. As if the person on the other end of the line had no choice but to follow his instructions to the letter. And it was in the way he carried himself. Yes, he was gorgeous, sophisticated, and undeniably sexy. But that was what you saw on the surface. Allie had only known this new version of Hudson for a few weeks, yet already she could tell there was something deeper, something darker even, that commanded the respect of most everyone he encountered.

His chair spun around and his eyes met hers, tracking her every move as she slowly crossed the room and rounded his desk. She drank him in from head to toe. Feet bare and hair still damp from his shower, he looked relaxed and casual in jeans and a gray cashmere sweater, a total contradiction to the person speaking instructions into the phone.

Hudson reached for her and ran his hand up her bare thigh, his eyes flaring when he realized she was wearing a pair of his boxer briefs. He smirked and shook his head. Pressing the phone between his shoulder and his ear, he leaned forward and swept the underwear down her legs. She watched him with a growing fascination, seeing both her playful lover and the powerful executive. The combination took her breath away.

His hand glided up the inside of Allie's thigh, his fingers teasing her as they slid back and forth between her silky folds. She stifled a moan as first one finger and then another moved in and out, again and again. With his eyes locked on hers, he removed his hand from between her thighs and sucked his fingers into his mouth. Allie's lips parted on a silent gasp. His eyes gleamed wickedly as he responded to someone on the other end of the line. "I want to double those numbers by the end of next week."

Oh, so that was the game he was playing? Allie took his smug grin as a challenge. Turned on and wanting more than just the brief touch of his fingers, she climbed into his lap. Her feet barely touched the ground as she straddled him. She reached for the button of his jeans and toyed with it, searching his face as she tried to gauge his reaction. His eyes darkened, giving her all the encouragement she needed to unzip his fly and free his erection.

Allie never broke eye contact as she positioned herself above his thick length. Hudson swallowed hard as he watched her grasp the back of the leather chair and lower herself onto him, inch by delicious inch. The feel of him filling her was incredible and she had to resist the urge to groan at the sweet invasion.

Leveraging against the back of the chair, she rose up and down in a slow, fluid movement. Hudson bit back a hiss and gripped her waist. He tried to hold her in place but she rocked her hips, riding him with each silent glide of the chair. Up and down. Over and over. He glanced down to where they were joined, struggling to maintain his composure and keep a level voice as she tortured him with each measured stroke.

"Update me on Monday," he bit out, grinding back on his molars and practically throwing the phone in its cradle. "Fuck, Allie." He groaned and took her mouth with a furious need, his tongue moving fast and hot as it slid over hers. His hands were splayed, palming her behind as he rocked her in a strong and dominating rhythm.

Capturing Hudson's face between her hands, Allie held his mouth to hers as he worked her up and down. Her hands raked into his hair and she cried out into his mouth, her muscles clenching as an intense orgasm rolled through her. A groan vibrated in the back of his throat, mixing with her cries as his hips pumped up, riding out the spasms of his release.

Allie collapsed against Hudson's chest for the second time in as many hours. She lay there for a long while before regaining the ability to speak. "Sorry to interrupt your call," she finally said, her breathing still erratic.

"Don't be." He buried his nose in her hair. "You can top me like that anytime."

Confused, Allie lifted her head. "What?"

"What you just did, always a welcome interruption. Encouraged even."

"Are you finished?"

He flashed a salacious grin. "For a few minutes anyway."

"No." She rolled her eyes. "I meant are you finished with your work?"

"I'm all yours." Hudson slid his hand up the side of her throat. His eyes burned with sincerity as he brushed his thumb across her cheek. "Does this mean you've decided to stay?"

She knew she shouldn't—it would only make things harder in the end—but she seemed incapable of denying him anything. Biting her lip, she gave a small, shy nod.

"Good. What would you like to do today? I know what I'd like to do, and since a few minutes have passed . . ." Hudson flexed his hips, rolling his already hardening arousal against her.

"Give a girl a chance to catch her breath," she said with a laugh. Her fingers played with the hair at the nape of his neck as she considered their options. "What would you do if I weren't here?"

"Work," he answered matter-of-factly. "You?"

She shrugged. "Shop, go to a movie."

"Well, you've already *shopped* my closet." He hooked a finger in the neck of her borrowed dress shirt. "But I do have a home theater. Movie?"

"We never did get to see a movie together."

Hudson frowned. "I couldn't afford the price of the tickets back then."

"Well, now's your chance." Allie placed a swift kiss on the corner of Hudson's mouth before climbing off his lap. "If you're lucky, I might even let you hold my hand."

"Hold your hand? Oh, Miss Sinclair, I plan to do a lot more than just hold your hand."

18

*A*llie followed Hudson to the second floor of his penthouse. When they reached the top of the stairs she felt as though she was peering into a gallery at an art museum. She was dying to get a closer look at the oversize canvases lining both sides of the darkened hallway, curious to see what type of artwork Hudson had chosen to decorate his home, but he stopped at the first door, opening it and gesturing for her to step inside.

As she did, a dozen Art Deco wall sconces flared to life, revealing five rows of oversize leather chairs. Large speakers were camouflaged in walls that were painted a deep burgundy, and heavy velvet curtains hung on both sides of a silver screen. It was so reminiscent of the golden age of cinema that Allie half expected to find gilded balcony seating behind her. Instead she found Hudson, standing in front of a wet bar that ran the length of the rear wall.

"Would you like popcorn?" he asked, motioning to a professional grade, state-of-the-art popcorn machine.

She raised a skeptical brow. "Do you know how to use that?"

Hudson frowned at the machine. "No, but I can make this."

Reaching up, he opened a cabinet and pulled out a box of microwave popcorn. The sight of him—so strong and powerful and yet so completely befuddled by another high-end, high-cost appliance—was so amusing that she had to press her lips together to stifle a giggle.

"Or perhaps I can interest you in something sweet?"

Her eyes grew wide as he opened the next cabinet. Sno-Caps, Twizzlers, Skittles, Junior Mints. The list went on and on. Hudson's theater had a selection of candy to rival any Cineplex concession stand. Allie chewed her bottom lip as she considered her choice. "Can't go wrong with Swedish Fish," she finally said.

Hudson grinned and handed her one of the bright yellow bags. "One of Nick's favorites." He grabbed an iPad from its charger and took her by the hand, leading her down the carpeted aisle and into a row of chairs. Once they were settled, he swiped his finger across the touch screen, accessing an impressive library of films.

"What do you want to watch?"

"I don't care," she said, already tearing into her candy. "You pick."

"*Pirates of the Caribbean*? If memory serves, that was the movie you wanted to see that summer." He tapped the icon featuring Jack Sparrow and smirked. "Had a crush on Johnny Depp, if I recall."

Allie's mouth popped open. "I did not!"

He held her stare, teasing her with his you-are-so-busted smile until her cheeks heated. She tucked her chin down, muttering to herself while digging a candy fish out of the bag. "And anyway, it was Orlando Bloom."

Hudson chuckled as he hit play. With the push of another button he dimmed the lights. "No difference, still one hundred and forty-three minutes in the dark." He set the iPad on the vacant seat next to him and leaned toward Allie. His voice was a low whisper. "You know, I would have made out with you the moment the lights went down."

"You mean you would have *tried* to make out with me."

"And succeeded."

"Shh," she hushed him. "It's starting."

About the time Elizabeth Swann yelled "parley", Hudson gave an exaggerated yawn. He stretched his arms high above his head, and when he lowered them, one managed to land smoothly around Allie. She glanced down to see his hand resting on her shoulder and gave a small smile as she popped another piece of candy into her mouth.

After a few minutes Hudson's hand moved toward her breast. Not taking her eyes off the screen, Allie reached for his hand and discreetly placed it back on her shoulder. But even with her eyes forward, she caught a glimpse of his amused grin. Clearly he was a man who enjoyed a challenge, and something told her he'd just declared "game on."

Sure enough, after a few more minutes passed, his hand once again began to wander. But this time he stopped halfway and waited. He watched her out of the corner of his eye, and when she made no protest, he slowly extended one finger, leisurely drawing a circle around the taut peak of her breast. Allie remained impassive, merely covering her hand with his and sliding it back to her shoulder.

Hudson leaned closer and let his lips drift up the column of her throat. "I know what you're doing," he whispered against her ear, grazing the lobe with his teeth.

Still not taking her eyes off the screen, Allie inclined her head towards his. "I have no idea what you're talking about."

His tongue traced the shell of her ear. "Fine. If that's how you want to play it."

Allie felt the knuckles of his free hand brush the bare skin just above her knee. She glanced down to see the fabric of her borrowed shirt inching higher as his broad palm glided slowly up the inside of her thigh. Her breath hitched and yet, like any good girl would, she pressed her legs together to halt his progress.

Hudson groaned in protest as he sucked on the sensitive skin below her ear. He was driving her positively mad—licking, sucking, nipping—but she was determined not to give in to his advances. This movie was about enjoying something they'd never had the chance to experience in the past. Seventeen- year-old Allie would have never let nineteen-year-old Hudson feel her up in a movie theater.

But he was damn well going to try.

His hand was back on her knee in minutes, leaving a trail of goose bumps in his wake as his fingers traced the hem of the linen shirt. Featherlight touches moving back and forth. Back and forth.

"Hudson." His name came out on a breathy whisper.

"Yes, Allie?"

"I want . . ."

She felt his rough stubble on her skin as he smiled against her neck. "Want what?

"Popcorn."

Hudson's hands and lips stilled. He lifted his head and the expression on his face had her biting the inside of her cheek to keep from smiling. After a few shell-shocked beats he got up, cursing under his breath as he adjusted the erection so obviously straining against the fly of his jeans. Allie waited until she heard the opening of cabinets before peeking over her shoulder to spy on him through the space between the seats. In the flickering light she saw him rip open the plastic wrapper on the popcorn before tossing it in the microwave and jabbing at the buttons. He waited impatiently, running his hand through his hair before leaning down to watch the carousel through the glass. He popped the door open the minute the microwave chimed.

"Fuck!" He dropped the steaming bag on the counter and shook his fingers. "Shit!"

Allie clasped her hand over her mouth to contain her giggle. She watched Hudson pick up the offending bag with a napkin and then straightened in her seat so as not to be discovered. He'd just made it to their row when he halted midstride and made a quick U-turn back to the concession area. She heard the sound of a refrigerator door open and then close, and a moment later he was back at her side.

"Had a feeling you'd ask for this next," he said, holding out a can of Diet Coke.

She took the can from him, genuinely concerned but unable to hide her smile. "Are you okay?"

"Nothing a skin graft won't fix," he grumbled, tearing open the bag and offering her some of the popcorn.

Allie helped herself to a handful, then turned her attention back to the movie in time to catch one of her favorite shots of the handsome Will Turner.

"I don't see the appeal," Hudson said.

She rolled her eyes and reached back into the bag of popcorn. "You're a guy, you wouldn't understand."

"Try me. It's the leather pants, isn't it?"

She whipped her head around to look at him. "Why, do you have a pair?"

He grinned. "No, but consider it my first order of business."

His arm draped across Allie's shoulders once again, only this time she snuggled against him. For the next two hours Allie watched sword fights between pirates and skeletons while Hudson continued his amorous assault. One step forward, two steps backs. He was relentless and she loved every minute of it.

The moment the credits rolled she was tugged across his lap. His mouth found hers and he kissed her fiercely. As if he had to. As if the past one hundred and forty-three minutes had been the longest of his life. And despite her game, she kissed him back.

Her fingers wound into his hair, holding him close as he deepened the kiss. His hand slid over her bare thigh and she felt the prod of his erection digging into her behind. He gripped her waist, shifting her so she straddled him, and with a flex of his hips pressed himself against her. *Oh yes, just like that.*

His lips moved lower, nibbling her neck, and she let her head fall back on a soft moan as he flexed up once more. She closed her eyes, reveling in the delicious friction as he slowly rubbed her through the worn denim of his jeans. If he kept it up, she'd be reaching for his fly in no time. It would be so easy. A few popped buttons, a subtle shift of her hips . . .

"Hudson?"

"Hmm?" he answered against her skin.

"What's for dinner?"

He lifted his head. "Dinner? Now?"

"Yes." She tried her hardest to keep a straight face. "Movie dates usually include dinner."

"Christ, woman, you're making my balls bluer than you did ten years ago." He flashed her a hopeful grin that made him look every bit the horny teen she remembered. "Can we eat in bed?"

She laughed. "In bed? On a first date?"

The noise he made was somewhere between animal and human. "Way past first dates, Allie." Moving her off his lap, he reached into the pocket of his jeans and pulled out his cell phone.

"Who are you calling?"

"Any place that will deliver in thirty minutes or less."

19

*A*llie couldn't remember the last time she had pizza for dinner. She lifted a second slice out of the cardboard box and took a bite. Mmm, delicious. Her eyes drifted shut for a moment, and when she opened them Hudson was staring at her, one brow slightly raised.

"No placemats, plates, or fine silver? When did you become the type to eat straight out of the box?"

"Are you forgetting the picnics we used to have when your shift was over?" Eating greasy food out of takeout cartons was something Allie had never done before she met Hudson. In fact, she'd done a lot of things with him that were outside her norm. And yet, they always felt so right.

"That was a long time ago."

A beat of silence passed between them.

"And what about you? When did you become the type to wear a suit and tie every day?"

Hudson reached for the nearly empty bottle of merlot and split the remainder between their two glasses. "I'm still not, but Wall Street continues to equate success with the ability to strangle oneself with a five-hundred-dollar tie." He leaned against the back of the barstool and took a sip of his wine. "All part of a strategic and well-crafted game."

"One you obviously play quite well. This place is amazing. I can't believe you have a movie theater upstairs." She narrowed her eyes at him as she reached for her glass. "What else do you have hidden behind closed doors?"

Hudson leaned closer, a wicked gleam in his eyes, and dropped a kiss to her lips. "Eat up and I'll show you."

When they finished eating, Allie followed him to the foyer. "The study you've already seen, as with my bedroom." He smirked at her before gesturing to a split staircase. "Downstairs are guest rooms, a gym, and staff quarters. But the rooms upstairs are my favorite."

She took his offered hand as he led her up the same staircase they'd taken on their way to the theater. Only this time they continued farther down the wide hallway, affording her a full view of the artwork she'd been so curious to see. The paintings she passed were bold, brightly colored abstracts with heavy textured strokes, a few of which she was sure she'd seen hanging in the Art Institute at one time.

Halfway down the hall Hudson paused in front of a set of carved wood doors standing at least ten feet tall. "This," he said, pushing them open, "was Hefner's office."

The room took Allie's breath away. A ceiling that soared upwards of fifteen feet with elaborate plaster designs; walls that were covered in recessed mahogany panels; a herringbone wood floor polished to a glossy shine; a limestone fireplace flanked by leather wingback chairs; and velvet drapes framing French doors that led to a stone terrace with potted palms. The entire room looked to be in its original 1920s condition. It was as if she'd stepped out of the Palmolive building and straight into the pages of *The Great Gatsby*. She was so enthralled by her surroundings that it took a few moments for Hudson's words to register.

"Wait, did you say Hefner's office?"

He nodded. "Fully restored."

"What . . . how?"

"This was his office when he launched his magazine in the fifties. A few years later he opened his first club here as well."

Allie gaped at him. "You live in the Playboy Club?"

"Yes. Interested in wearing a bunny outfit, Miss Sinclair?"

She smiled coyly. "Particular fantasy of yours, Mr. Chase?"

"Second only to Princess Leia's gold bikini." He flashed her a heart-stopping, panty-dropping grin, and in that moment she was quite sure he could talk her into wearing either if it meant his hands and mouth touching her. "Come," he said as if reading her mind. "There's more."

He led her to the very end of the hallway and yet another set of double doors. "This is my favorite room of all." Allie didn't think anything could top the room she'd just seen. But then Hudson swung the door open and she realized she'd been wrong. "The game room," he said.

Allie whistled through her teeth. "Quite the man cave you have here."

Like the previous room, this one was decorated in warm, rich colors. Dark hammer beams spanned the vaulted ceiling, spaced every six feet or so with trusses that came down to meet the walls where they divided the arched, floor-to-ceiling windows. Travertine tiles were covered with thick oriental rugs, and a large pool table sat front and center. Allie's hand trailed along the table's red baize as she admired the intricate bevels on the amber light fixture hanging above it.

"The room doesn't get much use unless Nick's here."

She looked up at him, surprised.

"If I'm home, I'm working." His mouth curved into a knowing smile. "With the exception of this weekend."

Hudson leaned his hip against the side of the pool table, casually crossing his arms as he watched her move farther into the room. She smiled back at him before turning her attention to the mahogany bar. A flat screen television was mounted to a stone-covered wall behind the bar, flanked on either side by glass shelving with enough high-end liquor to stock Tavern for the weekend. In front of the bar two leather chesterfield sofas sat facing each other, and on the wall across from them hung a dart-board worthy of any Irish pub. A giggle escaped her lips as she pictured the boy who'd tried to impress her by besting a game of carnival darts on his brother's behalf.

"Something funny, Alessandra?"

"I was just remembering that carnival dart game. The look on your face every time you had to hand over another dollar." She giggled again. He must have gone through a week's worth of tips that night.

"You think you could have done better?" he asked, pushing away from the pool table and sauntering toward her.

She shot him a teasing grin. "Well, I think I could have popped three green balloons in less than an hour, that's for sure."

Hudson cocked his head to one side. "Less than an hour, eh?" It was a rhetorical question, one he considered for a moment before strolling over to the board and lifting the six darts from their holes. "A game of Five-O-One?" He smirked as he approached, offering her three of the darts, feather tip forward. "You don't even have to beat me in less than an hour."

She tilted her chin up, holding his stare as she took the darts from his hand. "Challenge accepted."

He smiled down at her, his eyes shining with amusement, before tucking his darts into the back pocket of his jeans and heading for the bar. "Would you like another glass of wine? I can open a bottle."

"Trying to get me drunk? Compromise my abilities, perhaps?"

"Simply being a good host." He feigned politeness, but she knew it was an act. If there was one thing she'd learned about the modern-day version of Hudson Chase it was that he would go to any lengths to get what he wanted. But he was about to find out that he wasn't the only one who played to win.

"I'll take a bottle of whatever you're having."

Hudson's brow shot up. "Well, you're full of surprises today, aren't you?" He yanked open the glass door of a fridge displaying rows of every beer imaginable and grabbed two Heinekens. "Would you like a glass?" he asked, popping the tops off the green bottles.

"Nope, bottle's fine. Maybe some music?"

"Won't break your concentration, will it?"

She could see he was fighting a smile. *We'll just see who's laughing when this is over.* "Appreciate the concern, but I think I can manage."

"U2 okay?"

"Perfect."

He reached for a remote control and a moment later "Mysterious Ways" filled the room. She watched him move toward her, Allie's senses bombarded by the seductive beat of the music and the mesmerizing swagger of his walk. By the time he was standing in front of her, she'd completely lost her train of thought. He offered her one of the bottles and she took a long sip.

Hudson gestured toward the dartboard. "Ladies first."

Allie nearly choked on her drink as she recalled Harper's oh-so-tactful mention of that same phrase. After wiping her mouth, she set her beer on the bar and took her place in front of the board. She planted her feet solidly on the floor and raised her elbow to take aim, only to have Hudson walk up behind her and snake his arm around her waist.

"Oh no, baby, from back here," he said, tugging her farther.

She couldn't say for sure, but she suspected he'd pulled her far beyond the regulated distance. A devious smile formed on her lips. Perhaps she'd give him something to think about during his first toss, even the playing field a bit. Her hips swayed in his grasp as she shimmied against him to the beat of the music.

Hudson groaned. "Keep doing that and this is going to be a very short game." He gave her ass a quick smack before strolling over to the bar and sliding onto one of the padded leather stools.

Once again, she positioned her feet. Raising her right arm, she released the dart in a smooth motion, breaking out in a wide grin when it landed in the inner ring of the ten. She tossed the next two in quick succession. One landed on the outer ring of the eight and the other squarely in the nine. "I believe that's fifty-five points for me, Mr. Chase." She stepped aside, motioning for him to take his turn before retrieving her darts from the board.

"Well done." Hudson took a drink from his beer before setting it on the bar.

"Thank you." She waited for him to take his place before continuing. "It's all in the fingers, you know." He raised his arm, but his gaze drifted to her hands as she absentmindedly slid a dart between the pad of her thumb and her fingertips. His eyes flared ever so slightly before refocusing on the board. "How you grasp the shaft," she added when he began to throw.

The dart slipped from his hand, landing haphazardly on the two. Hudson turned to face her and raised a brow. "We'll test that theory later with a demonstration." Recovering, he tossed the next two darts with milder success, landing the second on the fifteen and the third on the outer ring of the six. "Twenty-nine points," he said, pulling his darts out in quick jabbing motions. "You're up."

Allie was enjoying every moment of his torment, and when her next turn yielded an inner five, a straight-up three, and a bull's-eye, she had to fight the urge to break into a happy dance. As it was she clapped her hands together and grinned like a fool. "Yes!" she yelled. "Sixty-eight points."

"Lucky toss," he mumbled as she sashayed passed him.

She pulled two darts out of the board and then paused with her hand on the one in the bull's-eye. Looking over her shoulder at him, she smiled innocently. "Do you want to get this one? See what a bull's-eye looks like up close?"

Hudson moved into position. "Savor it. May well be your last."

Allie leaned against the bar, sipping her beer and taking a moment to admire the view. Nothing beat the sight of Hudson Chase's ass in a pair of tight jeans . . . except maybe naked . . . his muscles flexing . . . her heels urging him deeper. . . .

"Like what you see?" he asked.

Her head snapped up to find him grinning at her like the Cheshire Cat, and her cheeks burned crimson. Ignoring his question, she turned her attention to the board where Hudson's dart had landed on the outer twenty. She heard a low chuckle just before he tossed the next dart. It landed on the inner fifteen, followed quickly by the third, which landed on the eight.

"One hundred and two," he announced. "It's all about not jerking the release and following through."

She smirked at him. "Oh, don't you worry, I wouldn't dream of jerking a release."

The corner of his mouth quirked up and he shook his head.

"Well done, by the way." She added his score to her mental tally. "Although I'm still in the lead." She raised her elbow, preparing to take her next turn, when he came up behind her.

"Not by much." His hands moved over her hips before pushing between her thighs, widening her stance. "Spread your legs for me," he murmured. Her breath hitched and she felt him smile against her temple. "Thatta girl, now you're in the correct position."

The hard ridge of his arousal pushed into her behind and Allie felt a hot rush between her legs. She wanted to push back, grind herself against him, but he stepped away. "Whenever you're ready," he said.

She raised her arm, inadvertently shifting her weight to one foot and dropping her shoulder. The dart arched upward and landed so weakly that it barely managed to cling to the board. Allie frowned over the measly three points.

"Your balance seemed a bit off."

"Oh, really? I wonder why?"

"Try relaxing your legs."

She raised a single brow. "I don't think my stance was the problem."

"Debatable, Miss Sinclair. But either way, I don't see how this is my fault."

"If you would behave yourself I could beat you blindfolded."

"Is that right?" His mouth twisted in contemplation. "Wait here a moment," he instructed before leaving the room. He returned a few minutes later with what appeared to be an airline sleep mask. As he drew closer he stretched the elastic wide and lifted the mask over her head.

Laughing, she took a small step back. "It was only a figure of speech."

"Afraid of the challenge?"

She rolled her eyes, but when she made no further protest, he slipped the mask over her head. The room went dark and then his hands were on her shoulders, turning her in a circle.

"I'll even point you in the right direction," he said.

On her next two tosses she heard the darts thud against the wall, then clatter to the floor.

"I'm not familiar with all the rules, Alessandra. Does the floor count as negative points?"

She could hear the smug amusement in his voice. "Okay, you made your point. Can we get back to the real game now?" Anxious to put an end to the pointless exercise, she reached for the edge of the mask.

"Wait," he said. Her hand froze in midair. Hudson suddenly behind her again, his lips hovering at her ear. "Keep it on."

"Keep it on?" Why on earth did he want her to keep the blindfold on? *Oh . . .*

"I want to take you further." His voice was low and full of dark promise. "Will you let me do that, Allie?"

Her mouth went dry and she swallowed hard. When she spoke it was barely a whisper. "Okay."

"Good. Don't move."

Allie heard footsteps followed by the creak of the door. And then nothing. All she could hear was the sound of her own blood rushing in her ears. When had the music stopped playing? She inhaled slowly, trying to calm her erratic breathing as she waited. And waited. She fidgeted, wondering what was taking him so long. But more importantly, what was he going to do to her? *He's probably a little kinky, too.* A tremor of uncertainty ran through her as Harper's words replayed in her head.

The door shut behind her and she jumped. Hudson was in the room. She couldn't see him but she could feel his presence. It made her skin tingle. The sound system hissed to life and a few seconds later the hypnotic rhythm of U2's "Moment of Surrender" wafted down from speakers above her. She listened intently, trying to decipher where he was, what he was doing. The unknown was driving her crazy.

Something brushed her hair aside and her head jerked. His fingertips—no, his lips—touched her shoulder, then her neck. "I won't push you any further than I think you can handle." His words sent a mixture of anxiety and excitement coursing through her veins. "If it gets to be too much, all you have to do is tell me to stop. Do you understand, Allie?"

Her heart pounded in anticipation. "Yes."

"Then let's start by getting you naked." He ran his fingers down the buttons of her shirt, unfastening each one at an excruciatingly slow pace. When he finally finished he pushed it off her shoulders and tossed it aside. His fingertips traced the edge of her bra cup and she shuddered. Her nipples tightened against the white lace, eager for his touch, but he left them bereft and straining against the rough fabric.

"I already removed these once," he said, hooking his thumbs into the waistband of her borrowed boxer briefs. She felt him drop to his knees in front of her as he swept them down her legs. "Don't make me do it again." Reaching out blindly, she steadied herself on his shoulder as he lifted one foot and then the other. "I want you ready for me to have anytime and anywhere I wish." He gripped her hips with both hands and yanked her closer. She gasped as he nuzzled the apex of her thighs, inhaling deeply. "Turn around."

She complied immediately and felt his knuckles brush the length of her spine. It was as if every nerve in her body sprang to attention. He unclasped her bra, then let his fingers skim her shoulders, leaving a trail of goose bumps in his wake as he slipped the straps down her arms.

The blindfold might have denied her the sight of him, but her other senses were keenly aware as he pressed in close behind her. The sound of his breathing, the smell of his skin, the heat radiating from his body. All of it was brought more sharply into focus.

His hand fisted in the hair at the nape of her neck and he pulled. Angling her head to the side, he ran his tongue up the side of her exposed throat before softly kissing the skin beneath her ear. "I want you to think of nothing but what I'm doing to you," he whispered, his voice hot and impassioned. "Don't feel anything but me."

Everything below her waist tensed with need as a wave of lust and want seized her.

"Do you trust me?" he asked, releasing her hair.

"Of course." She answered without hesitation, and as she spoke the words she realized that, despite her earlier concern, she did trust him. Completely.

He cupped her elbow and led her across the room, turning

her so that her back was against the wall. "I'm going to cuff you now."

Allie inhaled sharply. *Cuff me?* This was so beyond anything she had ever experienced, or even imagined. And yet she couldn't deny the excitement pulsing between her legs.

"Give me your hands." She held them out and he took her right hand in one of his, kissing the inside of her wrist before securing the cuff. "They're soft, so they won't hurt."

She had expected some sort of metal handcuffs, but what Hudson strapped around her felt like a wide band of fabric. Leather, maybe. Something hung from the end of the cuff and she felt it brush against her naked thigh. She assumed it was the other cuff but there was something else as well; something cold, like metal. A chain? Her breathing grew shallow as longing and desire mixed with nervous anticipation.

"Hands above your head," he ordered. His voice had taken on a hard, authoritative edge. She quickly did as she was told, and whatever was attached to the other end of the chain now dangled by her shoulder. She felt him reach for it and a moment later heard the sounds of something rough sliding over wood. The image of the beams spanning the ceiling before arching down to meet the walls flashed through her head, and at once she realized she was being chained to one of the trusses. She pressed her thighs together, shocked at the dampness she felt there over the thought of being chained to Hudson's ceiling, completely at his mercy.

Hudson took her left wrist and brought it to his lips before lifting it back above her head and securing the second cuff. He was standing closer now, so close she could feel his warm breath on her face. So close she could lean forward and run her tongue along the soft stubble on his jaw. So close her lips could find his. She inclined her head ever so slightly but he stepped back, leaving her feeling vulnerable and exposed.

The sultry beat of the music was the only sound in the room

and yet she knew he was still there, watching her. Even blind-folded she felt the heat of his stare. The thought of those piercing blue eyes drinking in every inch of her made a warm blush wash over her skin.

"You look beautiful like this," he said. Then his arms were around her, hauling her against him as his mouth claimed hers in a deep, possessive kiss. "Remember," he rasped over her lips, "all you have to do is tell me to stop." He kissed her again and she went lax in his arms. "Do you want me to stop, Allie?"

"No." Her answer was more breath than voice.

"Good."

Allie felt him pull back and she longed to wrap her arms around him and keep her chest crushed against his. She tugged on her restraints but it was no use, and just like that, he was gone again. She heard the slow metallic sound of a zipper opening, followed by the shuffling of fabric, and she knew that he was naked. Her heart thudded faster as she waited for his return.

"You teased me endlessly for one hundred and forty-three minutes. It's only fair that I return the favor."

"What are you going to do?" She turned her head toward the soft voice that had crooned in her ear, but a moment later it was on the other side.

"I'm going to make you come until you can't breathe. Until you're begging to have me inside you."

Hudson's fingers glided over her rib cage and her back arched, pushing her breasts into his hands. He palmed the soft flesh before rolling her nipples between his thumb and forefinger. Her body trembled with anticipation as he kissed his way down her neck, nipping and licking his way closer to the tight peaks. She groaned when he finally wrapped his lips around one of her nipples and drew it deep into his mouth.

"Please . . ."

"Please, what?" he asked, working his way across her chest.

"Touch me."

She felt him smile against her skin. "Oh no, baby, tonight we're following my rules." And with that his mouth closed over her other nipple, sucking until it grew hard and long against his tongue, then gently blowing across the sensitive skin before claiming it once again. He kept up the delicious torture, teasing her breasts with his talented fingers and lips until her head fell back on a groan. Then his teeth tugged hard on one nipple while his fingers pinched the other, and the sweet sensation echoed through her core. Pulling against the restraints, she cried out, her body convulsing and shattering into a thousand pieces.

"I love how you look when you come," he growled. "It makes me so fucking hard." Hudson's thumb pressed against her chin, forcing her mouth open as he thrust his tongue deep inside her mouth in an unforgiving kiss. His hand moved between her legs and his fingers slid back and forth over her slick flesh, stroking and teasing her as he expertly worked that sensitive place between her thighs.

"Does that feel good?" he asked, slipping a finger inside her.

She whimpered and rocked against his hand. "Yes."

His finger eased in and out, perfectly matching the music's steady, unhurried rhythm. "You're so ready for me, Alessandra. Open your mouth."

She parted her lips, completely seduced by the touch of his hand. She expected to feel the sweet invasion of his tongue once again and was shocked when instead it was his finger that pushed into her mouth. "Suck," he said in a low, commanding voice. "Taste how hot you are for this."

Her mouth closed around Hudson's finger and she sucked, tasting her own arousal.

"Don't stop sucking me." His words ignited the ache between her legs and she moaned around the fullness in her mouth. She sucked harder, then let her tongue swirl over his finger as she drew back. She heard his sharp intake of breath and a second later he lunged at her, crushing his lips to hers and sliding his tongue into her with lush, velvety strokes.

When he finally broke their kiss her breath left her in a wordless rush.

"You taste so good," he murmured. "My tongue knows your taste already."

She tugged against her restraints, trying to absorb the multitude of feelings overwhelming her senses.

"Do you want to come again?"

"Please . . ." She panted, her chest rising and falling with each heavy breath.

"How?"

"You know how."

His nose brushed against hers. "How, Alessandra?"

"Touch me," she whispered.

"Like this?" Two fingers pushed into her on a sleek glide and she gasped.

"Yes . . ."

"You sure?" His voice was low and measured but his breath was rough at her ear.

"Yes, Hudson." She was hanging on the edge, near mindless with her need for release. "Please, make me come."

The tempo of his fingers quickened and she threw her head back, lost in the delicious friction.

"That's it, baby. Just feel it. Let yourself go."

Her body began to climb as he rolled the pad of his thumb over the top of her sex, taking her higher and higher until she fell apart in his hands.

"I'm right here," he murmured. His arms banded around her as her knees buckled and she sagged against him. "I've got you."

Her head wilted against his chest as she melted into his embrace. The aftershocks of her orgasm made her entire body shudder, and she moaned softly. Hudson slipped the blindfold off Allie's head and she blinked up at him as her eyes adjusted to the light of the now dimly lit room. Unbuckling the cuffs, he released her wrists and moved her closer to the chesterfield. The soft leather cushions looked like heaven to her. A nice rest on the couch was exactly what she needed.

But instead of leading her to the front of the sofa, Hudson guided her to the side and folded her over the padded arm. Allie's eyes grew wide, and any fatigue she'd been feeling was instantly erased by the sudden rush of adrenaline.

"I've been waiting all afternoon to bend you over and fuck you deep and hard." His words were an erotic threat and her body responded, clenching tightly as a fresh wave of desire consumed her. He pulled her hips back with a sharp tug and pushed his foot against hers to spread her legs wide. "Grip the couch and don't let go," he ordered, his voice hoarse and urgent.

Allie's arms felt weak but she did as he asked. She braced herself for his assault, her fingers digging into the supple leather. His hands squeezed her hips and she felt the blunt head of him slipping against her as he guided himself to where she was wet and ready.

His length pushed deep inside her and her mouth dropped open. "Fuck, Allie, I can't get enough of you." He pulled back slowly, and with a shift of his hips, slammed back into her with a powerful surge. "You feel so good around my cock."

Over and over he plunged into her, jolting her forward against the arm of the couch with each punishing thrust. "Hold on," he ground out between clenched teeth. She tightened her grasp on the cushions as he yanked her back to meet his hips.

His drives were merciless, and in no time her insides began to quicken in surrender. Then his palm was on her shoulder, pulling her upright so that she felt every hard inch of him thrusting inside her. His lips found her neck and then his teeth grazed her ear. "Come for me again. I want you with me."

Her body exploded with pleasure as the sweet release of her orgasm rolled through her. Hudson jerked against her, shouting her name on an explosive breath as he joined her in release. She was vaguely aware that they were sinking to the floor, but to her it felt as though she were falling, spiraling as she lost all sense of self.

When she regained her senses she was in Hudson's lap, cradled in his arms.

"You okay?" he asked, covering her face with tender kisses.

"Hmmm." She leaned her head against his chest, murmuring her assent, and felt his low chuckle vibrate against her cheek.

"Is that a yes?"

She looked up at him and nodded shyly. "I'll play darts with you any day."

"I'm always up for a challenge, Miss Sinclair." His arms tightened around her and he pressed a soft kiss to the top of her head. They sat like that for several minutes before he rose to his feet, hauling Allie up with him. "Come," he said. "I have a rain check I plan to cash in."

overing over Allie, Hudson smoothed the hair away from her damp face. "I could get used to this, waking up in you." His erection was still twitching inside of her as he dipped his head and brushed his lips to hers.

"Not a bad way to start a Monday morning." Allie's lips curved into a lazy grin. "And unless that was a very erotic dream, I believe I woke up the same way during the night. In fact," she slid her foot along his muscular calf, "I think you've spent most of the weekend inside me."

"Hmm . . . I've been incredibly greedy with you" He withdrew from her, rolled over onto his back, and pulled Allie across his chest. "I'm making up for all the times you said 'no' ten years ago."

"You were very persistent, I'll give you that."

He smiled. "I was beginning to think 'no' was the extent of your vocabulary."

"What did you expect? I was a good girl." She rested her chin on her hands. "And you, Hudson Chase, were every bit the bad boy back then."

His brow lifted. "Back then? And now?" His tongue traced

her bottom lip before tugging it between his teeth for a long erotic moment. "Have I lost my touch?" His finger caressed the contours of her spine.

"Hardly. But you know what I mean. That swagger . . ." Her voice wavered at the end as his hand smoothed over the curve of her ass.

Hudson chuckled. "Swagger?"

"Yes. And the way you looked at me." Her eyes dropped for a split second, then met his. "From the moment I saw you, I knew you were nothing but trouble."

"And I knew you were a spoiled, uptight pain in the ass."

Allie's jaw dropped and she playfully hit him on the chest.

"And the most beautiful girl I'd ever laid eyes on." Hudson gently tucked a strand of hair behind her ear and his eyes roamed over her face. "What would you ever want with a guy like me?"

"Because when I was with you," her voice softened, "no one ever made me feel so alive. I couldn't stay away."

"Yet you still said no."

Allie smiled shyly at him. "I almost said yes."

He pushed up on an elbow. "You did?"

She nodded. "The night you took me out on the water taxi, just the two of us. I always wondered if you had permission to take the boat out that night."

"It might have been a slight misuse of company property." He eased back against the pillows and smirked.

"I suspected as much." She laughed. "Well then, I guess it's a good thing I said no. Could you imagine if we'd been caught?"

Hudson shifted to his side, wrapped his arms around Allie's waist, and hauled her against his hard chest. "With our pants down? Not a terrible image."

He nuzzled the back of her neck and sucked the skin at the nape. God, he wanted her again. He wanted her nails scoring his back and her tongue in his mouth as she writhed beneath him.

Then when they were through, to sleep with her in his arms once again.

His fingers splayed on the flat of her stomach as he pressed his heavy cock into her behind. Allie let out a soft moan and her body arched back to meet his. "What do you want, Allie?"

"You," she murmured, her hips slowly rocking against him.

"Show me where you want me to go." In a slow sweep, Hudson ran his palm down her arm and laced his fingers with hers. As he did, he felt the facets of the rock on her hand dig into his finger. His eyes closed. The juxtaposition of where they'd been moments ago and the reality of how this might inevitably end slammed inside his skull.

"I have to get ready for work." He flung the covers back and dropped his legs over the side of the bed. Pushing to his feet, he scrubbed a hand down his face and strode to the bathroom. He stood in the center of the room for a moment and breathed deeply, taking a time-out like a fucking toddler. He was pissed. He hated that ring on her finger. He hated the dandy prick who put it there. The more he thought about it, the more it ratcheted up the possessive male in him. He was an idiot to think one lost weekend with her would ever sate his need, though he wished like hell that it had. He wanted more and he was willing to take the time, for now. He'd use the next two weeks to show her how good they were together. But then he had to do it. Before that Julian what-the-fuck-do-you-need-a-title-for returned, he had to lay out his demands for her to choose.

The hell if he was going to be the other man in her life. He wanted to be *the* man in her life.

Fighting the impulse to go back in there, he yanked the glass door of the shower open and cranked the faucets on full blast. Not bothering to wait for the water to reach steaming, he stepped under the spray. The frigid water hit his chest and sluiced down his abs to his aching erection. He hoped the cold water would shock it into some flaccid state.

No such luck.

He braced his palms against the granite and allowed his head to drop forward, shoving whatever thoughts he had to the side and focusing on the hot water hitting the back of his neck and shoulders. A moment later he heard the shower door open and felt Allie's arms slip around his waist.

"Please," she said, pressing a trail of tender kisses along his back. "Don't ruin this."

Despite his temper and the strain of keeping his mouth shut doing a number on his brain, he wanted her.

Hudson dropped his arms and turned around. Their eyes met and suddenly he didn't care anymore about the thoughts poisoning his psyche. His hand slid up the side of her throat and into her hair. As his fingers fisted into the silky blond curls, he slanted his mouth over hers. His tongue parted her lips, going deep and taking over.

Allie arched into him and he groaned into her mouth at the feel of her nipples brushing against his chest. His hands roamed all over her tight body, from the gentle slope of her breasts to the curve of her waist and the top of her hips.

Maneuvering Allie against the glass, his fingers dug possessively into the flesh of her thigh and he curled her leg around his hip. His erection brushed between her legs as he positioned himself. He sucked in a sharp breath. She was so fucking hot and wet.

Primitive instinct taking over, he curled the end of his spine, joining their bodies. A breathless cry escaped her mouth and her core tightened, taking him deeper. She gripped his shoulders and her eyes fluttered closed as she gave herself up to him.

"Open your eyes," he demanded. "See what you do to me." His hips flexed forward and pulled back, sending a vicious ache up his cock to be back inside her. "You've stripped me raw."

Allie met his stare as she rocked into each of his thrusts. In that moment he knew she needed this as much as he did. It wasn't going to help them get through the words that needed to be said, but for now this skin-to-skin contact was what they had. He pushed into her again, staking his claim, and he knew with every fiber of his being that he wanted to be with her.

Forever.

21

*A*llie's stomach plummeted as the elevator whisked her to the top of the Palmolive building, but not from the force of gravity. She had a wicked case of nerves. Hudson had been in such a foul mood that morning, and even though their physical connection had been every bit as mind blowing, he'd still seemed somewhat distant when she'd left for work.

The image of him in the shower, his head down as the water pulsed over his tense shoulders, had haunted her all day. She knew what he wanted, and if she was honest with herself, she'd admit she was starting to want the same thing.

If only it were that simple.

And it wasn't just the fact that invitations had already been sent out. Yes, her mother would be humiliated to cancel "the event of the holidays," as she'd taken to calling it; but the ramifications of Allie's actions would run much deeper than that. There was Ingram Media to consider as well. Accepting Julian's proposal not only meant the joining of two people, but the merger of two empires as well. Her father had worked hard to ensure a seamless transition when Julian took the helm after their wedding. The two of them had met with nearly every subsidiary over the past month. Deals had been made, contracts had been signed. Wheels were in motion that had far greater implications than simply canceling a caterer.

But the ultimatum was coming. It was only a matter of time. And if that morning was any indication, it would be soon, possibly even tonight. She knew it was selfish of her to want to hold on to him as long as possible, but she couldn't help it. She was an addict and Hudson Chase was her drug.

Allie closed her eyes and tried to calm her erratic breathing, but it was no use. Not knowing what to expect when the doors slid open had her heart accelerating with each passing floor.

The musky scent of flowers washed over her the moment she stepped off the elevator. At least two dozen long-stem roses filled a vase on the round, dark wood table that sat in the center of the foyer. She paused in front of them, her fingers gently cupping the velvety petals of one of the deep red blooms.

"Good evening, Miss Sinclair," Hudson said. He was in the dining room, lighting the last of the crystal votives that lined the center of the table.

As she drew closer, she realized there were candles adorning nearly every surface. Their flickering light reflected off the wall of glass and lit the entire room in a soft glow. Her eyes drifted back to the table set with white linen, fine china, and crystal goblets.

"This is beautiful, Hudson. What's the occasion?"

His gaze met hers and his mouth curved into a shy smile. "My way of apologizing for being an ass."

"You cooked dinner for me?" she asked, unable to hide her surprise.

He chuckled. "Don't give me too much credit. I'm not much of a cook, and since I extended my housekeeper's impromptu vacation, you'll have to settle for something out of a delivery box."

"It smells amazing." Allie set her purse on the back of the couch. "Where's it from?"

"Spiaggia."

She frowned, glancing at him over her shoulder as he helped her out of her coat. "Spiaggia doesn't deliver."

He looked down at her with a smug grin stretched across his face. "For the right price, anyone will deliver, Alessandra."

"You know I would have been happy just ordering a pizza."

"I know, but I'm trying here." Hudson draped her coat over the couch and placed his hand on the small of her back. The gesture, so simple and yet so intimate, sent a shiver up the length of her spine. "Come, sit."

He guided her to the table and pulled out her chair. She sat, unfolding the linen napkin and placing it in her lap. Her mouth watered as one by one he removed sterling silver domes from a half dozen plates of food. It was far too much for just the two of them. As she watched him she realized the table was also set with at least eight different glasses of wine.

"I wasn't sure what you'd like, so I went ahead and ordered the tasting menu." He leaned down and his voice deepened as his lips grazed her ear. "I want to learn what pleases you."

Allie felt her face heat as all manner of erotic images filled her mind. "I believe we've already covered that."

"While I do know your taste," he smirked, "I want to know what you like." Hudson took a seat in the chair next to hers and picked up his knife and fork. "First we have Mediterranean sea bass with marinated Nantucket scallops." He sliced into the tender fish and then paused with a perfect bite suspended in midair. "Allow me?"

"I can feed myself," she began to protest.

"That's not the point. Open."

Feeling slightly foolish, she obliged, opening her mouth and allowing him to feed her. "Mmm . . ." Was that caviar with a hint of lemon? Her eyes drifted shut as she savored the mouthwatering bite. "That's delicious."

Hudson lifted a crystal goblet of a white wine and held it to her lips. "The restaurant pairs it with the 2010 Gavi."

"It's wonderful," she said after sampling the white wine. As Hudson moved the sea bass aside, she was suddenly aware of the soft strains of classical music wafting from the speakers mounted flush with the ceiling. "I didn't know you liked Tchaikovsky."

"It serves more as background noise. To be honest, it all sounds the same to me." He drew another plate closer. "A particular favorite of yours?"

"Absolutely. The Chicago Symphony Orchestra is doing a limited engagement of his Fourth Symphony right now. I had hoped to go, but they're sold out." She watched him prepare the next bite of food, ravioli in cream sauce. "Aren't you going to try any?" she asked when the fork once again hovered over her lips.

"Not yet. I enjoy watching you eat."

She managed to swallow the pasta before rolling her eyes at his comment. "Surely it's not that exciting."

"More than you know." His gaze was dark and penetrating. "The way your lips wrap around the fork. The noises you make. Your eyes fluttering shut as if memorizing every taste." Hudson's words were more intoxicating than the wine, and as he raised the next glass she realized her lips were already parted in anticipation. "Try it with Corino's 2007 Barolo." His eyes never left hers as she sipped the garnet-colored wine. When she finished he cocked his head to the side. "More?"

"Yes, please," she said, her breathless reply revealing a desire for more than just wine.

He offered her another sip before moving the ravioli aside and reaching for the next selection. "Spiaggia is known for their perfect risotto." His lips curved into a wicked grin. "Firm in the mouth and creamy on the tongue."

Oh, this could be fun.

She licked her lips and saw him pause momentarily as he lifted the next forkful. His jaw fell slack as he eased the bite into her mouth, keeping his eyes focused on her lips as she slid the risotto off the fork.

When she was done he offered her a sampling of yet another red wine. She sipped it slowly, relishing the warm, full-bodied flavor. A small drop remained at the corner of her mouth and she gently wiped it with her finger. He inhaled sharply as she pressed her finger to her lips, letting her tongue swirl around the tip before drawing it into her mouth. She moaned in quiet appreciation as she sucked the last bit of wine from her fingertip.

Hudson moved quickly, surprising Allie by locking his hand on the back of her neck and dragging her mouth to his. His lips were demanding against hers, kissing her as if he had to. As if her mouth churning with his was the only thing keeping him alive.

"Ah, God Allie," he groaned, deepening the kiss as his tongue swept over hers in firm, lush strokes. He gripped her around the waist and lifted her out of the chair as he stood. She raised her arms, her aching breasts rising and falling against his chest as her fingers weaved into his hair. His hands slid down her back, cupping her behind and urging her against him, every hard inch of him straining to get closer as his body pressed the length of her.

She was vaguely aware of movement; an arm sweeping out, the sound of dishes and silverware crashing to the floor, and then the table was at her back. "You're making a mess," she panted against his mouth.

"Fuck the mess," he growled. His body arched over hers as he kissed and licked his way down her throat. "I've been thinking about this all day." He dipped his head and his teeth caught her nipple through the fabric of her blouse. She gasped as he tugged hard, the sensation echoing through her core.

Hudson shifted fast and smooth, sweeping Allie's panties down her legs before dropping to his knees. He lifted one leg over his shoulder, spreading her wide, and dragged his tongue up the heart of her. She raised her head and heat pulsed through her veins as she watched him move between her thighs. There was an intensity in the way he consumed her, as if driven by an overwhelming need to give her pleasure.

He gazed up at her with dark, hungry eyes. "I could spend hours between your thighs." His tongue fluttered across her sensitive flesh. "Teasing you . . . tasting you."

She groaned, half afraid he planned to do just that. The stubble of his beard was rough against her skin as he continued his relentless torture. Licking, nipping, sucking. Her head dropped down with a thud and her leg flexed, urging him closer as her stiletto dug into his back.

"Oh no, baby, not yet," he murmured. His breath fanned over her warm, wet skin and she moaned. Her fingers wound through his hair, trying to hold his mouth to her, but he kept her on the brink, changing rhythm whenever her body began to quiver.

"Please, Hudson," she whimpered.

There was nothing gradual or gentle about the way his arms circled her hips, pulling her onto his thrusting tongue. She rocked against him, her hips moving restlessly in a desperate need for release.

"That's it, come for me." His deep drawl vibrated against her and she cried out, splintering apart in a mind-blowing orgasm.

Hudson stood in a rush with her leg still draped over his shoulder. She heard the sound of a buckle and glanced down to see him yank open his fly. Her body still trembled with aftershocks but the sight of his erection springing free had her clenching with need once more. Gripping the back of Allie's thigh, he lifted her other leg over his shoulders and surged forward, entering her on a solid stroke.

His breath hissed between his teeth. "Fuck."

Her hands gathered the white linen as her fingers curled around the edge of the table, holding herself in place against Hudson's relentless drives. He leaned closer, bending her legs under him as he worked his length in and out with each posses-sive thrust. Her grip on the edge of the table tightened and a moan escaped her lips. She felt herself climbing higher and higher. Hudson's pace quickened and her head arched back as an orgasm rolled through her body, obliterating everything else around her and numbing her senses.

"Christ, I'm going to come so hard." His hips jerked in powerful, unforgiving thrusts as he rode out his release. He shouted her name on an explosive breath and then collapsed on top of her, his head resting against her chest.

She cradled his head in her arms and felt the pounding beat of his heart keeping time with hers. They lay like that for a long time, neither one speaking as their collective breathing slowed. Allie closed her eyes, memorizing the feel of his body draped across hers. She wanted to freeze the moment in time. Some-where in the back of her mind she knew two weeks with this man would never be enough. And when he finally lifted his head and smiled, her heart twisted at the thought of saying good-bye.

22

All eyes were on Hudson as he flipped the pages of the contract his lawyers had drafted that afternoon. He could sense their collective flinching with each stroke of his red felt tip. The thing was a fucking mess. It was taking every ounce of restraint to keep from hurling the POS with enough force to defy the laws of physics, making his legal team play 150-page pickup.

In his peripheral vision, the skirts and suits shifted in their seats as if their asses were in a frying pan. The striped tie checked his watch, the gray skirt her cell phone. His jaw tightened. He was in no mood for bullshit. And it wasn't just the scrap in his hands that was frustrating the hell out of him, but his personal life as well. As if picking up on his vibe, gray skirt carefully set the phone front and center.

Good call.

Reaching the last page, he tossed the phone book–size contract down the length of the glossy conference table. The thing looked like it was bleeding to death as it skidded to a stop in the center. Hudson's tone was clipped and impatient as he rose out of his chair.

"I need the amended contract by morning."

His lawyer glanced down at the carnage. "Those changes will take hours. Even if I keep the whole department—"

Hudson cut off the whining. "I don't care if they're here till dawn." This acquisition, more like an assault, would launch Chase Industries to the top. No one was leaving until he was satisfied.

He leaned forward and planted his palms on the mahogany. "You're not going soft on me, are you?" He'd hired the guy because he had a pair. But since he'd gotten married he seemed to have handed his nuts over to his wife and tucked his dick between his legs.

"We've been at it for over forty-eight hours, Mr. Chase . . ."

Hudson's blue eyes narrowed. Lawyer guy seemed to relocate his brain and snapped his mouth shut. Riding a crest of aggression, Hudson pivoted away. With his back to the door and his muscles coiled tight, everything about him resonated get-the-fuck-out. "You have work to do."

In the window, Hudson watched his lawyer's reflection as he grabbed the decimated file from the center of the table and fled with the rest of his staff. When the room was empty he went over to the bar, poured himself a few fingers of scotch, and loosened his tie. Making his way back to his desk, he eased into his chair and swiveled toward the tireless view. He gripped the glass and stared out the window at a city that was his for the taking. The move to Chicago was proving beneficial. The deal that had brought him here was ahead of schedule, his name was blasted into stone on the goddamn building, and the press couldn't keep their lips off his ass. Hell, he'd even pushed Rahm off the front page of *Crain's*.

But when he thought of Allie, he felt like his life was spinning out of control.

That woman was a distraction that left him perpetually hard. And he had no time for distractions when a multi-billion dollar deal was on the line. But fuck, he wanted to see her, and the fact that she was attending a pretentious gathering her mother was throwing in the name of charity was riding him raw.

Of course she couldn't take him with her. Not that he'd wanted to subject himself to another glad- hand event, although he would have. To see her in her element. To watch the secret blush color her cheeks when he whispered all the ways he wanted to possess and pleasure her. To stand beside her and support her. He wanted that privilege.

This was his time with her. A fucking two-week window to prove their connection extended far beyond the bedroom.

The ultimatum he almost gave her when she broke the news of her mother's little party would have laid it all on the line. He'd been so tempted to put an end to this bullshit and make her choose. But he'd made the conscious decision at the start of this to wait the two weeks.

And timing was everything.

So he choked on his words to avoid ruining a night that started with dinner and ended with her for dessert. She'd been so beautiful spread out on his dining room table, her skin flushed with arousal and her body bowing off the surface. He tossed the rest of his drink back and the liquid slid sinuously over his tongue and down his throat. As it did, he thought of how his tongue had teased her swollen flesh and pulsed inside her as she came against his mouth.

Hudson let out a curse and tugged his shirttails out of his pants. With his free hand he reached for the phone and dialed Allie's number, waiting to hear her voice before his palm fused to his cock.

23

*O*nly Allie's mother could convince Chicago's A-list to drive all the way to Lake Forest on a Tuesday night, let alone get the weather to cooperate. But when Victoria Sinclair decided to throw a party at Mayflower Place, no one dared decline. Not even Mother Nature.

She'd determined a gathering was in order—"something intimate, a dinner perhaps"—when the final numbers revealed that the museum gala had far exceeded expectations. The target of a spring groundbreaking was all but guaranteed and Allie's mother thought the board of directors at Better Start should be thanked for their efforts.

What had begun as a simple affair for the board and a few key staff members had turned into a full- blown event. Valets greeted guests as they rounded the fountain court. Tuxedo-clad waiters passed hors d'oeuvres on silver trays. And a string quartet played under the glow of tiny lights strung above the limestone terrace.

So much for an intimate dinner.

Victoria had relented at the last minute and, at Allie's urging, extended invitations to the entire Better Start staff. They'd spent countless hours ensuring the event's success and deserved a show of appreciation far more than someone who simply lent their name to the program. Of course Allie knew they would have never exceeded their goal without one very generous donation pledged in exchange for a dance.

Her heart sank as she pushed through one of the many French doors spanning the rear of the house, and in a moment of clarity she realized why. It wasn't because she was dreading the customary small talk with board members or her mother's constant attempts to work Julian and the wedding into every conversation. It was because she already knew the person most deserving of thanks, the one whose face she suddenly longed to see, would be nowhere in sight.

Allie walked to the edge of the terrace and leaned against the stone balustrade. The grounds of the estate were still in full bloom thanks to the unseasonably warm weather, and the sweet scent of jasmine hung in the air. Copper lanterns lined the stone steps, their flickering candlelight leading to an expanse of perfectly manicured grass. In the distance, Allie could make out the silvery shores of Lake Michigan just beyond the esplanade. She took a deep breath. Watching the water ebb and flow usually soothed her, especially on nights like this when her mother was in high gear. But as the small whitecaps crashed on the sand, she couldn't help but wish she was enjoying the view of the lake from Hudson's penthouse.

She needed to get a grip. It was only one night. But if this was how she felt spending one night without Hudson Chase, how would she ever endure a lifetime?

"I have to hand it to Vicky, she certainly knows how to throw a party." Harper was suddenly behind her. She was wearing a tailored floral sheath dress that would have surely caught Don Draper's eye, and from the looks of it, had just relieved a waiter of several salmon crostini. "Find out what caterer she used and let's call them for our next event."

"Food's that good?"

"No, the waiters are that hot."

Allie laughed at her friend's ability to see every situation as her own personal version of match.com. "I thought you were planning to marry the waiter at Tavern."

"Found out he was still in college," Harper mumbled as she crammed an hors d'oeuvre in her mouth. "I'm all for dating younger men, but I have to draw the line somewhere." Allie could practically see the lightbulb turn on over her head. "Hey, Mr. Moneybags doesn't happen to have a younger brother, does he?"

"Harper!" Allie checked to see if anyone was in earshot.

"Oh relax. No one knows which Mr. Moneybags I meant. Look around," she said with a snort. "The place is crawling with them." Harper grabbed a flute of champagne from a passing waiter. "You can't keep dodging me. Sooner or later I'm getting the scoop," she said before taking a sip.

"I haven't been dodging you."

"Please, for the past two days every time I've come near your office you've either been conveniently on the phone or dashing out the door to some mysterious meeting."

Allie didn't mean to hurt her friend's feelings. But how could she explain her roller coaster of emotions when she didn't understand them yet herself? She was about to assure Harper it was nothing personal when she heard someone call her name. The unmistakable voice sounded like fingernails on a blackboard. *Oh great.*

Allie and Harper turned as one to find Hillary Prescott, heir to the country club throne.

"There you are! Your mother told me you'd be here." She greeted Allie with an air kiss to each cheek. "I've been looking everywhere."

"Well here I am." *Trapped.* Allie caught sight of Harper smiling over the top of her champagne glass as she drifted away.

Hillary reached for Allie's left hand. "Let me see that ring your mom keeps bragging about." She cursed under her breath and yanked the ring closer. "So you're really marrying a duke?"

Allie would have corrected her former classmate if she'd given her half a chance.

"How are the plans coming? It must be horrible trying to balance wedding planning with a full-time job. No wonder you look so exhausted." She lowered her voice. "I have a face guy who works miracles. Call me and I'll give you his number."

"Thanks, but—"

"Oh my God, that reminds me. Have you seen Meredith since she got back from the spa?" Hillary emphasized the last word with a harsh laugh. "Right, a spa that doubled her cup size."

"How was your game this summer?" Allie asked, desperate to change the subject. A smile spread across Hillary's face. "Club champion again this year. You know, if we team up next summer, I bet I could take the doubles title, too."

"Oh thanks, but with work I couldn't—"

"Work?" Hillary grimaced as if she had a bad taste in her mouth. "After the wedding? I just assumed—"

"Sorry to interrupt," Allie said, a smile plastered across her face. "But I see my boss and there's something I really need to discuss with him."

"Oh, sure. Call me, we'll do lunch."

As she walked away, Allie almost felt bad for lying. Almost. And besides, it wasn't a total lie. She *had* seen her boss. He was standing off to the side shifting his weight from one foot to the other and looking as uncomfortable on her mother's terrace as he had at the museum gala. Bob Ellis was a man committed to seeing underprivileged kids get the education they deserved, and as the director of Better Start, he knew that fund-raising was essential. But that didn't mean he had to like it. In fact, he once told Allie that even after decades of working for nonprofits, he'd still rather have a root canal than talk a prospective donor into parting with their cash. When Allie came onboard as the head of fund-raising, he'd welcomed her to the team with open arms.

He smiled as she approached, his warm brown eyes crinkling around the edges. "Now there's a familiar face." For a moment he looked as though he might try to extend his hand, awkwardly juggling a small china plate and a glass drained to only ice. Allie came to his rescue by way of launching into conversation.

"Did you try the beef Wellington?" she asked. "Harper was raving about the caterers."

"Wonderful. Everything is just wonderful. And very kind of your mother to invite the entire staff." A waiter passed by with an empty tray and her boss handed him his plate and glass. Realizing too late that he still had his napkin, he crumpled it and shoved it into the pocket of his khaki pants. "The gala was a lot of work. You should be very proud of how well it turned out."

"Thank you, Mr. Ellis."

"You've done a terrific job, Alessandra. And not just with the gala. We're certainly going to miss you."

"Miss me?"

"Yes, your mother said you wouldn't be returning after the wedding. At least not on a daily basis." He tugged on the knot of his knit tie, loosening it ever so slightly. "I must say, I was sad to hear it."

Allie's face flamed. Overruling her on wedding details was one thing. Allie couldn't care less what flowers were in the center-pieces or if the ballroom chairs were covered in silk. But tendering her resignation? That was a step too far, even for Victoria. "Will you excuse me, Mr. Ellis? I just remembered my mother asked me to check on the wine. Can't have the caterers running low, now can we?"

She tried to mask her anger with the same saccharine smile she'd used on Hillary. She'd had a lifetime to perfect the expression and yet struggled to keep the facade in place as she weaved through the crowd in search of her mother. She found her chatting with one of the ladies from the club—Hillary Prescott's mother, to be exact—her delicate laughter barely audible above the quartet.

"Mother," Allie interrupted, not caring if she'd think her rude.

"Oh, Alessandra, perfect timing. I was just telling Elizabeth all about the wedding plans."

"Your mother tells me you've moved the wedding up to the beginning of December." Allie watched as Mrs. Prescott's gaze swept over her, tensing when it lingered a bit too long on her stomach. "It sounds like it will be lovely, dear. Late enough for the decorations to be up but still plenty of time before we all flee the dreadful cold on holiday."

Victoria nodded in agreement. "That's exactly what I was telling her. The lights on Michigan Avenue are beautiful that time of year, and wouldn't it be perfect if the park in front of the hotel had a fresh blanket of snow?"

Allie gaped at the two women as they discussed how much snow they'd like to see—*enough to cover the grass, but not freeze the lake*—and when they'd like it to fall—*so enough time has passed to clear the roads, but not so long that it turns black at the curb.* When she could take no more, she cut them off with a crisis sure to attract her mother's undivided attention. "The caterer needs to speak with you, Mother. Something about a substitution on the brand of caviar."

Her mother sighed. "Honestly, if it isn't one thing it's another."

"Always something," Mrs. Prescott said. She brushed cheeks with Victoria before joining another group of women.

"Did he say what brand, because I specifically ordered—"

"Relax mother, there's no caviar emergency."

She looked utterly confused.

"Did you tell Mr. Ellis I was resigning after the wedding?"

If it weren't for the recent injections, Victoria's eyebrows would have shot up in surprise. "*That's* what all this is about?"

"You had no right to speak on my behalf," Allie snapped.

Victoria turned to ice. "Watch your tone." Her voice was much louder than Allie expected, but she regained her composure quickly. The smile returned to her face, and when she spoke again her tone was hushed, though just as lethal. "I'm your mother. I will not have you speaking to me in that manner." Taking Allie by the arm, she led her away from the crowd. "I'm sorry you didn't get the chance to tell Bob about your plans. The subject came up and I mentioned it. Simple as that."

The last line was said with complete finality. Allie knew from past experience her mother considered the conversation over, but she was far from done discussing the matter. "I haven't decided what—"

The sound of Allie's cell phone stopped her midsentence.

Victoria's face lit up. "Oh, is that Julian? Be sure to tell him how much he's missed this evening."

The screen read "private caller," but Allie seriously doubted the call was from Julian. Other than the message he'd left on her answering machine, she hadn't heard from him since he arrived in Paris. "Hello?"

"Excuse yourself." The sound of Hudson's deep voice sent a chill down her spine.

"I . . . um," Allie's eyes darted to her mother. "I'll need to call you back later."

Victoria tsked. "It's late in Paris. Talk to the man."

"Tell whomever you're with that you need to take this call," he instructed. "Move to some place private."

Allie waited until her mother drifted out of earshot. "Can we discuss this after the party?"

"No."

"Hudson, I can't—"

"I'm not a patient man, Alessandra. Don't keep me waiting."

She turned away from the crowd and lowered her voice. "There are people everywhere. Where exactly do you suggest I go?"

"I'm sure there are at least a dozen rooms upstairs," he said through clenched teeth. "Pick one."

"I can't just disappear. My parents are hosting the event." She stole a glance over her shoulder. "They'll be looking for me"

"Do. It. Now."

His command made her knees go weak. What was it about this man that could be so aggravating one minute and so unbelievably hot the next? Allie gave a resigned sigh and, against her better judgment, started toward the house. She kept her head down, trying not to draw attention to herself as she weaved through the mingling guests. Fearing her mother might be consulting with the caterer, she avoided the kitchen and dining room altogether and slipped through the glass doors of the conservatory instead.

When she reached the foyer she paused briefly to make sure no one was watching before dashing up the stairs to her childhood bedroom. It looked exactly as it had when she was a little girl: French provincial furniture, lace bedspread, porcelain dolls. God, how she'd hated those porcelain dolls.

"Okay, I'm in my old room. What was so important I had to—"

"Take your panties off."

"*What?*"

His voice dropped. "You heard me."

Allie felt her face flame. "Hudson . . . I can't do that."

"After some of the stuff we've done, don't get squeamish now. I had you cuffed to my ceiling, Alessandra. Something I hope to do again." His words were more promise than threat. A promise she suddenly found herself wanting to hold him to. "Or maybe next time I'll cuff you to my bed, every inch of your fuckable body at my disposal."

His possessive tone sent of rush of heat through Allie's body and a flood of erotic images along with it. She envisioned herself tied to Hudson's bed, completely at his mercy and delirious with pleasure.

"You're picturing that, aren't you?"

"Yes."

"Good. Because right now I can't stop picturing you bent over my desk, naked and wet. Your hips lifting in anticipation, greedy to have me inside you. The hell if my assistant is mere feet away, because it has to be here. It has to be now."

A small gasp escaped her lips. "You're at work?"

"Yes. I kicked everyone out of my office in the middle of a deal."

"You did?" Her heart beat faster. "Why?"

"I started thinking about last night, how you were spread out on my dining room table, rocking against my mouth. Fifteen hundred dollars an hour for the best legal opinions money can buy and I couldn't focus on a damn word they were saying. All I could hear were the sounds you make when I'm inside you, those little moans of pleasure when you're about to come."

Allie's breath hitched. His confession shocked her and at the same time she found herself incredibly aroused. She pressed her thighs together, amazed at how a simple phone conversation could have her aching with need.

"I cleared the room to call you and at the moment I'm looking out the window with my cock laying hard against my stomach. Does that turn you on, Allie, knowing my cock is out and ready for you?"

"Yes." Her voice was barely a whisper as she pictured him stretched back in his chair. Jacket off, tie loosened, pants unzipped.

"Now do as you're told and take your panties off."

Allie drew a deep breath and reached under her dress. Her

fingers trembled as she hooked her thumbs into her lace panties and swept them down her legs.

"Are they off?"

"Yes."

Hudson's voice was low and rough, but his tone turned sensual. "Lie down on the bed."

She flipped the lock on the door, the small click echoing in the darkness. A sliver of moonlight guided her to the bed, where she followed his instructions, lying back against the ruffled pillows.

"Pull your dress around your hips."

Her fingers curled into the green fabric as she inched her dress over her hips. Cool air rushed against her naked core, making her feel vulnerable and exposed. She knew what he wanted, what he would ask for next, and she braced for his instructions.

"Touch yourself. Feel how hot and wet you are."

Allie hesitated before tentatively brushing her fingers up the inside of her thigh. The sound of laughter floated up from the patio and she tensed. Even if she could somehow manage to block out the rest of the world, it wouldn't be enough. The ache between her legs begged for *his* touch, not hers. "I can't," she whispered.

Hudson groaned. "Fuck, Allie. I've never been so hard and thick. I need my fist gripping and stroking my cock like I'm inside you."

The thought of Hudson pleasuring himself sent an unexpected wave of excitement coursing through her. She swallowed hard. "What's stopping you?"

"Because I want you right there with me, baby. We'll take it nice and slow. Close your eyes and caress your hands down your neck, let them cup your breasts. Feel how perfect they are."

Allie's eyes drifted shut. She followed his directions, letting her hands glide down her throat past the neckline of her dress. Her breath caught as she cupped her breasts.

He was quick with his next command. "Squeeze them how I would."

She did as he described, and in the darkness he was with her. His warm body pressed against the length of hers. His hands squeezing and kneading her breasts. His lips trailing down her neck.

"That's it. Get your nipples nice and hard for my mouth." His deep voice resonated through her body, magnifying every sensation as she drew her fingertips across her breasts. Her nipples strained against the thin fabric of her dress as she slowly circled them. "Pinch them, as if I'm dragging my tongue from one to the other and pulling them between my teeth."

She trapped her nipples between her fingers and thumbs, imagining Hudson's teeth grazing her skin as she tugged and pulled.

"Now feel my hands sliding over your stomach and trailing soft kisses as I go." Her breathing grew louder as his words caressed her skin. "That's it, baby, I can hear how turned on you are." Every inch of her body hummed with anticipation. "Now touch yourself for me. Feel my fingers parting you, sliding over your skin."

Music wafted up the stairs, a distant reminder that they weren't alone, but Allie no longer cared. She was far beyond shyness or shame. She was lost in the moment, focused solely on Hudson's voice as she slid her hand between her thighs. She gasped from her own touch and moaned his name.

"Tell me what you feel, Allie. Are you ready for me?"

"Oh God, yes." She was so wet, so ready. She needed him there with her, filling her, possessing her.

"Stroke yourself, feel my cock rubbing against you." His voice was tight with restraint and she knew he was fighting his own release, waiting for her to join him. "Let me hear how good it feels. You want me inside you, don't you?"

"Please," she moaned his name and was lost, surrendering to each of his commands as he brought them both closer to the edge.

"Come with me, Allie." His words pushed out on an explosive breath. "Fuck."

White knuckles gripped the bedspread as searing pleasure ripped through her. She turned her head toward the pillow, letting it absorb her cries.

"This is what you do to me, Allie." Hudson's breath was still harsh in her ear. "You have the power to make me come harder than anyone and yet it's never enough. Come to my place tonight, I can't wait until tomorrow."

"Yes," she managed to say, still trying to collect her wits. Allie sat up and ran her fingers through her hair. She didn't need a mirror to know her face was flushed.

"Oh, and one more thing, Alessandra." She could hear his grin through the phone. "Enjoy the rest of the party."

24

The limo moved at a crawl down Astor. Hudson straightened his tie for what must have been the tenth time since they'd turned down the street. When they finally came to a stop in front of Allie's brownstone, he forced his hands to give the tie a rest and gripped the lever on the door at the same time his driver opened his.

"I got this, Max."

"Yes, sir." Max nodded and pulled his door shut.

Hudson got out of the limo and buttoned his jacket. God, he was nervous. Like first date, sweaty palms nervous. He moved toward the brownstone in powerful strides, taking the stairs two at a time until he was standing in front of her door. He punched the doorbell, then ran a hand through his hair.

The door swung open and Hudson's breath came short and fast at the sight of her in an elegant, charcoal-gray gown that was clinging for its life to each of her lush curves. He wasn't sure what was holding it all together as his eyes drifted over every inch of Allie's exposed skin. He couldn't tear his greedy gaze away from her, and his thoughts immediately went to the images that had been permanently burned into his mind. What she looked like under him with her blond hair spilling over the pillows; over him with her hands splayed on his chest as she took him; or in front of him as he pushed in deep from behind. Christ, he could practically feel her soft ass against his groin as he moved in and out of her tight, hot body. He was getting hard just thinking about it. Thank fuck he buttoned his jacket so his dick didn't arrive at the door before he did. He wanted tonight to be about her. To be perfect.

Allie pinched the diamond chandelier earring dangling from her left lobe between her fingers. "Hi."

"Hi, yourself. You look beautiful. That dress is making me want to either cover you up or revise our plans for the evening."

"Your message was very mysterious, Mr. Chase. Why did I need to get so dressed up?"

"It's a surprise." Hudson took the wrap from Allie's hands and draped it around her shoulders. He pulled her hair out from underneath it, and when his index finger grazed the back of her neck he had to fight the impulse to press his lips to her nape.

His hand fell to the small of her back, skin-to-skin, and he led her to the limo where Max was waiting with an open door. Allie slid across the bench and Hudson moved in beside her. As he did, he became acutely aware of how incredible she smelled, and it was doing nothing to ease the ache between his legs. He dragged in a deep breath. This was going to be a long night, and he wasn't exactly the kind of guy used to keeping his hands to himself. Especially when she was looking sexy as hell in a dress that was begging to be unzipped.

Allie stared out the window as the limo picked up speed. Hudson could sense her wheels turning, trying to figure out where he was taking her based on their location. Nervous anticipation crackled between them as he watched her try to put the pieces of the puzzle together in her head.

He reached for her, curling his fingers around her hand and rhythmically brushing his thumb over the inside of her palm. It was a simple gesture meant to soothe her and reassure him, but all it did was drive him crazy and make him focus on the potential disaster waiting to knock him on his ass.

The limo rolled to a stop. Traffic surrounded them and pedestrians parted around the car, all squinting to figure out what hotshot was in the ride while trying to play it cool as they did so. Allie ducked her head, peering out the window at the front of a large building with Mozart, Beethoven, and Bach blasted into stone. Recognition spread across her face and she turned to him and smiled. "The symphony?"

Hudson breathed a silent sigh of relief at her reaction. "I was able to pull a few strings and score tickets."

Allie leaned across the seat and pressed her lips against his. "Thank you."

His index finger caressed her jaw, then slipped underneath her chin. "It's my pleasure." Taking advantage of the tinted windows, he slanted his mouth over hers. Her lips parted and his tongue slid inside, savoring her softly and slowly. He heard the muted click of her seat belt, the equivalent of a green light, and tugged her into his lap. She was the most incredible thing he'd ever known. He groaned into her mouth, deepening the kiss— licking, teasing, tasting. And it made him want to kiss her elsewhere with the same eagerness. His hands slid down the bare skin of her back as her fingers raked into his hair, pulling just how he liked it.

On the verge of losing control, he dragged his mouth away from hers. His breath was harsh against her lips. "Christ, Allie, I need to get you out of this limo before I tell my driver to keep going."

She hesitated for a moment with her lips hovering over his before sliding off his lap. Hudson hissed as she shifted over the erection beating like a drum against his fly. He adjusted himself and thought how he'd misjudged in thinking this was going to be a long night. It was going to be excruciating.

The door opened, and when she stepped onto the sidewalk he was right behind her, catching her wrap as the wind blew it off her bare shoulders. He draped it across her and then placed his hand discreetly beneath it, stroking his thumb down her spine. His fingers lingered at the top of her zipper and all he could think about was peeling her out of that dress, laying her back on the leather seats, and spreading her wide. Fuck. He ran a hand through his hair and slammed the door to the limo shut to keep from yanking her back into the car and enjoying the hell out of her in the middle of Chicago.

Walking up to the brick and stone orchestra hall, Hudson placed his hand on the small of Allie's back. When he did, he couldn't help but notice the sudden stiffness in her body.

"Don't," she murmured under her breath.

He held the door open and dropped his hand from her back. The tension in her shoulders visibly eased as if it was his hand that had held it there. As they crossed the gold CSO emblem hammered into the marble tile, he reminded himself that this kind of place was as regular a joint to her as McDonalds had been to a guy like him.

They started up the stairs and Hudson watched her hand drift up the varnished banister. He wanted her gentle hand to be on his arm, her delicate fingers curled around his bicep. God, he wanted that connection; to feel her hand close the distance he suddenly felt between them. But he understood her trepidation. Being here with him and displaying anything other than a professional front was guaranteed to make the damn society pages. She was an engaged heiress and he was the playboy billionaire. A dark secret once again.

When they reached the top, Hudson guided her through the mingling crowd, all humming about this year's "season." Man, the people surrounding them were colder than the ice they wore on their ears and around their necks. When her gaze swept the room, his followed, stopping short on the bar across the room. He dipped his mouth to Allie's ear.

"Would you like a drink?" He straightened back up. "I know I could use one." Or five.

Allie nodded.

"Be right back."

Women turned as he walked through the room, their stares following him to the bar; no doubt curious about all the recent press or wagering his net worth. To them he'd just gotten lucky. Funny how the harder he worked, the luckier he seemed.

"Pinot Grigio and Blue Label, neat."

When the bartender set his order on the bar, Hudson curled his fingers around a crystal glass filled with the finest scotch, and yet he still felt like he was holding a can of Budweiser. He tossed back his drink and ordered another, the heat of the recognizing stares burning into his back.

Fuck, this was becoming an increasingly bad idea.

He dropped a fifty on the bar and worked his way back through the throngs of people. The closer he got, the more he could see the nervousness on Allie's face, the way she fidgeted with her clutch.

"I'm sorry if this was a mistake," he said, handing her the glass of white wine.

Allie's eyes shot up to his and softened. "I love that you surprised me with these tickets, that you remembered . . ." Her voice trailed off. "It was very thoughtful of you."

"We can leave if you'd like."

"No, I want to be here."

"Would you rather I leave? I can pick you up after the show if that—"

She placed her hand on his forearm. "I want to be here with you."

The contact was casual, but the intimacy made his chest hurt as she if she was squeezing his heart. He lowered his head and everything around them faded. The clanking of glasses, the murmurs of conversation, the sounds of the orchestra warming up. All of it disappeared. In that moment she was his whole world.

His lips inched closer to hers, and at the same time she lifted onto her toes.

The overhead lights began to flicker the five-minute warning, and all sound returned to the room. Allie dropped smoothly back on her heels and Hudson straightened. What the fuck was he doing? They were in public, for Christ's sake. Yet with her, everything around him evaporated.

"We better get to our seats," Hudson said. He waved in the direction of the box but refrained from laying his hand on her back. Once inside the private box, he pulled the door closed and ducked around the red velvet curtain to join Allie at their seats.

Hudson walked up behind her plush red chair, the vantage point affording him a spectacular view. She crossed her legs and the slit of her dress fell open. Sweet Jesus, those legs. The next three hours were going to be one helluva practice in self-control.

He dropped his mouth to her ear. The movement was innocuous enough, someone attempting to speak to another over the sound of bows warming over strings in the orchestra pit. His lips brushed against her ear as he whispered, "I can't wait to get you home. And naked." He took his seat and flashed her a salacious grin. "Then again, all manner of things happen in the dark."

*A*llie's mouth gaped open as the lights of the CSO dimmed. All eyes were on the conductor as he took his place at the podium. All eyes but hers. She was far too busy staring at Hudson's impassive profile to pay much attention to a waving baton. Alexander Borodin's "In the Steppes of Central Asia" had always been one of her favorites, but not even the rousing French horn could capture her attention.

All manner of things happen in the dark.

Surely he was joking. He wouldn't really try something in the box. Out in the open. Where anyone could see. He wouldn't dare. She swallowed past the lump in her throat. Or would he?

As it turned out, she had nothing to fear. Hudson was a perfect gentleman during the first performance, and when it came to a close, Allie found herself feeling more than a bit foolish for expecting otherwise. And if she were really honest with herself, a tad disappointed. *Jeez, Sinclair, get a grip.* Where was all this coming from? She thought about it and realized that what she was really hoping for was a bit of reassurance that she hadn't hurt his feelings. After the way she behaved when they arrived, it was a wonder he was still in the building. She had totally overreacted. What difference did it make if someone saw them together? It wasn't a big deal to go to the symphony with a friend. She snorted softly to herself. Yeah right—a friend who's spent the past week taking her on every surface imaginable.

Khachaturian's flute concerto served as the second portion of the evening's entertainment. Allie stole a glance at Hudson as it began, hoping he wasn't bored out of his mind. Their eyes met and to her great relief, he smiled. A warm blush spread across her cheeks. What was it about this man that could make her feel so uninhibited one minute and so unbelievably shy the next? He held her stare and slowly his gaze began to shift. It became darker, more heated, and she found herself squirming from the sheer intensity.

Allie looked away, staring blindly at the stage in front of her. Hudson shifted so his hand was on the armrest next to hers, not touching her, but close enough that she could feel the radiating warmth of his body. And then, with a subtle shift of his wrist, there was contact. It was small, hardly visible to the eye, but it felt as though a current of electricity passed between them at that one tiny point where skin touched skin.

A blare of trumpets signaled the start of Tchaikovsky's fourth symphony, and a hush fell over the crowd. Hudson inclined his head toward hers ever so slightly. "Put your wrap over your legs," he told her in a low, raspy voice.

Her eyes flashed to his and found them alight with some wicked thought. She hesitated, his words both exciting and terrifying. The balcony wall shielded them from prying eyes, but still . . .

"Do it," he mouthed.

Allie's heartbeat quickened as she pulled the wrap from her shoulders and arranged it carefully across her lap. Her body hummed with anticipation as he casually lowered his hand to his own right thigh, now pressed tightly to her left. She waited with bated breath for . . . nothing. The first movement ended as it began, with Hudson paying rapt attention to the tuxedo-clad musicians and Allie squirming, untouched, in her seat.

Perplexed, she exhaled and crossed her legs, right over left. His movement was so subtle that she never even noticed his hand leave his thigh. Instead she felt it. His fingers slipped under her cashmere wrap and brushed lightly over her calf. Allie startled and his fingers stilled. When she relaxed he continued, stroking and caressing as he slowly worked his way higher. He paused to draw lazy circles around her kneecap before letting his fingers drift back down her calf, only to start the tortuous circuit all over again. He continued the same pattern, stroking up, then back down, while Allie tried desperately to keep her erratic breathing under control.

The music swelled and his hand dropped to the back of her knee, gently nudging it. Her wide hazel eyes met the silent entreaty of his blazing blues, and she slowly uncrossed her legs.

His fingers parted the slit of her dress. The wide pashmina covered him, but still Allie adjusted it. Her heart pounded as he stroked her bare skin, going higher and higher with each brush of his hand. Back and forth. Back and forth. The steady rhythm perfectly matched the music of the second movement, and as the conductor transitioned to the third, so did Hudson. Without warning, his hand delved between her thighs. His fingers slipped beneath her panties, and she heard a faint hiss when he discovered the evidence of her desire.

The music slowed to a hush as he brushed his fingers right where she was wet and aching for his touch. Then a long note from a flute penetrated the hushed room and two thick fingers pushed deep inside her. Her eyes darted to his and he held her gaze, his unmoving fingers filling her, stretching her. Slowly, he began to move in deliberate, even strokes, careful not to draw attention with any sudden or repetitive movements that could be seen above the balcony wall. With a flick of his wrist his fingers twisted, expertly finding that sweet spot that had her melting in his hand.

Allie stifled a moan as his thumb suddenly skimmed the top of her sex, moving in rhythmic circles while his fingers continued their provocative caress. Her gaze swept the crowd below, but all eyes were following the conductor's mad gestures, completely oblivious to the explosion building in the private box above them.

She felt the weight of his stare, watching her reactions. She knew from the heat of her cheeks that her face was flushed. But could he see her heart hammering against her chest? Had he noticed the wild racing of her pulse? Or the way her lips had parted on a silent gasp? Her hands gripped the velvet armrests as she tried to quell the riotous feelings inside her, but it was no use. The ache between her legs was becoming unbearable as he pushed her closer and closer to losing all control.

And yet there he sat, seemingly unaffected.

As if reading her mind, Hudson took her hand and surreptitiously placed it on his lap, careful to shield her with his program.

"Touch me," he whispered. "Feel how hard I am for you."

His erection strained against the fabric of his suit pants, and with a slight shift of his hips, he flexed into her palm. He wanted her, and at any cost, it seemed. It was too much. She'd maintained a modicum of control up until then, resisting the urge to rock against his questing fingers. But feeling the hard evidence of his arousal, his blatant need and desire, shattered her sense of reason. In a bold move, her fingers curled around his length and squeezed. His eyes closed briefly, and when he opened them, they were burning with need.

"We're leaving," he said, as the fourth and final movement began. He stood, taking Allie by the hand and pulling her to her feet. He yanked the velvet curtain back, dragging her toward the door, but when he reached for the handle, the curtain fell back into place, shrouding them in near total darkness.

Hudson stopped and spun on his heel. In one swift move he lunged at her, pushing her against the wall of the box. Her mouth fell open on a gasp and he took full advantage, kissing her ferociously with long, deep sweeps of his tongue. His taut body pinned her, enveloped her, overwhelmed her, and she moaned with a desperate hunger as her hands raked into his hair.

"I can't wait until we get home." He moved away for a handful of seconds and she heard the faint clink of his belt buckle. "I'm going to fuck you. Here. Now."

His erotic, untamed words thrilled her, and a surge of pure lust coursed through her veins.

"Someone could walk in," she panted.

"I don't care."

And in that moment, neither did she. Not even a little. There were hundreds of people below them, all listening intently as Tchaikovsky's fourth movement wafted through the symphony hall, and yet all she could think about was the how badly she needed to feel him inside her.

His hands shifted from his fly to between her thighs, lifting her dress higher until he found the soaked satin of her panties. He groaned as his fingertips brushed the wet material, and then his grip tightened around the edge. Allie felt a sharp tug as the delicate fabric was shredded from her body, and then a rush of cool air against her aching core.

She reached for him, pushing his pants just low enough to free him from his boxer briefs, and then he closed the distance between them, grinding his mouth against hers and pressing her between the wall and his hard, muscular body. She felt the throb of his erection straining hard and hot against her, and she shuddered. Once he was inside, she knew it was going to be a fast, fierce ride.

Hudson's hand smoothed up the back of her thigh. He lifted

her leg, spreading her, and hooked her knee around his hip. The heavy curtain afforded almost total darkness, but in the thin strip of light coming from beneath the door, she could see a haze of lust clouding his bright blue eyes. He bent his knees and pushed into her in one long thrust that had her sucking in a sharp, gasping breath. He pulled back and thrust again, forcing his way deeper until she was utterly impaled and it was impossible to tell where he ended and she began.

Her head fell back against the wall as he moved inside her in slick, relentless drives that had her moaning at how perfectly they fit together. No one had ever come close to igniting her passion the way Hudson did. He was what she needed, what she craved.

The sound of pounding drums surrounded them, a fiery rhythm pushing them higher and higher as his thrusts grew wilder and more desperate. Her fingers clutched the shoulders of his jacket, holding on tight as a white-hot rush threatened to consume her.

The music swelled to a crescendo and her entire body began to quake. Rippling tremors started in her core and then pulsed like waves throughout her body, in perfect time to the clashing symbols on the stage below. Drums pounded their way through the finale and Allie dropped her head, burying her face in Hudson's neck to muffle the keening cry that escaped her lips. Her climax washed over her and her teeth sank into Hudson's neck. He groaned as she marked him and his body jerked, driving to the hilt one last time as he came.

Once the tremors subsided, Hudson lowered her carefully back to her feet. She wobbled on her heels and he steadied her with an arm around her waist.

"I believe I'm starting to develop an appreciation for classical music," he said.

Still short of breath, she managed a slight laugh. "I thought it all sounded the same to you?"

"This one is different." His expression grew serious as he brushed the pad of his thumb over Allie's swollen lips, but then he quickly flashed a wicked grin. "In fact, I need to go home and listen to it a few more times."

Allie pushed through the brass revolving doors of the Drake Hotel and hurried up the stairs. The concierge glanced up from his desk as she passed, but Allie didn't need directions. She'd been to the Palm Court dozens of times over the years.

The harpist was at her post, same as she was every day during afternoon tea. Her carefully plucked notes wafted through the air in perfect harmony with the tranquil fountain at the center of the room. Chiffon-draped columns framed the scene and divided the restaurant into cozy seating areas of plush velvet couches and white linen chairs. Allie scanned the room and found her mother in one of the chairs, her back to the fountain as she set her china teacup on the white marble table in front of her.

"You're late," Victoria scolded. She tilted her head in invitation. Despite her aggravation, Allie obliged, careful not to smudge lipstick on her mother as she pressed her cheek to hers.

"I have a job, Mother. I can't drop everything just because you leave a voice mail summoning me to tea."

Her mother bristled. "You were not *summoned* to tea,

191

Alessandra. I simply needed to discuss a few items with you and this seemed like the perfect venue."

A tuxedo-clad waiter greeted her the moment she settled in on the dark brown sofa. "Welcome to the Palm Court," he said. "What can I start you out with this afternoon?"

"I'll take the Earl Grey. Decaf please. No cream or sugar, but I'd love some honey on the side." As an afterthought, she added, "Oh, and an orange twist instead of lemon, if you have one." The waiter backed away with a nod and Allie turned to her mother. "What was so urgent?"

"Elizabeth Prescott called me yesterday. She tells me Hillary asked you to be her doubles partner next summer."

Allie dug her nails into the palm of her hand. Had her mother really interrupted her workday to talk about tennis? Even if she was somehow under the misconception Allie was interested in league play, the season was still a good six months away. "Mother, if you called me here to discuss—"

"She also invited me to be her guest at the symphony last night." She gazed at Allie, her facial expression giving nothing away.

Allie tried to keep her voice level. "She did?"

"Yes, seems her husband had something come up rather last minute and she was kind enough to offer me the extra ticket. They were good seats, too. Main floor, center aisle." Victoria lifted her teacup to her lips and took a small sip. "Of course, I would have preferred box seats." She moved slowly and methodically, setting her cup and saucer back on the small table. Allie's heart thudded in her chest, yet she held perfectly still, doing her best to remain impassive as her mother studied her face for any hint of a reaction. Her eyes never left Allie's as she dabbed the corner of her mouth with a cloth napkin. When she was done, she folded it neatly and smoothed it across the lap of her mint-green St. John suit. "Did you enjoy the performance, Alessandra?"

The waiter arrived with Allie's tea, giving her a few precious moments to collect her thoughts. Denial was pointless. Her mother had obviously seen her in the box with Hudson. The only question that remained was how much had she seen. Her stomach rolled at the thought. *Keep it together, Allie.* All she had to do was drink her tea, make a bit of small talk, and get the hell out of there.

"Very much so." Allie reached for the small dish of honey, just as she had on countless other afternoons. Only this time there was a small tremor in her hand as she dabbed a spoonful into her tea. Hopefully her mother hadn't noticed. "I was invited by one of the foundation's patrons. I met him at the museum gala last month."

"Yes, I saw you dancing with him that night."

Was there anything this woman missed? "He's new in town and asked me to be his guest. You know how disappointed I was to discover Julian had forgotten to get tickets. Plus, I thought this would allow me the opportunity to discuss the work we do at Better Start in greater detail, possibly secure another donation." Allie paused, suddenly aware her words were coming out in a high-pitched rushed. She drew a calming breath through her nose. "We never would have reached our initial goal without his pledge."

"I'm well aware of the generous check Mr. Chase wrote."

She knows his name? "You are?"

"I make it my business to know who all the major players are, Alessandra, and I'm not only referring to the foundation."

The waiter set a three-tiered, sterling silver stand on the table between them. Each level held a china plate displaying an array of finger sandwiches, fruit breads, scones, and French pastries. He hesitated for an awkward moment before hightailing it to the kitchen. *Lucky bastard.*

"I just love this place. It has so much more character than those new flashy hotels they're building these days." Her mother helped herself to a delicate offering of cucumber and tomato on crustless bread, but didn't bother taking a bite. Instead she placed the small sandwich on her plate and lifted her chin. "There's no substitute for lineage, Alessandra. You'll do well to remember that. A few lucky investments do not put that man in the same class as Julian."

"There's also something to be said for respecting a self-made man, Mother. Some people aren't fortunate enough to be born with a title or family fortune. They have to work hard for what they want in life. Everything Hudson Chase has was earned, not inherited."

Victoria's nostrils flared ever so slightly. "That's quite a passionate defense of someone who's merely a donor." She leaned closer, her voice a lethal whisper. "Don't think you can play me for a fool, young lady. You're hardly the first woman to enjoy a walk on the wild side, Alessandra." Her hand smoothed an already immaculate French twist. "Lord knows Paolo brightened more than a few of my afternoons."

Who the hell was Paolo? Allie's mind raced, processing information before screeching to a dizzying halt as the face of her childhood tennis instructor flashed before her eyes. "The tennis pro?"

Her mother arched a single brow. "His private lessons did wonders for my swing, but I would have never let him escort me to a social event."

Allie's heart sank at the realization that her mother was a walking, talking cliché. Her voice wavered when she asked, "Does Daddy know?"

"Your father and I reached an understanding years ago. This is the world we live in, Alessandra, but you're hardly in a position to expect that sort of latitude." Victoria's eyes flicked down to the ring on Allie's finger. "Wait till you're wearing his wedding band, have given him an heir to the family title— but even then you must learn to be discreet. Men are willing to overlook certain . . .

hobbies, as long as their needs are met. But no man will tolerate the sort of embarrassing display you put on last night."

Every muscle in Allie's body tensed as she wondered exactly how much her mother had seen. The balcony wall would have shielded Hudson's hand from view. And her wrap had been across her lap. Had she caught a glimpse of them behind the curtain? *Oh God.* Allie thought she might be sick.

"Honestly, it was nothing short of a miracle Elizabeth didn't see the way you were looking at that man last night."

All she saw was a few heated glances? Allie would have exhaled in relief if it weren't for her mother's piercing stare.

"I won't be humiliated by your indiscretions, Alessandra."

The waiter eased toward their table. Victoria gave him a tight smile and asked for the check before turning her attention back to Allie. "I think this will be a lovely location for cocktails, don't you agree?"

Allie's brow knit together. "Cocktails?"

Her mother gave a small nod and took another sip of tea. "Yes, before the reception. They clear the couches and chairs out of the way and bring in a few high-top tables. Of course we'll have them draped in silk, dress them up with votives and fresh flowers. The catering manager suggested a pasta bar or a carving station, but I went with passed hors d'oeuvres. Silver trays and white gloves are so much more elegant than a line forming in the corner. This is the Drake, not the Sizzler, for heaven's sake."

Victoria continued to describe her vision of the perfect wedding reception. Staring straight ahead, Allie noticed she had a clear view of the doors to the ballroom in the distance. The words "Gold Coast Room" seemed to float over her mother's head as she covered everything from the height of the centerpieces to the size of the dance floor. Every detail had been carefully planned, right down to the location of their meeting.

Allie listened without really hearing, somehow managing to

nod at the appropriate moments. She rubbed her palms on the velvet couch. Where the hell was the waiter with that check?

She made her escape as soon as the bill was paid, practically running down the stairs. The gust of fresh air was a welcome relief until she looked across the street at the entrance to the Palmolive building. Her chest tightened. She had to end things with Hudson. Postponing the inevitable was getting them nowhere, and it was only going to be harder the more time she spent with him. And now that her mother was suspicious. . . .

"Taxi?" the doorman asked.

"Yes, please." Her phone pinged with a text and she looked down at the screen.

It was from Hudson. `Cleared my schedule. Early dinner at my place?`

Only four thirty and Hudson was willing to ditch work. For her. She glanced up at his building. Was he already there, waiting?

"Ma'am?"

She turned to find the doorman holding open a taxi door.

"Still want the cab?"

Allie looked back at her phone and quickly typed a reply. `Can't. Lots of work. Call you later.`

Without looking up, she pressed send and ducked into the cab.

"*D*rink this. You look like you need it." Hudson offered Allie a squat glass. She shook her head and continued her pacing from the fireplace to the couch, looping back for a scenic route along the windows. "Then I need it, because I have a feeling I'm not going to like whatever it is you have to say."

"I can't keep running over here with my toothbrush and a pair of panties in my purse."

"I'd offer you a drawer, but that's not the issue, is it?" When there was nothing but silence, he continued. "This is when you tell me what's really going on." Hudson took a long drink from his glass, his throat working on a swallow. He tracked her movements, willing to go all in that this had something to do with the horseshit text she sent him about having to work late. "Spill it."

She stopped by the fireplace. "I can't do this anymore."

"You don't get to decide that." He tossed back the rest of his scotch, leaned over, and set the glass down on the coffee table a little harder than intended. "Not this time."

"My mother summoned me to the Drake today, Hudson. Apparently she saw us at the CSO and felt the need to discuss it over tea and scones."

"I see."

"She's going to be watching my every move."

Any trace of levity drained from Hudson's face. Victoria Sinclair was taking up more space in the room than he was. Fuck that, she saturated it. "Your mother's playing games within games, Alessandra."

Allie's face clouded over and she turned toward the fire.

Hudson stepped closer. His tone softened as he slipped a finger under her chin, turning her head to meet his gaze. "You have the power to take control of your life."

The simple words lingered between them, and as the weight of them settled, he realized he needed to pull Allie out of the eye of the shit storm. She was ready to run, he could see it on her face. Hell, she already had one foot out the door. But words were not going to be enough. He was going to have to show her, make her see that what she wanted was standing right in front of her. "Go away with me this weekend. Just the two of us."

She shook her head. "I can't just disappear for the weekend."

"You're not falling off the face of the earth, and there is cell reception . . . in most places. Unless you think your mom is tracking your phone; then I'll see that it finds a new home at the bottom of the lake."

Allie laughed. "I don't think cell phone destruction will be necessary. Not that she wouldn't track me if she could, but the woman barely manages a text message."

"What do you say?" With his eyes he traced the delicate little crease that wrinkled her brow. The one she got when she was weighed down with uncertainty, confined by the pressure of indecision, or rankly pissed off.

"I don't know." Allied chewed on her bottom lip. "It's Thursday night, where would we even go on such short notice?"

"I have a little place a couple hours from here on Lake Geneva. It's beautiful this time of year when the leaves have all turned. We can go out on the lake or we can stay in so I can kiss every inch of your perfect body." He flashed a grin. "Besides, I miss my bike."

"Finally saved up enough to buy that motorcycle you wanted?" she teased.

"Managed to scrape a few bucks together. And I can't wait to take you on it." He dragged his mouth down her throat, leaving a trail of featherlight kisses in his wake. "There's an idea."

Allie tilted her head to the side. "It does sound tempting."

"It's settled, then." He lifted his head and pressed his lips to her forehead. "Now how about that drink?"

"Yes, please."

Hudson strolled around the breakfast bar, then yanked open the door of the wine fridge. The majority of his collection was stored downstairs, but he always had a few bottles on hand in the kitchen. He'd just pulled a California chardonnay from the rack when the phone rang. He set the bottle on the granite counter and snatched the receiver from the cradle. "Chase."

As Allie approached, Hudson did a tight 180 while running a hand through his hair. "Send him up." He hung up the phone and cursed under his breath before turning back to face her.

"What is it?" she asked.

His jaw tightened. "My brother."

28

"*N*ick's here?" The last time Allie saw Hudson's little brother he was all of twelve years old. Crooked grin, mop of unruly hair, and big brown eyes filled with hero worship for his older brother. Allie smiled. She couldn't wait to see him again.

"Yeah, but now is not the time for a reunion." Hudson moved quickly toward Allie and cupped her elbow. "I need you to wait in my room."

"What?" Allie frowned. "Why do I need to wait in there? It's just your brother." True, she'd just had a meltdown over her mother seeing them at the CSO, but this was different. This was Nick. He'd kept their secret ten years ago. She certainly wasn't worried about him blowing their cover now.

"You have to trust me on this one, Allie." Hudson's strides were long and measured as he directed her down the hallway toward his bedroom. Everything about his demeanor had changed since the doorman's call. Tension rolled off him in waves. When they reached the door to his room she heard the penthouse elevator ping softly in the distance. "Stay here," he said. "This shouldn't take long."

He turned to leave, pulling the door shut behind him.

What the hell was that all about? Hudson had hustled her out of the room so quickly. Allie's heart sank. Was that how she made him feel? Like she was ashamed to be seen with him? It couldn't have been further from the truth. Under normal circumstances she'd have been proud to be on his arm. But her situation was far from normal. The panic she'd felt earlier had nothing to do with who he was, or where he'd come from. Somehow she had to make him see that.

Allie sighed heavily, resigned to the fact there was nothing she could do at the moment but wait. Might as well get ready for bed. She hadn't planned on spending the night but after Nick's unexpected arrival and Hudson's bizarre reaction, there was no way she was leaving. Not with so many unanswered questions.

She grabbed a T-shirt from Hudson's dresser and headed for the master bathroom to change and brush her teeth. A new toothbrush lay in the drawer next to Hudson's. She unwrapped it, smiling at the gesture. Underneath that tough exterior was a sweet, considerate man. Of course he would hate that description if he heard it. Just picturing the look on his face made her laugh with a mouthful of toothpaste, but it was true. She'd seen his softer side more times than she could count, although it had never been more evident than in the way he treated Nick.

Hudson had always been so good with his kid brother. He was patient, putting up with the incessant barrage of question only a twelve-year-old could conjure. He was protective, always making sure Nick was home before curfew. And he was kind, letting Nick hang around the two of them despite constantly teasing Hudson about having a "giiiiiiiirlfriend."

So what had changed? Why was he insisting she stay in his room? Allie spit and rinsed her mouth, mulling the questions over in her head as she dried her face with a towel. Curiosity eventually got the better of her and she slipped quietly out of Hudson's room.

When she reached the end of the hallway, she heard a voice she assumed was Nick's. "You gotta help me, man."

"What the hell do you keep looking at?"

"Your elevator. Does that fucking thing close?"

"Private elevator, Nicky. Here, drink this." The exasperation in Hudson's voice was tangible, and although she couldn't see him, she could picture a deep furrow between his brows. "How many days have you been up this time?"

"Can't fucking sleep. I haven't even been home."

"Why not? Did you blow your goddamn rent again?" Hudson was practically shouting. "Stop looking at the mother-fucking elevator and sit the fuck down."

Allie poked her head around the corner and stole a glance at the two brothers. Hudson had his back to her, obscuring her view of Nick, who had apparently listened to his brother and sat the fuck down. Hudson ran a hand through his hair and moved toward the window, giving Allie her first glimpse of Nick. She had to cover her mouth to stifle a gasp.

Of course he looked different—he was older now, twenty-two, maybe twenty-three—she'd expected that. But what she hadn't expected was to find him so disheveled and agitated. He was tapping his heel, his leg bouncing at a manic pace as he fidgeted with a water bottle. *Cap off. Cap on.* And even from a distance she could see how badly he was sweating. *Cap back off.* Nick skipped the plastic cap across the coffee table and took a long drink. When he'd drained the bottle, he wiped his mouth with the back of his hand.

Hudson turned to face his brother and Allie was struck by the overwhelming family resemblance. She'd never really noticed it when they were young, but despite Nick's current condition, he looked so much like his older brother. Same jawline and nose, same dark wavy hair—although Nick's was considerably longer and, from the looks of it, hadn't been washed in a few days. Their most distinguishable feature, though, was their eyes. Hudson's were a clear blue while Nick's were a deep brown. Allie's chest tightened as she focused her attention on Nick's dark circled eyes. Once so warm and full of life, his eyes were now vacant as they darted anxiously around the room.

"They're after me. Bastard's probably got my place on watch."

"Look, you're crashing and not making any sense," Hudson said, but Nick didn't appear to be listening. All his attention was focused on scraping the label from his water bottle. Without warning he jumped up and began pacing like a caged animal. When he was within arm's reach, Hudson snagged him by the collar. "Come on, you can sleep it off downstairs or in the theater, take your pick."

Nick shrugged out of his hold. Hudson stared at him for a long moment and then shook his head as he turned away. Allie ducked back around the corner, afraid she was about to be discovered. She was inching toward the master bedroom when Nick's voice stopped her in her tracks.

"You're not listening to me!" he yelled.

"Hearing you loud and clear. What kind of money are we talking about?"

There was a lengthy pause, and when Nick finally spoke, his voice had grown quiet. "A shit ton."

"How much, Nick?"

Nick muttered a few words she couldn't hear.

"Fuck!" Hudson exploded. "How could you be so stupid?"

Allie flinched at the sound of a fist pounding into a hard surface.

"I didn't mean for shit to get real. I swear, Hudson, this is the—"

"Don't you dare finish that fucking sentence."

A cabinet opened in the kitchen. Glasses clinked. A bottle was set down with a thud. And then nothing but an uncomfortable silence.

When Hudson finally spoke, Allie could tell he'd used the

time to reign in his temper. His voice was level though his words were still razor-sharp. "You're going to listen to me carefully, because the terms of this deal are non-negotiable. I'll bail you out one last time, but you're checking into rehab. Tomorrow. Consider it repayment."

"I got this, bro. Don't need rehab."

"There's only one right answer here, Nick."

Nick mumbled his reply, and the next thing Allie heard was the sound of Hudson's footsteps on the living room floor. *Shit!* She scampered down the hall and was sitting cross-legged on the bed when he entered the room.

"Everything okay?"

"Fine." Hudson strode through the room without so much as a glance in her direction. His face was taut with tension as he stripped his watch from his wrist and tossed it on top of the dresser. Pockets were next. He emptied them, carelessly dumping his wallet, change, and cell phone into a pile. When he was done he yanked open a drawer and grabbed a pair of pajama bottoms before disappearing into the bathroom.

Clearly he wasn't fine.

Allie crawled up the bed and slipped under the covers. Exhaling, she leaned back against the headboard, crossed her arms, and waited. When Hudson emerged from the bathroom a few minutes later, his clothes had changed but not his mood.

He threw back the duvet and stretched out on the bed with his forearm resting over his eyes. Allie lowered herself to the pillow next to him, watching the heavy rise and fall of his chest. After a while it became clear Hudson wasn't going to say anything about his brother's late night arrival. It was up to Allie to address the elephant in the room.

She took a deep breath and confessed. "I was listening."

Hudson lifted his arm and stared at her, his expression unreadable. "Were you now?"

She nodded. "I'm sorry. You were just so upset . . ." Allie

fumbled with excuses as Hudson dropped his arm back over his face, offering no reaction or further explanation. "I had no idea."

"What? That my brother is a drug addict?" There was a quiet resignation in his voice and she couldn't help but wonder if it was the first time he'd ever admitted it to himself, let alone said the words out loud.

"How long has he been using?"

Hudson scrubbed a hand down his face. "Nick had a hard time." There was an overwhelming sadness in his eyes, and for an instant something else, something darker. "Especially after Mom died."

Their mom died? This was news to her.

It was a while before Hudson spoke again and when he did his voice had softened to barely a whisper. "Nick's the one who found her." His eyes drifted shut. "He was still trying to wake her up when I got there, shaking her, shouting her name."

Allie's throat tightened at the thought of the moppet-haired boy she once knew clinging to his dead mother. Her eyes welled up as she imagined how scared he must have been. No little boy should have to bury his mom, let alone discover her lifeless body.

A muscle in Hudson's jaw flexed. "This is all standard operating procedure for Nick—showing up late at night, asking for money—but tonight was the worst I've ever seen him." He drew an unsteady breath. "If he keeps going the way he is, he'll end up just like she did, overdosing on God knows what. Shit, I can't . . ." Hudson's voice trailed off and his body tensed. A moment later he cleared his throat, and when he continued it was with a steely determination. The CEO was back, handling the issue. "I need to get him some help."

"Did he take the deal, agree to rehab?" she asked. Her voice was thick with unshed tears.

"He said he'd go." Hudson didn't sound completely convinced.

"We should cancel our trip. You need to focus on Nick right now."

"No, I'll take him in the morning, then swing by and pick you up. Can you leave at lunchtime?"

"That should be fine." Allie studied his face, trying hard to gauge his expression. "Are you sure?"

"Not much I can do while he's in detox."

Hudson grew quiet again. She could only imagine how helpless he felt, because that was how she felt when she looked at him. Helpless to ease his worry and pain.

Allie shifted closer. Hudson wrapped his arm around her, welcoming her comfort by tucking her into his side and pressing his lips to the top of her head. She reciprocated, planting a soft kiss on his bare chest, and felt him relax beneath her touch. This was the comfort she could offer. If only for the night, he could lose himself in her.

Her hand slid across his stomach, gliding over the ripples of his abs as she left a trail of openmouthed kisses along the slope of his pecs. His chest expanded, and when her tongue flicked over his nipple, an appreciative groan vibrated in the back of his throat. Her mouth drifted further, softly sucking and nipping the skin along his ribs. Hudson ran his hand up and down her back as her questing fingers drew rhythmic patterns. She glanced up at him. His eyes blistered with heat as he watched her explore his upper body with her fingers and tongue.

Wanting more, she reached for the drawstring of his pants. When she tugged them open, his erection sprang free, hard and glistening at the tip. Featherlight touches teased him as her fingers traced the honed contour of his hips. He twitched when the back of her hand brushed the hard ridge of his arousal, and a satisfied smile tugged at her lips. Oh yes, she could do this. She could turn the tables on the game he played so well.

Allie pushed his pajamas lower. She dragged her fingernails down one thigh then back up the other. Then her hand swept across his stomach before repeating the same path, making sure her wrist brushed his straining erection before running her nails down his inner thigh. His hips flexed.

"Touch me," he whispered.

She pressed a wet kiss to his chest and finally took him in her hand. Hudson's breath hitched as she caressed him, so firm and yet velvety soft. His hips flexed again. Instinctively her grasp tightened, squeezing and stroking his thickening length. His eyes drifted shut, and when her tongue swirled over his navel, a low moan escaped his lips. It was the most erotic sound she'd ever heard. Her body ignited with a need for more. Touching every inch of him wasn't enough. She wanted to taste him. All of him. She leaned forward and took the tip of him past her lips.

His eyes flew open. "Allie . . ."

He gazed down at her, his eyes burning with desire as she flicked her tongue across the head of his erection. His hand gently cradled her head as her tongue swirled round and round. Her lips slid over him and she sucked tentatively, pulling him deeper as she found a rhythm with her mouth. His lids lowered and his breath hissed between his teeth.

"Ah, fuck, just like that."

Moving between his legs, she folded his erection against his stomach, running the flat of her tongue from root to tip before taking him fully. His hips flexed, thrusting him deeper into her mouth. She pushed him to the back of her throat then sucked hard as she drew him out. Her tongue swirled over the top before sliding him deep once again.

His fingers fisted in her hair. "God, Allie . . . that feels good."

A warm ache spread between her thighs. Hearing her name on his lips had her practically panting with need. She had no idea giving him pleasure could be such a turn-on. But as she looked up at him, she couldn't imagine anything more arousing than the feel of him in her mouth.

Hudson's eyes blazed with desire as he watched her take him

again and again. "Ah, Allie . . ." He ground the words out through clenched teeth. "You're going to make me come." He sucked in a sharp breath and exhaled a warning. "Stop now if you don't want me to."

Allie grabbed his hips, feeling his muscles tense beneath her hands. He twitched in her mouth and she knew he was close. She sucked harder, relishing in her ability to make him lose control. The fingers in her hair pulled tighter and the rhythm of his hips intensified.

"I'm gonna come." He pushed the words out between harsh breaths. He thrust deeply and then stilled, shouting out as his release filled her mouth. "Fuck, Allie."

She glanced up as the salty taste of his pleasure slipped down her throat. God, she loved watching him come. And knowing it was her touch, her mouth, that caused him to come undone made it that much sweeter. She sat back on her heels, a victorious smile spreading across her face as the tension drained from his body.

Hudson's chest heaved as he struggled to catch his breath. "That was quite unexpected," he said, pushing up on an elbow and bending one knee. "Exceptional, but unexpected." He pushed up further, holding Allie's gaze until they were sitting eye to eye. One hand supported his weight while the other began caressing her thigh. "Did it turn you on to do that?"

The simple act of his hand on her skin made her belly tighten. "What do you think?" she asked. His palm slid between her knees and she opened herself to him, spreading her legs as his hand moved higher. Her breath caught as his fingers brushed over the silk of her panties.

"Oh, I think it did. I think having my cock in your mouth made you ache to feel it between your thighs." His crude words sent a rush of heat through her core and her entire body pulsed with need. His fingers kept up their relentless torture, stroking the damp fabric. Her eyes drifted shut as she concentrated solely on the sensation of his fingers rubbing back and forth. Back and forth. Before long her hips began to rock against his hand. "Am I right, Alessandra, are you aching to have me inside you?"

She gasped as his finger slipped under the edge of her panties. "Yes."

He surged forward, his tongue plunging into her mouth at the same time his finger thrust inside her. Desire coursed through her veins. She reached for him, grabbing fistfuls of his hair and holding him to her. His tongue stroked over hers, mirroring the rhythm of his finger as he massaged a spot deep inside of her.

Her back arched as his hand cupped her breast, his thumb brushing her hardened nipple as it strained against the fabric of her T-shirt. He groaned into her mouth, then broke away, whipping her shirt over her head and lowering her onto the bed.

Hudson hovered over her. He dipped his head and took her lower lip between his teeth, tugging gently before kissing her long and hard. She welcomed his kiss, wrapping her arms around his neck and urging him closer. His body glided over hers until every inch of her skin was covered by him. And yet it wasn't enough. She needed more. Desperate for friction, she lifted her hips only to have him shift to his side.

She whimpered at the loss of contact, then shivered as his hand slid down her stomach and under the delicate fabric of her panties. The ache between her legs spread throughout her body as his fingers pressed and released. He moved lower, pausing at her entrance. Circling, caressing . . . driving her wild.

She cried out as first one and then two fingers pushed inside her. His voice rasped in her ear, telling her how good it felt to have her lips around him and how badly he wanted to feel her body's wet heat around him now. He accentuated his words by pressing his growing erection against her hip while his fingers continued their steady rhythm. Her muscles tightened around him, his fingers and words pushing her closer to the release she craved.

His tongue traced the edge of her ear and then his lips were on her neck, slowly kissing his way down her body. He traced leisurely circles around her taut nipple before scraping it with his teeth. She writhed beneath him, near mindless with need.

"Please, Hudson . . ."

She felt him smile against her stomach. "Oh no, baby, quid pro quo."

"What?" Panting, she lifted her head. Hudson looked up at her from beneath dark lashes. His eyes were full of salacious intent as he dragged his tongue from one hip bone to the other.

"You were relentless in your pursuit, Alessandra." His hands gripped the sides of her panties, easing them down as he worked his way lower. "Now it's my turn."

29

*A*llie yanked open the bathroom drawer and began gathering items by the handful. Toothpaste, makeup, lotion. She didn't stop to sort through them, just tossed them into a cosmetic bag. The last thing she needed was for her mother to stop by unannounced and find her packing for a weekend getaway. And now that Victoria's antenna was up, anything was possible. Of course she'd offer some perfectly logical excuse—*I was in the neighborhood and just had to show you these swatches* —but it would be nothing more than a pretense. The sooner she got Hudson out of her apartment, the better.

She'd tried to get him to wait in the car, offering a seemingly innocent, "No need to come up. I'll just be a few minutes."

Yeah, that went well.

"The hell I'm waiting in the car," he'd said.

Judging by his success in the corporate world, there wasn't much that intimidated Hudson Chase. Not a ruthless competitor in the boardroom and certainly not an irate mother in a living room. What Hudson failed to understand was that if Victoria Ingram Sinclair felt her family's image was at stake, there was no telling how far she'd go to protect it. On the surface her mother might have appeared the flighty socialite, but in reality, she was a shrewd and powerful player among Chicago's elite. Allie's reaction to tea with her mother had run far deeper than a simple mother/daughter test of wills. She also worried what would happen to Hudson if he became the target of her mother's rage.

Allie shoved her hair dryer and hiking boots into the duffle bag and quickly zipped it closed. She hoisted the bag off the bed and carried it into the living room just in time to see Hudson putting his phone back in the breast pocket of his coat. Without even asking she knew he'd been calling his brother again.

They'd woken that morning to find Nick had left sometime before dawn, and Hudson had been trying, unsuccessfully, to reach him ever since. He'd even gone by Nick's apartment while Allie was at work, but said from the looks of things, Nick hadn't been there in days.

"Any luck?" she asked, dropping the overstuffed duffle bag on the couch.

Hudson ran a hand back through his hair before pulling his tie loose. "Voice mail again."

"Are you sure you don't want to cancel?" she asked him for at least the tenth time.

"I'm sure. Nick's probably coming down. He'll be sleeping his high off for a couple days."

She considered his response for a moment. Part of her still thought they should postpone the trip so he could look for Nick, but Hudson was probably right in assuming he'd crashed somewhere. The poor kid looked exhausted. And besides, if Nick was ready to get help, he wouldn't have snuck off in the middle of the night.

Hudson picked up Allie's suitcase. "Ready?"

"Almost; let me just finish packing."

His brow shot up. "You have more?" The amusement in his voice was obvious, and for the first time all day he cracked a smile. He'd been so quiet and withdrawn since discovering Nick had bailed on their deal. But now, as he looked at her in feigned dismay, his frown lines relaxed into a genuine smile that touched his blue eyes.

"Just two." She turned back toward her bedroom and gazed at him over her shoulder, trying her best to look innocent as she held up two fingers. "They're small."

As she scurried back down the hall, she heard her duffle bag drop to the living room floor with a thud. A moment later Hudson was standing in the doorway of her room.

"Christ, Allie, we're only going away for the weekend."

Her hands settled on her hips as she surveyed the clothes spread out all over her bed. "I don't know how many outfits I'll need."

Catching her by the waist, Hudson wrapped his arms around her and hauled her back against him. "I don't plan on letting you stay dressed long enough to consider other outfits." He nuzzled her hair. "I want this body ready for me at any time."

His words were intoxicating, and everything below her waist suddenly clenched with need. If he kept up what he was doing— tracing her ear with his tongue, tugging the lobe between his teeth, *oh yes, just like that*—they were never going to leave her bedroom, much less Chicago.

"Hudson, I'm serious. I don't know where we're going or what we'll be doing." She wriggled out of his arms and into her walk-in closet. When she emerged a moment later with an armload of sweaters and jeans, she found Hudson lounging across her bed. He was leaning back on one elbow, wearing that sexy smirk of his, and looking all kinds of tempting. The sight of him stopped her in her tracks. She couldn't help but picture the last time he'd lounged on that bed . . . naked . . . with the moon casting shadows across the hard contours of his chest as he moved over her . . . under her . . . inside her. . . .

"I think you know what we'll be doing, Alessandra," he said

in a low drawl, interrupting her delicious memories as if reading her mind. "As for where? My bed, the hot tub—"

"Oh, hot tub! I need my swimsuit." Allie dumped the pile of clothes on the bed and headed for the dresser. She pulled a bikini out of the bottom drawer and shoved it in her bag, only to have Hudson promptly pull it out and toss it to the side.

"You won't be needing that. In fact, you won't be needing half of this," he said, pulling articles of clothing from her bag one at a time until something of interest caught his eye. "Is this what you envision wearing in the woods?" He sat up, a black lace garter stretched between his thumbs, and flashed a wicked grin. "It would look remarkable on the back of my bike."

Allie rolled her eyes as she snatched the garter out of Hudson's hands. "That's not supposed to be in there."

"Suit yourself. But this," he said, smirking as he held up her pink lace baby-doll nightgown, "is definitely making the trip. A survival necessity."

"Give me that." She tried to swipe the skimpy nightgown from him but he pulled it out of reach.

"Oh no, this is coming with me. For safe keeping." Hudson pulled Allie between his legs. His broad palms swept over her rib cage before cupping her breasts. "Unless you'd like to put it on now?"

His hopeful grin made her insides melt like warm honey. She grinned back at him as she pulled away. "If we start this now, we'll never leave."

"True. And the sooner we get there, the sooner I'll have you naked." Hudson stood and swatted her playfully on the ass. "Pack it up."

Allie leaned her head back against the black leather seats of Hudson's Range Rover Autobiography. They'd been driving for about an hour, and the farther they got from the city limits, the more she felt herself relax.

It had been so long since she'd been out of the world of concrete and glass that Allie had forgotten how beautiful the countryside was this time of year. A few of the trees were still green, but most had begun to turn despite the warm temperatures. Vibrant shades of gold, orange, and red dotted the landscape like Mother Nature's own version of Monet.

As they grew closer to the town of Lake Geneva, the rolling hills gave way to luxury resorts, lush golf courses, and riding stables surrounded by white wooden fences. The town itself was quaint with brightly colored shops and restaurants lining the water's edge. It was the kind of place where city goers shelled out big bucks to "get away from it all," and there were dozens of retailers more than willing to help them spend their money. Art galleries, antique shops, and jewelry stores filled both sides of the street, along with a few high-end sporting goods stores catering to outdoor thrill seekers. A sign advertising zip-lining hung in one of the windows. Allie's stomach plummeted at the thought. She glanced at Hudson, hoping that dangling from a harness in the woods wasn't his idea of enjoying the great outdoors.

"Anything special you'd like to do while we're up here?" she asked.

Hudson raised a curious brow and cut his eyes at her. "Are you giving me carte blanche, Miss Sinclair?"

She felt her face flame. "I meant something more along the lines of golfing or riding horses. That sort of thing."

Hudson chuckled. "I prefer my Harley to a horse." The Range Rover rolled to a stop at a red light and Hudson's dark gaze met hers. "As for the rest of the time we're up here, I believe I made my intentions clear back at your brownstone."

His eyes never left hers as he reached for her hand and pressed a soft kiss to her knuckles. The feel of his lips against her skin had her shifting in her seat. She wanted to feel that mouth on every inch of her skin; kissing her, licking her, making her come. Hudson's eyes widened infinitesimally as she squirmed under the heat of his stare. He knew exactly what he was doing to her. But instead of being annoyed by his look of smug satisfaction, she found herself fighting the urge to slide his hand up the inside of her thighs so he could feel for himself just how right he was.

The light changed and Hudson gave her hand a gentle squeeze before releasing it to place both of his on the wheel. His foot pushed down hard on the accelerator and the car surged forward, pressing her into the supple leather. She turned toward the window to hide her grin. If the speed of the car was any indication, she wasn't the only one fighting urges.

Allie gazed across the water as the SUV sped along the shoreline. The sun was just beginning its descent and the late afternoon rays made the surface of the lake sparkle like silver glitter. In the distance, the paddle wheel of a double-decker steamboat churned through the water. The old-fashioned riverboat looked like it would be more at home on the mighty Mississippi than a nine-mile lake, but it was charming nonetheless.

"We're here," Hudson said. The Autobiography took a sharp left through a set of stone walls flanking either side of a winding drive that led to a clearing at the top of a hill. Allie peered out the window. A wood and stone house towered above her with a high-peaked roof and windows that soared over two stories. Hudson parked the car in front of the house alongside a wide staircase. At the top was a wood plank door with a glass inset. Allie leaned forward, her eyes following the lines of a wide deck that wrapped around the entire house. When she looked back, she found Hudson watching her expectantly.

"It's lovely," she offered.

The corner of his mouth turned up in a shy smile. "I can't wait to show you the rest. Wait there." A moment later he was at her door, taking her hand as she stepped out of the car. He led her up the stairs with an almost childlike excitement, but stopped abruptly when they reached the top. Allie heard the faint buzzing of a cell phone as Hudson reached into the pocket of his jeans. He frowned when he read the screen, then silenced it with a push of his thumb. Clearly not the call he'd been hoping for.

"Give me a minute to grab the bags and check my messages, then I'll show you around." He unlocked the door and flipped on a few lights before disappearing down the stairs with his phone pressed to his ear. Allie hoped he'd be able to reach Nick, even if only to hear his voice and know he was okay. But as she thought the words, she realized the odds of that were slim. Nick wasn't ready to accept Hudson's help. She shuddered at the thought of how much worse things might get before he was.

Allie wandered around the great room as she waited for Hudson to return. The modern rustic style was the complete opposite of his sprawling penthouse. Dark beams of distressed wood crisscrossed overhead while wide planks spanned the length of the floors. A fireplace made of tan and gray stones ran the full height of the two-story ceiling, as did the windows that looked out over the treetops. A row of bookshelves held an impressive collection of hardbacks, but the centerpiece of the room was the oversize leather sectional that curved around a tufted ottoman. It was weathered brown leather, the kind she knew without touching would be buttery soft, with tapestry pillows piled on each end.

To her right was the kitchen. The beamed ceiling and planked floors flowed into the open space, and the same stones that were on the fireplace created a similar hearth around a twelve-burner cooktop. A large island sat in the middle of the room with copper lights strung from the ceiling above it. There was a slab of marble on top that was bigger than most dining room tables, and six barstools were arranged around two of the sides. It was obvious the house had been designed for entertaining.

A set of glass doors led to an expansive deck off the kitchen.

Allie opened them to find a cluster of teak chairs with green-and-tan cushions facing an outdoor fireplace. There were gas torches placed at intervals along railing posts, and in the corner a large hot tub sat perched atop a platform.

Bet that could tell some stories.

An unwelcome pang of jealousy twisted in her stomach and she turned her attention back to the view. The sun was beginning its descent and the fading rays cast a gold reflection on the lake below. She sighed. It was the perfect romantic getaway. She knew it was ridiculous, but as she leaned against the railing and gazed out over the tops of the pine trees, part of her couldn't help but wonder how many other women had enjoyed the same view.

The door opened behind her. "There you are," Hudson said.

"Gorgeous view. How long have you owned the place?"

"About six months. I bought it in the spring about the same time I bought the penthouse."

"Must be a hit with all the ladies." The words slipped out before she could stop them. She was about to tell him she was sorry and that it was none of her business when his answer left her with nothing but a gaping mouth.

"You're the only person I've ever brought up here."

He held her stare for a long moment, so much going unsaid between them, until Allie broke the awkward silence. "How about that tour?"

His lips pressed together in a thin line and he nodded. "Right. A tour."

She followed him through the kitchen, where he pointed out more high-end appliances she suspected got little to no use, and back into the Great Room. He showed her the two guest suites that made up the rest of the main floor and then held out his hand.

"Would you like to see the upstairs?" he asked. Seven words that held such promise.

She placed her hand in his and he gave it a gentle squeeze

before leading her up the staircase to the master suite. Hudson's bedroom had the same devastating view as the great room, even more so given the added height. Leather club chairs sat in front of a fireplace that opened on the other side to what she presumed was the master bathroom, and an acoustic guitar sat propped against the hearth. She would have asked if that was an instrument he actually played, but her thoughts were interrupted by the sight of his larger-than-life bed.

The headboard and footboard were covered in rich dark-brown leather that was tufted to mimic a chesterfield sofa. As she trailed her hand over the rolled padded edge of the footboard, she couldn't help but think how similar it looked to the arm of the sofa in Hudson's game room. Images of blindfolds and leather cuffs consumed her thoughts, and her heart began to pound. A hand touched her shoulder and she jumped. Hudson was suddenly behind her, sweeping her hair to one side as his lips found the curve of her neck.

"Put this on." He held out his arm and her babydoll nightgown dropped down from his hand. "And when you return, I want to tie you to my bed."

A soft moan escaped her lips as he ran the tip of his tongue up the column of her throat.

"Look at the bed, Allie." Her heart raced with a mixture of excitement and anxiety. "Imagine yourself completely at my mercy. Now go change."

*A*llie kept her eyes closed, doing her best to block out the sunlight flooding the room. She wasn't ready to wake up. Not when her dreams brought images of silk ties and satin blindfolds. And had that been a feather? And ice? The barrage on her senses had been overwhelming, exhilarating . . . mind-blowing. Her blood began to heat from the memories, and a sleepy smile stretched across her face. She reached out, her hand sliding across the cool sheets, but found nothing but an empty bed.

She blinked a few times as the room came into focus, then stretched her deliciously sore muscles. Allie had always prided herself on keeping in good shape, even in college when pizza was its own food group, but the past week with Hudson had brought its own unique form of exercise. And speaking of Mr. Insatiable, where was he?

The bathroom door stood open, with no sounds of running water coming from inside. In fact, the whole room was quiet except for the intermittent chirping of a few birds.

And a revving engine.

What the hell?

Allie sat up, the sheet slipping from her naked body, and

looked toward the large picture window. All she could see from her vantage point was a clear blue sky. She peered over the bed where her lace nightie lay in a pile on the floor. Hudson had been so intent on bringing it with him and then had barely left it on her.

Looks even better on my floor. His words distracted her until the engine revved again.

With no bathrobe in sight, she wrapped the sheet around her and climbed out of bed to investigate. A pair of French doors led to a small balcony, and when she opened them she discovered Hudson sitting on the driveway below her. On a Harley. Wearing leather.

Allie's mouth went dry. Up until then she'd only seen him dressed like a CEO in custom suits or cashmere sweaters. But now he looked like a bad boy from the wrong side of town. Her skin warmed at the sight of him; from his motorcycle boots to his faded jeans to his black leather jacket. She knew she was gawking, but she couldn't help it. Below her, straddling that sleek black and chrome machine, was the boy she once knew. Only now he was powerful, in control, and if possible, ten times hotter. It was like Hudson Chase 2.0.

He cut the engine and smiled up at her. "Good morning, sleepy head."

"Good morning." Allie dropped her chin and tucked a stray piece of hair behind her ear. For some reason, she found herself feeling incredibly shy. Perhaps it was being outside in her current state of undress, or perhaps it was their night of raw, uninhibited sex. She felt her face flush just thinking about the things he'd done to her the night before; things she'd like him to do again. She cleared her throat and tried her best to keep her voice level. "So that's the bike I keep hearing about?"

"The very one." He shifted the motorcycle back to engage the kickstand and climbed off. "Get dressed. We're going for a ride."

A thrill shot through her. "Be right down."

Allie hurried back into the house, quickly changing into jeans and a lightweight sweater. She brushed her teeth and pulled her hair into a haphazard ponytail before grabbing her leather jacket and flying down the stairs. She was going for a ride on Hudson Chase's Harley! When she reached the gravel drive she found Hudson leaning against the bike seat with a helmet in his hands. "I was beginning to wonder if you were ever going to wake up."

"Must be all the fresh air."

He raised a brow as he straightened and stepped away from the bike.

"Well, I would have been up earlier if you hadn't kept me up all night."

"I clearly remember being given specific instructions." He drew her against him and let his hand glide over the curve of her ass, holding her tight as his hips rolled against hers. "Don't stop, Hudson. Oh God, don't stop."

Heat pooled between her legs as her traitorous body responded to his despite her embarrassment over her wanton behavior. Placing both hands on his chest, she gave him a playful shove. "Well, you can stop now."

Hudson chuckled. "Here," he said, handing Allie the helmet. "Put this on."

Allie took the helmet from him and eyed it skeptically. "I don't think it will fit over my ponytail."

"It's not up for debate. But you might be more comfortable with your hair down." He reached up and gently tugged the hair tie loose, letting her long blond curls cascade around her shoulders. His knuckles brushed her cheek. "You look beautiful."

His touch ignited her skin. She looked up at him from beneath her lashes and began to wonder if they'd make it back in the house, let alone on a bike ride. If he wanted to take her right there on the gravel, she'd probably let him.

"So how does this thing work?" she asked, breaking the connection. Her hand trembled as she lifted the helmet in the air.

"Let me." He carefully lowered the helmet and buckled the chinstrap. When he deemed it sufficiently secure he reached for her jacket, yanking the zipper up to her chin. "It can get cold on the bike."

She resisted the urge to roll her eyes. One moment he was reducing her to a puddle on his driveway, and the next he was fussing over her as if she were a child.

"So where are we headed?" she asked.

"Thought we'd ride north, grab a bite to eat, and maybe hit one of the wineries. There's one in a restored mill that looks interesting, and it's not too far." Hudson mounted the Harley, strapped on his own helmet, and then started the bike. The engine roared to life. "Get on, baby."

Allie took his offered hand and climbed onto the seat behind him. She wrapped her arms around his waist, her body molding against his, and inhaled deeply. Fresh pine mixed with the scent of his body and the rich smell of leather. She couldn't think of anything sexier.

Hudson turned the bike toward the driveway. Once on the road, they took off like a shot. Allie squealed with delight. The power of the engine rumbled through her body and she pressed her thighs tight against his hips. God, this was a turn-on. Why did anyone ever drive a regular car when they could ride a motorcycle instead? She giggled as her naughty thoughts answered her own question. Because they'd end up having roadside sex, that's why.

The bike hugged the north side of the lake for a few miles before veering off into a more wooded area. Brightly colored trees lined both sides of the small lane, but the sun still managed to peak through every so often. Allie closed her eyes, tilting her face toward the warm rays. Her hands slipped inside Hudson's leather jacket and splayed across the fabric of his black T-shirt. She loved the feel of his muscles flexing beneath her hand. She loved the fresh country air and the winding open road. But most of all she loved that Hudson was sharing something with her that obviously meant so much to him.

They stopped for lunch at a diner, eating greasy food out of paper baskets, and then rode to the winery Hudson had mentioned back at the house. Covered with ivy and trimmed in Wedgewood blue, Stone Creek Winery exuded an old-world charm that made it look as though it had been plucked straight from the French countryside. Hudson pulled the Harley to the front of the limestone building, turned off the bike's ignition, and rocked it back onto its kickstand. Allie held his arm as she climbed off the bike, and had just unstrapped her helmet when she heard his cell phone ring.

Hudson fished the phone out of his pocket and frowned at the screen. "I need to take this."

"Nick?" she asked. For a moment she was hopeful, but he shook his head.

"Chase," he said into the phone. He turned his back to her and wandered a few paces away. "Time isn't going to improve the offer. Their financial projections are horseshit. They're out of moves." He glanced briefly at Allie, who stood by the bike watching him. "Now's not a good time. Deal with it," he said, ending the call.

"Everything all right?"

"Fine." He offered nothing more as he took Allie's hand in his. "Ready to taste some wine?"

"Lead the way."

Hudson led her to the entrance of the winery where he purchased two tickets for the tour and tasting. It turned out he'd been right about the building being a restored mill. Built in the 1860s, it had once housed looms and knitting machines, but in later years the cool underground cellars had proved the perfect environment for fermenting and aging wine.

After explaining the modern-day process—everything from stemming the grapes to corking the bottles—the guide led their group down a narrow staircase to a cellar full of oak barrels standing over six-feet tall. Small doors sat at the bottom of each barrel and the guide explained how these were once used as a means for winemakers to climb in and clean out the sediment. He opened one, asking if anyone wanted to try squeezing through the tiny hole and offering advice to the takers. "You'll need to get in a side-plank position, slide in feetfirst, then one arm . . ."

"No way am I getting in there," Allie whispered.

Hudson cocked a brow at the miniature door. "Good, because I wouldn't be able to come in after you."

"It might be fun if you did. Just the two of us, alone in the dark." The words popped out without much thought, but she went with it and flashed him a devious smile. "Think they'd realize we fell behind the rest of the tour?"

The corner of Hudson's mouth quirked up and he shook his head. Apparently she wasn't the only one wondering what had come over her. He hooked his arm around her neck, pulling her close and kissing the top of her head. "Tempting."

The tour concluded in a tasting room overlooking Stone Creek. Allie wandered over to the large windows to watch the rushing current channel through the mill's open-flume water wheel. "It's beautiful," she said. "Reminds me of the Little House on the Prairie books."

Hudson dropped his mouth to her ear. "Can't say that's the first thing that comes to my mind."

She tilted her head to the side, almost afraid to ask. But as was the case with everything when it came to Hudson Chase, she was unable to resist. "And what would be the first thing that comes to your mind?"

He wrapped his arms around her from behind and nuzzled her hair. "Laying you out on a blanket creek-side and making out."

Allie turned in his arms and looked up at him incredulously. "Making out?"

His answering smile melted her heart. "For hours."

No telling how long they would have stood there grinning like fools if the tour guide hadn't interrupted, directing them to the bar. "Ladies and gentlemen, the tasting is about to begin."

*T*he tour guide motioned for everyone to get a little closer. "Squeeze in. We're all friends now." Hudson pressed in behind Allie, caging her with his arms as his hands casually gripped the bar. She tilted her head back against his chest and smiled up at him. That simple smile wrecked him every time.

"Pay attention. I plan to quiz you later." His lips brushed her ear and his voiced lowered so only she could hear. "Answer wrong and you'll get a spanking." He felt the warm flush of her cheek against his and smiled as she began to fidget with her wineglass, a habit he'd observed when she was unsure of what to say or how to respond. She was given a reprieve by the start of the presentation.

"We're going to start off with our Cranberry Blush, a perennial favorite around here." The tour guide began working his way down the line, pouring a few ounces into everyone's glasses. He stopped to fill Allie's, then tilted the bottle over Hudson's.

Hudson let go of the bar and covered the glass with his hand. "No, thank you."

The guy continued down the line. "This is a sweet grape wine with a touch of fresh Wisconsin cranberry juice added to give it a nice blush color." He reached the end of the bar and set the bottle down. "Well, don't just stand there, drink up."

Allie twisted around to face Hudson, her lips perched on the edge of her glass. "Aren't you going to try any?"

"No, not when I'm driving the bike. However," his fingertips caressed her cheek, "I do enjoy watching you."

Allie took a sip of the wine. "It's almost too sweet," she whispered before proceeding to drain the glass.

He laughed. "Satisfying your sweet tooth? Here I thought it was only chocolate you'd crawl through fire for."

"Hmm . . . chocolate sounds good. We should stop at the store and pick up what we need to make s'mores tonight."

Hudson's teeth caught the shell of her ear. "I'd like to lick melted chocolate off your beautiful body." He heard Allie's breath catch in her throat and was about to elaborate when the tour guide interrupted.

"Next we have our Waterfall Riesling," he announced. Starting at the opposite end of the bar, the guide began pouring wine from a bright blue bottle. "It has a light, semidry sweetness and has won many awards, including the Chairman's Best of Class last year."

Hudson watched intently over Allie's shoulder as she lifted the white wine to her lips. "How's that one?"

"Let me take another taste and I'll tell you." She took another sip. "Delicious. Very crisp. You can really taste the pear."

He smirked. "Pear? Such a sophisticated palate, Miss Sinclair."

Allie looked up at him, her cheeks pink and her eyes slightly glassy. "The key is to swirl it in your mouth, let it roll across your tongue." Her tongue darted out and slid across her lips.

Hudson briefly closed his eyes.

"Of course, a good finish is crucial," she continued. "I know some prefer not to swallow, but a good finish can make the experience even more enjoyable. Don't you agree, Mr. Chase?"

Oh, he so fucking agreed.

Hudson gripped Allie's waist, his fingers digging into her soft sweater as he urged her back against his thickening erection. "I think you need another taste," he suggested, if for no other reason than to watch her tongue moisten her lips again.

"I'd love one." She smiled over the top of her glass and then polished off the Riesling.

The sound of laughter and clinking glassware filled the room and the guide practically shouted to be heard. "Everyone ready for Bon Vivant?"

An uncoordinated "Yeah!" echoed through the tasting room.

The guide chuckled. "Ah, Lover of Life. And all of you certainly have taste and enjoy living." He started in the middle this time, pouring a generous sample in Allie's glass before continuing his never- ending speech. "In order to maintain the character of the grape, this wine doesn't age in oak. The result is a nice, easy red."

Allie lifted the glass to her lips, shifting her weight as she lowered it so that her hips brushed back against Hudson's. She was driving him completely insane, grinding against him after every sip. "It's been hours since I've been inside you." His voice was low and tight with restraint. "And you're making me inconveniently hard teasing me with your delectable ass."

Reaching behind her, Allie slipped her hand between their bodies, stroking him through his jeans as she finished off the glass of red wine.

Hudson hissed between clenched teeth and dropped his mouth to her ear. "Keep it up. I won't hesitate to buy this place out so I can fuck you on the bar." And with the black Amex in his wallet, he had the means to do it.

"The final selection is our Cabernet Sauvignon, a robust, full-bodied red that is aged ten months in oak barrels."

Allie removed her hand from between them and lifted the

wineglass to her lips as soon as the sample was poured. "Oh, I really like this one."

"Let me taste." Hudson buried his fingers in Allie's hair and pulled her head back. His mouth moved softly over hers and his tongue dipped inside, teasing her in an unhurried kiss. The scent of her invaded his senses and he groaned inwardly. When he finally broke away from her mouth, he looked at the tour guide. "We'll take a bottle of that one."

Hudson handed the guide his credit card and quickly signed the receipt. He grabbed the bottle by its neck and looked down at Allie, brushing his thumb across her bottom lip. "Ready to go?"

"So ready," she murmured softly.

"You didn't need to finish every last drop." His hand slid under the weight of her hair, massaging the nape of her neck as they made a beeline for the bike. "Though it might be to my benefit that you did."

"It would have been rude not to! You were on the tour, they made those wines themselves."

Hudson chuckled. "Yes, they have numerous women in skirts with scarves on their heads stomping grapes with their bare feet."

"Making fun of me?" Allie playfully elbowed him in the ribs. She lost her balance and stumbled into his arms.

"I wouldn't dare." He set her back on her feet. "You're not going to fall off my bike, are you?"

"Of course not. Where to now?"

"Back to my place." He secured the bottle of wine in the leather saddlebag on the side of the bike, then handed Allie her helmet.

"You read my mind," she said, pulling the helmet down over her head.

"I thought we'd take Snake Road back. It's beautiful this time of year."

Allie looked at him with her mouth hanging open. "Snake Road?" Her voice was a couple octaves too high.

Hudson laughed. "It's called 'Snake Road' because of the twists and turns." His hand slipped under her chin. "Lift up, baby."

Allie tilted her head back and he made quick work of her chinstrap. "It's not longer that way, is it?"

He dropped a firm, quick kiss on her mouth. "So eager to get me naked again." Grinning, he kicked his leg over the seat and put his helmet on. "Keep thinking those thoughts."

Hudson rose up and slammed down on all that horsepower. The Harley roared to life beneath him and he was suddenly desperate to have the freedom of the road with her on his bike.

He held out his hand. "On you go."

Allie placed her hand in his and swung her leg over, mounting the bike. Sliding forward, she wrapped her arms around his waist, her body becoming flush with his.

"You ready, baby?"

She nodded and her hold tightened on his waist.

Hudson cranked the throttle on the handlebar and the engine growled as they turned onto the road. He wound them down Snake Road for miles, the bike humming and throbbing beneath them as if it were alive. He took them over rolling hills and through valleys canopied by trees, where yellow leaves bled into orange, then flamed up red as they blurred by. They passed a couple bikers along the way, and one person stupid enough to tow a boat along the devil road, but otherwise they were alone. And with the open road ahead of them, they were almost untouchable. Hudson didn't want their time together to end. He was selfish and greedy, and wanted more than just a few days alone with her.

Allie relaxed against his torso. He could feel every inch of her pressed intimately against him. Her perfect breasts against his back, her legs cradling his hips, and her hands sliding down his waist and across his groin. Her intrepid fingers stroked him through the denim of his jeans and his cock hardened instantly.

He gripped the handlebars tighter. Soon all he could think about was the way the soft skin on the inside of her thighs would feel against his legs as he stroked in and out of her, slow and hard.

Hudson ground back on his molars. With each stroke of Allie's hand his emotions and need for her became more volatile. He shifted the gears with smooth coordination and veered down a narrow stretch of road, pulling into a secluded picnic area at the edge of the lake. Turning the bike off, he engaged the kickstand and hung his helmet from the end of the handle bar.

"Come here." Hudson slid an arm around Allie's waist and pulled her across his body, her legs straddling his thighs. He removed her helmet and let it drop to the ground. Her hair was tangled at the ends and her cheeks were flushed from the crisp October wind. "We're going to finish what you started." His palms cupped her face and he seized her mouth as if he were only alive to kiss her, his lips moving desperately over hers. The dark fruits and sensuous spices of the Cabernet permeated his tongue and he moaned at the decadent taste.

Allie shoved her hands underneath his T-shirt. His abs tightened in a sequential rush as her hands smoothed down the ridges of his stomach to the top of his fly. Her fearless fingers popped the buttons one by one, releasing him from the confines of his jeans until he fell hot and heavy into her palms. His hips flexed as she took him with both hands. God, it felt good. Every time she touched him, it felt so good.

Hanging on to the last vestige of his control, he caught her bottom lip between his teeth and shuddered as her hand twisted over the head of his cock. Her skin was like satin against his and it reminded him of just how soft the rest of her body was.

"Allie . . ." His fist clenched in her hair and he took her mouth in a bruising kiss, starved to have any part of her in his mouth.

"Squeeze me," he whispered hoarsely. Her hand tightened around him. "Again."

Allie squeezed and her hands stroked down his shaft. His breath grew louder and harsher and his hips rocked uncontrollably. He was completely at her mercy as his hard length slid through her fists, her hands slick from his arousal.

His eyes flipped open. "Enough," he panted. "Too close."

Hudson could barely think straight. All he wanted to do was be inside her again. The need was so potent it defied all reason. Part of him wanted to take his time savoring her, but they were outdoors, at the side of a damn lake. He'd explore her body later. Right now desire overrode all logic.

He gripped Allie and kicked his leg over the bike. Without pause he folded her over the seat, unzipped her jeans, and yanked them down along with her panties in one sharp pull. He dropped to his knees and his hands coasted up the back of her thighs, spreading them wide. "Oh yeah, this is what I want." Flattening his tongue, he licked right up the center of her and was blissfully lost.

His fingers dug into her ass as he captured her hot flesh with his lips. Allie let out a soft moan and her back arched, pushing herself onto his mouth. He brushed his stubble against her core, wanting her scent and taste on him until he was drunk with it, then sank his tongue inside. There was nothing better than being between her thighs, either with his mouth, his fingers, or his cock.

She cried out as his tongue lashed over her sex, devouring her with ruthless skill as if he were starving and she was the only nourishment that could satisfy him. Her thighs began to tremble under his hands. Without lifting his head he coaxed her with his voice and plunging tongue. "Let go, Allie."

Allie threw her head back as she came in a violent rush. The sweet taste of her coated his tongue and yet he was still greedy for more.

Rising up behind her, he took himself in hand and stroked the blunt head of his cock between her slick folds, spreading the moisture of her arousal. He rolled his hips, opening her up, and with a powerful thrust pushed inside her. His breath exploded out of his mouth. "I'm so fucking deep."

"Oh God, yes," Allie moaned. She clawed at the leather seat and pushed her hips back to meet his thrusts. "Fuck me, Hudson. Harder."

Hot damn, she was wild and untamed. And he loved it. Loved watching her let go of her inhibitions and shamelessly give in to her own pleasure. She was wet and on fire around him. For him. He was beyond fucking her; she was under his skin, the very breath in his lungs.

Leveraging at her hips, he powered into her with a single-minded ferocity, his body slapping against the curve of her ass. "Is this hard enough for you?"

"Yes," she breathed. "Please . . ." She reached down and gripped his hand on the side of her thigh, trying to pull him closer. Her eyes were closed, her lips parted. She was as out of control as he was.

"I can feel you getting ready to come." He arched over her, his breath harsh on the back of her neck. He slid his free hand to the top of her sex and massaged the swollen flesh while he surged into her again and again, taking what he wanted as she gave herself over to him.

Allie cried out as her core tightened around him. The instant he filled her again, his cock kicked hard and every sensation magnified as he followed her with his own release.

They were both panting and leaning heavily on the bike as their senses returned. Hudson was shocked as shit the Harley was still upright.

"Wasn't quite what I expected when I said let's go for a ride. Not that I have any complaints." He straightened, taking her with him. "Let's go home. I plan on doing that again, but slowly. I want to spend hours inside you."

Hudson swept her hair out of her face and pressed a lingering kiss to her mouth. As her lips yielded to his, a thought came out of nowhere: *I need you. Don't let us go.*

llie worked her way down the wall of bookshelves lining Hudson's living room wall. Most were about politics and banking, but there were a few fiction titles mixed in here and there. "Have you read all these?"

Hudson looked up from behind the breakfast bar. "Most. I deal with enough mindless chatter at the office. Last thing I need when I have a chance to get away is the godforsaken TV blaring at me."

A quick glance around the room confirmed there wasn't a television in sight. Come to think of it, Allie couldn't remember seeing one anywhere on the tour he'd given her. Of course she'd been a bit distracted by the sight of his bed. Not to mention the naughty intentions he'd whispered in her ear.

"Up here I like it quiet, just books and my bike." He turned and opened one of the cabinets. "The larger collection is in the library at my apartment."

Allie's thoughts drifted to the extraordinary library on the top floor of his penthouse. She imagined spending a lazy Sunday afternoon with him there, lounging in front of the fireplace, devouring books before devouring each other. *Mmm.* A feast for the body and the mind.

"Wine?" he asked, pulling her out of her daydream.

"I'd love some." A thought occurred to her as she reached for one of the books. "Oh! Open the bottle we bought today."

"I had every intention to. Looking forward to seeing if it's as good as it tasted." Hudson's gaze darkened with sensual promise and her nipples hardened under his stare. His eyes flared ever so slightly and she knew her reaction hadn't gone unnoticed. A warm flush spread across her face. *Jeez, what was with her tonight?* Maybe she'd had enough wine after all.

Allie quickly turned back to the bookcase, making a mental note to merely sample the next time she visited a winery, not chug. A knowing smile spread across her face. Then again, maybe her mood had nothing to do with wine and everything to do with the outrageously insatiable man in the kitchen.

She could feel his gaze follow her as she slowly moved down the bookcases. Heat swept through her body like a slow-burning fire. Stopping in front of the sound system, she pulled his iPod from its dock, stealing a glance at him while feigning interest in his playlists. Sure enough, he was watching her, never once taking his smoldering eyes off her as he twisted the opener into the cork. Her mouth went dry. Oh yes, she was definitely going to need that wine.

Grabbing the glasses, he strolled barefoot around the kitchen island. "Let me know when you get hungry and I'll show you my impressive collection of takeout menus." He handed her a glass and clinked it with his. "Cheers."

"Cheers." She studied him as she swirled the wine in her glass and then lifted it to her lips. Something was different. And it wasn't just his still-wet hair from the shower or his casual attire. She'd seen him like that before. He seemed relaxed, carefree almost. More like the Hudson Chase she remembered.

"Ah, very good," he said, lowering his glass. "You made an

excellent choice." He dipped his head and his tongue traced the contours of her lower lip. "Although I do believe it tastes better on you."

"Better try a bit more, just to be sure." She lifted to her tiptoes and felt a vibration against her hip. Hudson frowned, digging in his pocket for his phone and glancing at the screen.

"If you need to get that . . ."

He held the power button down with his thumb, turning the phone off before shoving it back into his pocket. "It can wait."

"What if Nick calls or there's a problem at work?"

"He's not going to. And he won't until the next time he needs something. As for the office, they can manage without me for twenty-four hours." His gaze drifted to the iPod in Allie's hands. "See anything you like?"

"Quite a few, actually." She scrolled through the list of artists. "You have very eclectic taste, Mr. Chase."

"I have varied interests, Miss Sinclair." He smirked at her over the rim of his glass before taking a sip of his wine.

Hmm, like kinky darts.

Allie turned her attention to the iPod before her shameless nipples decided to put on another show. A bat-winged skeleton stared up at her from the screen. "Avenged Sevenfold?"

"When I'm pissed off. My salvation on those challenging days."

"I guess the skull on the cover should have been my first clue." Her finger slid across the screen. "Mumford & Sons?"

"Dig a righteous group of banjo players."

"And Journey?"

"Oh come on," he feigned insult, flattening a palm over his heart. "A classic."

"Fair enough." Allie glanced down and a smile tugged at the corner of her mouth. "What about Madonna, another classic?"

He held up his hands in innocence. "Oh no, that's all Nick."

She laughed. "I suppose Nick likes Carly Simon, too?"

Hudson grew quiet, focusing his attention on his glass of wine. "My mom's favorite," he murmured. Some dark emotion clouded his face. It went far beyond sadness. It was something more, something deeper. Allie tried her best to decipher what it was, but then he took a sip of wine; when he lowered the glass it was gone.

Lifting the iPod out of her hands, he quickly shuffled through the artists. "Then there's Frank." He placed it back on the dock and "Summer Wind," the song they danced to at the Field Museum, filled the room. "Timeless."

Hudson took her wineglass and placed it alongside his on the table. "Dance with me?"

He held out his hand and smiled. It was that same shy smile from long ago. The one that never failed to melt her heart. Even now, after all this time, it still had the same effect. With damp hair and not a trace of makeup on, Allie knew she was looking far from glamorous. But the way he looked at her made her feel like she'd spent the day at the salon getting ready for a black-tie affair.

She placed her hand in his. "My pleasure."

"Good thing," he said, snaking his arm around her waist, "because I didn't bring my checkbook."

She pulled back to look at him. "Checkbook?"

"A million dollars, the going rate for a dance with you. You drive a hard sell, Miss Sinclair." He grinned down at Allie, then swept her into his arms, whirling her around his living room. She was breathless when he finally brought them to a stop.

Caught up in his playful mood, she smiled coyly at him through her lashes. "You knew I was high maintenance when you met me."

Hudson's head fell back and he laughed. "Alessandra, you bring new meaning to high maintenance."

Allie's mouth dropped open. "Is that so?"

"And I wouldn't change a thing." His eyes were lit with warm amusement. "I love the way it takes you an hour to order a cup of coffee."

She pursed her lips, but it was no use. His you-can't-stay-mad-at-me grin was impossible to resist. And even though she was pretty sure she should have been offended by his comment, Allie couldn't help but be won over by the obvious affection in his voice. She smiled and shook her head. "Glad I amuse you, Mr. Chase."

"Always, Miss Sinclair. Always." He brought their bodies closer together and his hand flexed against the small of her back.

"Thank you again, by the way. We never would have met our goal without your donation."

"I was glad to help. You should be feeling some sort of triumph with your obvious success. And you managed to break the monotony of old fogies with a herd mentality clustered around tables."

His words of praise touched her. Allie had put a lot of work into making her event different from the typical fare served in a run-of-the-mill ballroom. The fact that Hudson had noticed meant the world to her.

"Do you plan these types of events frequently?"

"The museum was my first major fund-raiser."

"Well, you've set a high standard. I look forward to attending any future events you plan."

She opened her mouth to speak but then closed it again.

Hudson didn't miss a beat. "Out with it."

"The Harris Group offered me a position planning fund-raising events full-time."

His eyebrows shot up. "Impressive. That's a prestigious organization." He spun her away and then yanked her back against him. "Are you taking the job?"

She shook her head. "I turned it down. But Mr. Harris said the door was always open if I changed my mind."

"And have you?"

"No. Although it was certainly a tempting offer. I can't just leave the foundation. I made a commitment and people are expecting me to see it through."

"Let me ask you this—what do *you* want?"

She chewed on her bottom lip as she considered her reply. "I love my work at Better Start. The people I've met there are amazing, so committed to helping kids. But I also loved putting together that event. All of it, even the aggravating details. With this new position I could still raise money for the foundation, but I could also help so many other worthy causes." She paused and her voice grew softer. "For the first time in my life I feel like I've found something I'm actually good at. Me. Not my family's name or money. Just me."

"It's your life, Allie." He tugged her closer, curling his fingers around her hand and pressing it against his chest. "You should do what makes you happy."

She leaned into him, not entirely sure they were still talking about her job. They swayed gently from side to side as Sinatra crooned about a summer of young love. The lyrics conjured images of sandy beaches, entwined hands, and lingering kisses. But just like the song said, all summers come to an end, and so had their dance.

"Hmm, the summer wind." Hudson pressed his cheek to her temple and his warm breath fanned over her ear. A delicious tingle swept over her skin and she shivered. "Cold?"

"A little." It wasn't a total lie.

He ran his hands up and down her arms, soothing the goose bumps that had formed. "Sit. I'll get a fire going."

Allie sat on the rug in front of the fireplace while Hudson stacked several birch logs on the grate. "So what about you?" she asked, drawing her knees up and leaning back against the couch. "Is running an empire what you've always dreamed of?"

"Not exactly. But then again, dreams change." He lit the

starters and then closed the screen, staring into the stone fireplace as the white bark crackled with flames.

The question was meant as nothing more than a lighthearted inquiry, and his sobering reply surprised her. She waited for an explanation, but none was offered.

"How so?" she finally prompted.

He came to sit with her, sliding in behind her and pulling her between his legs. "Well for starters, I never saw myself going to college, much less owning my own company."

She wondered what had altered Hudson's path in life. Obviously something had since he was now one of the most powerful businessmen in the country. But during the summer they spent together, he never showed any interest in college whatsoever.

"What changed your mind?"

Hudson picked up Allie's hand and fit it into his palm. "It was either that or continue to work on the docks. Driving that damn boat and running with the same old crowd was obviously getting me nowhere."

Allie turned in his arms, not quite sure how to ask the obvious. "How did you—"

"Afford it? Loans, work study. I took whatever jobs they gave me, but usually I was stuck washing dishes in the cafeteria. On the weekends I hustled as a barback." He cracked a slight grin. "More dishes."

She settled back against his chest. "Doesn't sound like you had much time for fun."

Hudson frowned. "I wasn't there to have fun."

The flames shot higher as the logs caught. She watched them and couldn't help but think about her own college experience. Being invited to the right parties had been almost as important as getting into the right classes, maybe more. And paying tuition had certainly never been a concern. Hudson had gone to college to work hard and change his life. All on his own.

"What made you decide to take on Wall Street?" she asked.

"I landed an internship and discovered it was a place where I excelled. Moving in on vulnerable companies, cultivating serious ins with private resources, leveraging billions of dollars or killing deals at the drop of a hat. . . after a while, it all became a game. A sport, really. "

"Your very own version of Monopoly?"

He chuckled. "I suppose. And I liked the power and control that came with having money." His arms tightened around her. "Although none of it could make up for what I'd lost."

"You mean your mom?" she asked softly.

"And Nick."

"Nick?"

Hudson nodded. "They took him away from me."

What? Allie sat up. "Took him? Who took him?"

"The county." His words were barely audible. "Not five minutes after telling us our mom was dead."

Hudson closed his eyes and his brow creased as if he were in pain. He was quiet for several moments and she began to wonder if he would continue. But then his eyes opened and his body tensed. He turned his head to look at her and she saw unthinkable horror reflected in his eyes. Allie held her breath.

It was all coming back to him.

"When the doctor came out, he had the sheriff with him and some lady from DCFS. He told us he was sorry, that they'd done all they could."

"Nick must have been so scared," she said, her voice mirroring his.

"I'll never forget the look in his eyes when he realized what was happening. He started screaming, begging me not to let them take him. Christ, I think the whole damn hospital heard him."

Her heart clenched as she imagined a frightened young boy losing his mom and then being taken from his home. "Did they give you a reason?"

"They gave me a load of crap about how it was all in his best interest." He ran his hand through his hair and exhaled a harsh breath. "Yeah, fucking best interest."

"Next thing I knew the sheriff was trying to take Nick out to the car, but his hand locked down in a vise grip on my arm. The more the sheriff pulled, the harder Nicky held on. He kept screaming for me to do something but the sheriff was already unsnapping his cuffs like he was expecting trouble from me." Hudson's face grew pale, and when he spoke, the sound was more gravel than voice. "There wasn't a damn thing I could do except pry his fingers off my arm."

A log in the fireplace shifted and a spark popped. Tears burned Allie's eyes as she watched Hudson stare blindly at the flames in front of him. His pain and anguish was palpable. In the end, he had been the one to tear his brother away. He had been the one to break his heart. She couldn't even begin to imagine how hard that must have been for him.

Silence stretched between them. Once again Allie found herself wondering what had become of Hudson's father. She'd asked about him when they were teens, but Hudson's terse reply had made it clear his father wasn't a subject he wished to discuss. And as much as she wanted him to open up to her, she refrained from asking. Instead she merely held his hand and waited, letting Hudson reveal what he wanted at his own pace.

Long moments passed before he cleared his throat and continued. "After that Nick was dumped into foster home after foster home. He'd call, beg me to come and get him, threaten to run away. I tried to get him released into my custody, but who would give a young kid to a fuckup?"

"You were just a kid yourself, Hudson."

He gave her a sideways glance. "I should have had my shit together. My brother needed me, but I didn't have the means to get him out of that defective system." He sighed, and in a quiet voice added, "The way things played out that summer gave me a cold, hard look at my life. Everything I've done since then has been driven by my need to never feel that helpless again."

Allie placed her hand on Hudson's cheek, urging him to look at her. "What happened to Nick wasn't your fault. It's obvious how much you love your brother, Hudson, but there wasn't a lot you could do back then. You're trying to do right by him now; that's all that matters."

"You saw for yourself, he's a train wreck. I've done nothing but fail him in every way."

"You'll get him the help he needs. Even if we have to camp out at his apartment, he's going to rehab."

He gave her a halfhearted smile and pressed a soft, quick kiss to her lips. "I appreciate that, but Nick's my responsibility, not yours."

In that moment Allie realized Hudson had always seen Nick not just as his responsibility, but also his failure. As she listened to his story, she couldn't help but feel as though she shared part of the blame. If she hadn't disappeared from Hudson's life without so much as a good-bye, would she have been someone he could've turned to? A friend when he needed one the most? He'd had to face his battles alone then, but it didn't have to be that way now.

"Hudson, you've taken on so much already. Let me help if I can. I just . . . ," she choked back a sob. "I wish I could go back. I'm sorry I wasn't there for you. I'm sorry I hurt you."

His fingers touched her cheek. "No need to apologize, Allie. I've never regretted any of the time we spent together. Those days with you were the best of my life." He cocked a slight grin. "You were the first woman I cared about and didn't just want to take for a ride."

Allie smiled and shook her head. *Ever the bad boy.* "I'd be lying if I said I hadn't thought about that last night on the boat a time or two over the past ten years. Or the night we rode that Ferris wheel about a dozen times." She snuggled against the warmth of his chest. "I don't think I've ever been happier than I was that summer."

"And this?" His hand stroked up and down her back. "This feels good, doesn't it?"

Allie tensed, knowing he was asking so much more than a simple question, and Hudson stilled.

"Don't answer that," he said, sliding out from behind her. He stood and jogged up the stairs. When he returned he had something in his hand and that shy smile on his lips.

"I believe this is yours." He held out his hand and a delicate string of shells dangled from his fingertip.

Allie's mouth fell open on a gasp. It was a shell anklet, *her* shell anklet. She recognized it immediately. To her, that anklet represented all they had once shared. She'd been devastated when she lost it on their last night together, leaving her with nothing to remember him by.

"I never thought I'd see that again." Her eyes filled with tears. "You kept it all this time?"

"I did." Hudson sat down beside her on the rug and gently pulled her foot into his lap. The shells slid along the clear string, filling the spaces of ones lost over time as he wrapped them around her leg. When it was clasped, his hand lingered and his fingers caressed her skin. Allie wondered if, like her, he was remembering the night he first put it there.

Gently, he lifted her leg and pressed a soft kiss to the side of her ankle. "You made me feel hopeful," he whispered.

Allie slipped her leg out of Hudson's grasp and moved into his lap, her thighs straddling his hips as she held his face between her hands.

"Hudson . . ." Her voice trailed off. There was so much they needed to discuss, so much she wanted to say. But in that moment, the words escaped her.

He reached up and brushed her cheek with his knuckles. "What's wrong, Allie?"

251

Her eyes drifted shut and she leaned into his touch. When she opened them, his fierce blue eyes searched hers as if her were trying to see not only into her thoughts, but her very soul. Her heart lurched and she was lost. The only thing that mattered was this man, this moment. She needed to show him with her body all her heart could never say.

She drew a stuttering breath. "Nothing's wrong. Make love to me, Hudson."

His hand curled around her nape and he pulled her to his mouth, kissing her long and slow and deep. Allie's fingers slid into his hair and she held him to her as his tongue slid greedily over hers in lush, dragging sweeps. With a soft moan, she kissed him back, matching his strokes with her own. Exploring, tasting, consuming.

This kiss went on and on like a seductive dance until Allie thought she might come from the sheer pleasure of his lips moving with hers.

Running his hands down her back, Hudson cupped her ass and squeezed. Allie gasped as he yanked her forward, bringing her in intimate contact with the impressive erection straining the front of his jeans.

"What you make me feel . . . ," he whispered in a low, ragged voice. He held her gaze as he flexed his hips. The thin fabric of her yoga pants offered little barrier, allowing the thick ridge of his arousal to hit that sweet spot between her thighs. His mouth slanted over hers once more, and with a roll of his hips, he pushed into her again and again, mimicking the motion of him inside her until she writhed restlessly in his lap.

Hudson reached down, lifted the hem of Allie's sweater, and pulled it over her head. Her breath hitched as his fingers traced the lace cups of her bra before curling around the straps and sliding them down her arms. He leaned forward, nuzzling her hair as his hands followed the band to her back. With a flick of his wrist he released the clasp, letting the bra fall wherever it landed.

Lowering his head, he pressed his warm, wet mouth to her shoulder, then dragged his tongue along her collarbone. Anticipation thrummed hot and heavy through Allie's veins, and she arched her back in silent entreaty. Hudson palmed her breast in one hand, brushing the pad of his thumb over her erect nipple, and flattened his other hand on the middle of her spine. With his fingers splayed wide, he pressed against her, urging her to bend farther back.

"So beautiful," he murmured. His tongue flickered across one nipple, then he kissed his way to the other, leaving a trail of damp heat on her sensitive skin. He laved her slowly, drawing lazy circles around the hardened peak before suckling it deep into his mouth. Her body shuddered and a helpless moan escaped her lips as he tugged the tender tip between his teeth.

Wanting to feel his skin against hers, Allie slipped her fingers under the edge of Hudson's T-shirt. The palms of her hands glided across his taut stomach and chest, leisurely exploring his muscular contours as she worked the fabric higher.

Gathering the cotton fabric in her fingers, she lifted it over his head and tossed it to the side. Her hands moved over his broad shoulders before drifting lower. He sucked in a sharp breath as her thumbnails scraped across his nipples, and then suddenly his arms were around her, holding her close as his mouth claimed hers in a passionate kiss. This time when he pulled her into his arms, there were no barriers, no walls. Just skin against skin. Her breathing was ragged and aroused, her nipples brushing against his chest with every rise and fall of her breasts.

In a swift move he lowered her to the floor, sweeping her black yoga pants down her legs and tossing them to the side before stretching out next to her in front of the fire. His heated gaze raked over her from head to toe.

"No panties?" He licked his lips and she practically convulsed.

Dropping her hands, Allie caressed his erection through the soft denim of his jeans. "I prefer wearing yours." She tugged on his fly, popping the small buttons open one by one, and then slipped her fingers under the waistband of his boxer briefs. He twitched as she took him in her hand, gently squeezing and stroking him from root to tip until a deep groan vibrated in his throat. "In fact, I think I'll take them now if you don't mind."

A sexy grin curved his lips. "By all means."

He stared up at her, his eyes glittering in the warm glow of the fire as she tugged his boxers and jeans down his legs in one sweep. When his erection sprang free she reached for him again, curling her fingers firmly around his length. Hudson's eyes closed briefly and he flexed into her palm.

"Now what?" The amusement in his voice was gone, replaced by a raw, heated desire. His blatant need sent a rush of warmth through her body.

"I want you in my mouth," she whispered.

His answering groan was a sound of sweet misery.

Bending down, she teased him with soft laps of her tongue before parting her lips and taking him inside. Hudson watched her through hooded eyes as she slowly drew him back out, blowing a breath of warm air across his moistened flesh. He flexed his hips and she smiled. *Hmm, now who wants more?* Only too happy to oblige, she swirled her tongue across the tip, then ran it up and down his length as she moved him in and out of her mouth.

His fingers tangled in her hair and his body arched, pushing him deeper. "Yes," he hissed between clenched teeth.

The feel of him throbbing and pulsing in her mouth drove her wild. She loved that she could do this to him, make him lose himself in the moment, lose himself in her. Spurred on by his pleasure, she sucked harder, finding a perfect rhythm with her hands and mouth.

His stomach muscles tensed. "Enough. I want to be inside you when I come." The words came out in a rush. He curled toward her, pulling her up the length of his body and crushing his mouth to hers.

With a groan he rolled Allie onto her back, kneeing her legs apart and settling between her thighs. Bearing his weight on his elbows, he threaded his fingers with hers and held them on either side of her head. He gazed down at her and gently brushed his lips across her mouth. The kiss deepened as he brought their bodies together, licking his way into her mouth as he pushed himself farther inside her.

Once buried to the hilt, he stilled; the peace and tranquility of the room broken only by the sounds of their mingled breaths and the roaring fire.

"You're all I need," he murmured. Slowly he began to move, pulling back and then flexing into her with a deliberate, unhurried rhythm.

Allie moaned, loving the feel of him inside her, filling her, moving with her. She wrapped her legs around him, her heels digging into his ass as she urged him on.

"Slow," he whispered, running his tongue along her bottom lip before lazily pulling it between his teeth. "I want to take this slow."

He continued his leisurely torment, drawing back to the tip before gliding into her again. Allie's neck arched on a frustrated groan. His carefully timed thrusts were driving her wild. Heaven and hell all rolled into one.

She lifted her body into his and gasped as he slid deeper. "Please, Hudson . . ."

Gradually he increased his rhythm, and slowly but surely she began to climb. His body rolled against hers with measured determination as he drove her higher and higher. Allie felt her insides begin to quicken as his thrusts became shorter, sharper.

"That's it, Allie," he growled. "Come with me."

His words were her undoing and she came in a dizzying rush. Her orgasm went on and on, pulsing through her like waves as he stroked into her again and again.

Hudson's fingers squeezed hers and he came long and hard, his hips slicing forward one last time as he poured himself into her. With their hands still linked, he collapsed on top of her and buried his face in her neck.

When he released her hands, she wrapped her arms around him and held him tight, emotions welling up inside her like the tears that stung her eyes.

After miles of roping turns, Hudson maneuvered the Range Rover through the light Sunday traffic on I- 94, his grip tight on the wheel and the air in the SUV thick with silence. There was so much he wanted to say to Allie that his mind raced and his head pounded. But every time he opened his damn mouth, the threat to spill his guts was doing a jig on the end of his tongue. Being the other man wasn't in his nature, and whenever he thought about that marquis fucker his territorial impulses were triggered.

Headlights on the other side of the highway intermittently illuminated the car, highlighting her face and allowing him to steal a glimpse of her. His eyes glided over Allie's delicate profile before looking back at the road in front of him. Her attempts at making conversation with his monosyllabic responses had been getting them nowhere, but as the towering skyline of the city appeared in the distance, she tried again.

"Do you have a busy day tomorrow?" she asked.

"Shit." He reached for his phone and turned it on. The thing lit up like a goddamn Christmas tree with notifications of missed messages, e-mails, and texts. All that was missing were smoke signals.

Hudson hit the voice mail and Nick's panicked voice came over the speaker. "It's me. Call me as soon as you get this." There was a low, deep sigh, then his voice grew stronger. "Where the fuck are you?"

The message ended and another began to play, then another and another. With each one Nick sounded progressively worse, spiraling into a full-blown panic attack. Hudson cursed under his breath when the next message began to play and that raspy, heavy with nicotine voice filled the car.

"Hudson, my man, need to get your ass down here . . ."

He snapped the cell out of the cradle and pressed it to his ear. He could feel Allie watching him as he curbed the SUV in front of his building and shifted into park.

"I need to get Nick. Go on upstairs and make yourself at home."

"Do you want me to come with you?"

"No." His tone was insistent. "Wait for me." He lifted his hips, reached into the pocket of his jeans, and pulled a card out of his wallet. "For the elevator," he said, handing it to her. "It will take you straight up."

Her hand gripped the door handle. "Is Nick okay?" The worry in her voice was palpable. He wanted to take her face between his hands and tell her everything was going to be fine, but he didn't know that it would be.

"Yeah . . . I think." He pushed the speed dial on his phone and held it up to his ear as Allie reluctantly got out of the car. With a screech, he merged with the oncoming traffic. In his rearview mirror he could still see Allie standing at the curb, watching him.

When the call was answered he didn't wait for hello. "How bad?" he barked into the phone, speeding through a yellow light just as it changed to red.

The bar owner cocked his fingers like a gun and pointed in the direction of the back room as soon as Hudson walked through the door. His stomach turned as he made his way through the dingy establishment. The place never seemed to lose that stale beer stench and must have been breaking about a dozen health codes.

Cranking the knob, Hudson walked into the back room, only for his stride to falter. He stumbled back a step and shoved his hand into his hair. The gruesome scene was straight out of his recurring nightmare. Blood, lots of it, and front and center a man was sprawled unconscious. Not wanting to touch the guy, Hudson nudged him with his foot. Nothing.

He looked to Nick and found him pacing like a caged animal. There were a couple contusions already starting to swell on his face, and blood trailed from a cut below his eye, dripping off his chin.

Hudson's eyes dropped to the DOA with the cracked skull and the remnants of a broken chair beside him. Blood pooled under the guy's head, his greasy hair marinating in the dense liquid. As it began to ooze toward Hudson's shoes, images flashed in rapid succession. A gunshot. Blood-soaked jeans. His father shouting.

Turning his back on the scene, Hudson drew a deep breath and put a lockdown on his memories. He shut the door, then pegged his little brother with a hard stare. "What the fuck happened, Nick?"

"It was an accident, Hudson, I swear. The bastard was going to kill me." Nick paced back and forth, back and forth. "Fuck. Fuck. Fuck."

Hudson's eyes tracked Nick's movements. "Who is he?"

Nick stopped pacing and his shell-shocked eyes focused on Hudson. "He's . . . ah, just a guy I know."

Hudson's glare narrowed. "Bullshit. Who the fuck is he, Nick?"

"My . . . yeah, my dealer."

"What happened?" he said through gritted teeth.

"I don't want to get you involved."

"Too late." He grabbed Nick by the collar and pushed him into a chair. "Start talking. Now."

"I don't know, man, it all went down so fast. I guess he hit his head." Nick blew out a breath and wiped his palms on his thighs. "He wanted the money I owe him. I told him I didn't have it and he went crazy, started coming after me with a fucking chair."

Hudson's eyes flicked down to the broken chair, now suited for kindling.

"He was beating the shit out of me, bro. I'm pretty sure he woulda killed me if I hadn't pushed him."

"Fuck, Nick." Hudson knew his brother was on the up and up. When shit got real, Nick's instincts had kicked into gear, refusing to take a beatdown of the six-feet-under variety. But what a fucking mess. The press would have a field day with this one, and the DA would fry Nick just to prove relatives of the rich and famous weren't above the law. Hell if he was going to lose his brother to another system, one he'd have no chance of getting him out of even with his means and a team of lawyers.

The door creaked open and Hudson shot Nick a shut-the-fuck-up look.

"You two about done with the family reunion?"

Hudson heard the rasp of a lighter and turned to find the bar owner lighting up another one. "Anyone else know?"

"No, in this part of town you mind your own fucking business. Most of the guys in here have records as long as my arm." He took a long drag off his cigarette. "They're gonna scatter like roaches if the cops start poking around."

"Good. Keep it that way." Hudson flipped open his wallet.

"I'm sure in this neighborhood another dead junkie isn't breaking news."

"Yeah, you wouldn't believe the shit we find in the trash out back."

Hudson thumbed through a stack of benji's, counting them off while the bar owner watched like a salivating dog. "Consider this a down payment."

*A*llie was staring blankly at the television screen, mindlessly flipping through hundreds of channels, when she heard the distant *ping* of the elevator. *Finally!* It had been almost two hours since Hudson had left her on the sidewalk in front of his penthouse, and she was going out of her mind with worry.

She scrambled off the couch and flew down the stairs, reaching the bottom just as the elevator doors slid open.

Hudson stepped off first. His face was set in hard lines as he strode through the foyer without so much as a glance in her direction. Nick was tight on his heels with his head down and his hands shoved into the pockets of his jeans.

Self-conscious, Allie tugged at the hem of her borrowed T-shirt. With her suitcase still in the car, it wasn't like she'd had many options. But it had been ten years since she'd seen Nick, and although Hudson's shirt was plenty long enough, she wouldn't have changed for bed if she'd known he was coming over. Then again, this was hardly the typical reunion.

She hesitated for a moment, unsure of what to say, then cleared her throat and kept it simple. "Hi, Nick."

He stopped short at the sound of her voice. "Oh hey, Allie. I didn't know you were here."

Her hand flew to her mouth. "Oh my God . . ."

Nick's clothes were splattered with blood and his face had been horribly beaten. He stared at her like a deer in headlights before tucking his head back down and following his brother into the penthouse.

Allie was right behind him.

She found them in the kitchen. Hudson radiated a barely restrained fury, opening and closing cabinets with more force than necessary until he found a bottle of Blue Label. He poured himself a sizable shot while Nick stood quietly at the end of the breakfast bar, shifting from one foot to the other. Waiting for instructions, she presumed.

"What happened?" she asked him.

"Um . . ." Nick's bloodshot eyes darted to his brother.

Hudson paused with his glass halfway to his mouth. The look he shot Nick spoke volumes, not the least of which was "don't you fucking dare."

Allie let out an exasperated breath. The wall was back up. There was no way she was letting the subject drop indefinitely, but at the moment Nick's injuries were her main concern. "Let me see." She brushed his hair back from his face, trying to inspect the deep cut below his eye. "Do you think you need stitches?"

Nick winced and ducked out of her reach. "Nah, I'm fine. S'all good. Just need some soap and water."

"I think it needs more than that." She turned back to Hudson. "Do you have a first-aid kit?"

"He's a big boy, Alessandra. He can take care of it." The muscles in his jaw clenched as he glared at his younger brother. "Go to bed, Nick."

"Ah . . . yeah. It's been a long one." Nick licked at the dried blood in the corner of his mouth.

"Well at least let me give you some ice." Allie turned and

reached for a clean dish towel, filling it with a handful of ice cubes. "Here, this will help with the swelling."

He gave her a weak smile. "Thanks, Allie. Good seeing you again."

"Yeah, you too." She watched as Nick lumbered out of the room. He stumbled into the wall once but quickly righted himself before heading toward the stairs. Allie followed to make sure he made it down in one piece, then went to find Hudson.

He was in the living room, sipping scotch while staring out the window at the black shadow of Lake Michigan. Obviously he was upset by whatever he'd found when he went to get Nick, but what she couldn't understand was why he was acting so cold toward the younger brother she knew he loved. Not to mention the anger she felt directed at her. Hostility rolled off him in waves, and part of her couldn't help but wonder if it had something to do with his mood on the car ride home. Their weekend together had been perfect; but then everything started to unravel the moment they left the lake, and the closer they got to the city limits, the more she'd felt him pulling away.

When he'd drained his glass, he went to the kitchen to pour himself another. Allie waited for him to offer an explanation—or hell, say anything at all—but he merely turned on his heel and stalked out of the room.

She followed him into his office. "Are you going to tell me what's going on?"

He leaned against the corner of his desk and took a sip of the amber liquid. "How about you go first?"

"What do you mean?"

"This." He gestured between them. "This farce. After all these years I'm still your dirty little secret, aren't I?"

Allie stiffened. "Of course not."

"Sure as hell been acting like it. Your mother saw us at the symphony and your first reaction was to run."

"I couldn't tell her the truth."

"Right, because I'll always be the kid from the wrong part of town. Doesn't matter how much money I have, I'll never be good enough."

"That's not true," she said. Her voice was small. "I'm engaged, Hudson. You knew that from the beginning."

He contemplated her words with narrowed eyes, then tossed back the rest of his drink. "Fair point." His movements were smooth and methodical as he set the empty glass behind him and crossed his arms over his chest. When he spoke, his voice was menacingly calm. "Tell me, Alessandra, did he ask you to go with him to Paris? Two weeks is a long time to be apart. How many times has he called while he—"

Allie held up her hand. "Stop." Enough was enough. She turned to leave but he caught her wrist.

"Not until you stop lying to yourself and end this charade."

"It's not that simple," she shot back.

Hudson let out a harsh laugh. "Why, because the fucking invitations have gone out? Is that some rule of high society? No turning back once the announcement has run on page six? The rules you've lived by, the ones you had no say in creating no longer apply, Alessandra. If you continue to allow people to lead you down a predetermined path, then you're not the woman I think you are."

Tears pooled in Allie's eyes. "I don't know what you want from me." She took an involuntary step backward as Hudson pushed away from the desk. He stepped closer until he stood before her, the bookshelf at her back. His proximity and the intensity of his gaze overwhelmed her, and she looked away, torn between the urge to run and the urge to wrap her arms around him and never let him go.

He cupped her jaw and gently turned her head. His blue eyes burned with sincerity. "What I want is for you to ask yourself what makes you happy. Not your parents, but you."

A stray tear slid down her cheek and he caught it with his thumb.

"You have it in you to get what you want," he said, his voice low and coaxing. "You have all along."

Dipping his head, Hudson took her mouth in a tender kiss. His lips moved softly over hers, his tongue lightly tracing the seam of her lips until she opened for him. He entered slowly, reverently, teasing and tasting her with soft, shallow licks as her body melted into his.

He sighed deeply and let his forehead rest against hers. "I promised myself I wouldn't bring this up till next weekend, but I can't do this anymore, Allie. I can't keep pretending two weeks will be enough." His impassioned voice was barely a whisper. "The thought of you leaving tears me apart, a knife twisting into my soul."

His confession burned through her like fire, igniting her body with a desperate need. She grabbed him, pulling him to her and kissing him with all the pent-up emotion of the past two weeks. Every feeling, every desire, every unspoken word poured into that one kiss.

"I won't share you," he murmured against her lips. "I can't. And it's not just male pride."

Hudson leaned back to look at her, his eyes dark and smoldering. "The thought of another man touching you . . ." His hand smoothed over the curve of her waist. "Making love to you . . ." His fingers dug into her hip. "It's unbearable."

Grasping the back of her thigh, he lifted her leg, draping it over his as he placed his foot on one of the lower shelves. With a flex of his hips he pressed her against the bookshelf. "It's either me or him."

Her body moved of its own volition, pushing back against the erection straining the seam of his fly.

He watched her through hooded eyes. "If you can honestly tell me you want to walk away from this, I won't stand in your way." His fingers threaded with hers and he lifted her hand, pinning it above her head. "I'll leave you alone if that's what you decide."

Allie felt her engagement ring slip from her finger.

"But tonight you're mine."

Hudson moved fast and swift, undoing his fly and shifting her panties. In one lithe movement he thrust inside her, emphasizing his words with the force of his body. She moaned, relishing the feel of him, but then all too quickly he withdrew. The emptiness she felt brought an unwelcome ache.

"More?" His voice was thick and husky.

"Yes."

He groaned and drove to the hilt once more.

"Harder," she breathed, wanting all he had to give.

Allie gasped as he surged into her, claiming both her body and her mouth. Over and over he took her, his tongue stroking hers with the same ferocious passion as his thrusts. Her senses were overloaded. The scent of his skin, the feel of his body, the taste of his mouth. She was surrounded by him, inside and out.

His arm banded around her waist, pulling her down to meet his punishing drives, and she tilted her hips, trying to take more of him. She clung to his shoulders and felt the muscles in his back flex as he gripped the shelf above her head. With his foot leveraged on the lower shelf, he powered into her, practically climbing the bookcase as he tried to get deeper and deeper inside her.

Her eyes fluttered closed, memorizing the feel of him moving hard and strong inside her—filling her, stretching her, possessing her—and a hot tear slid down her cheek. The intensity of their connection was almost more than she could bear.

He moved faster, pushed higher, until finally it became too much. Her back arched against the shelves and her body exploded in a violent rush.

"Again," he growled, and with a roll of his hips drove her over the edge once more. Her head fell back on a desperate cry of his name as fierce tremors pulsed through her. Hudson was tireless, grinding into her with unrelenting thrusts until she came again and again, each orgasm rolling into the next as her core clenched and released.

With a long, deep groan he drove hard one last time, burying his face in her neck as he found his release. His breath was harsh and hot against her skin. "Never enough, Allie. It will never be enough."

Her body shuddered on a silent sob and she collapsed against his chest. Totally exhausted. Totally sated.

Totally his.

35

*S*hots rang out.

Like a fist out of the darkness, the nightmare seized Hudson with a fury. He couldn't move and his heart was hammering in his chest.

Sucked into the vortex of terror, he was on his knees, unable to speak. Death encircled him as the metallic stench of blood coated the back of his throat. It was splattered on his shirt and dripping from his fingers in rivulets.

Flashing lights descended on the convenience store and the image sharpened. They'd come back in for something. What had he foolishly wanted? Crippling grief haunted every cell of his body.

Wake up, damn it . . . wake up. Hudson fisted the sheets under him in his rising panic.

A weak hand captured his and held on. Everything was chaos. People ran around him shouting commands. His mother skidded to her knees, slipping through the viscous liquid that stained her legs, and wrapped her arms around him, clutching him to her chest. She was so cold, yet the room was stifling hot and he was sweating.

And as quick as a last breath, the hand clutching his let go. The sounds of his mother's scream ricocheted off the walls so loudly he thought the fluorescent lights above them would shatter.

He should be crying, shouldn't he? With a scream lodged in his burning throat, Hudson squeezed his eyes shut, straining to force tears out for someone he should be crying for. Why wasn't he crying? Why couldn't he cry for the one person who meant so much to him?

This was his fault . . .

All his fault.

"Hudson." Gentle cool hands landed on his chest. "Hudson, wake up."

White-knuckling the sheets, Hudson thrashed his legs and his chest heaved with a panting breath.

"Hudson. You're dreaming. Wake up."

He bolted upright. "What? What is it?" His eyes darted around the room.

"You were having a nightmare."

"Jesus." Closing his eyes, Hudson scrubbed a hand down his face, the remains of his dream clinging to him like a physical blow.

"Are you okay?" she asked. He could hear the concern in her voice.

"Yeah." Fuck no. "Yeah." He looked at Allie kneeling back on her heels beside him and thought how convoluted and screwed up her life was because of him. She didn't need someone like him fucking everything up the way he had with his own family, but the compulsion to be with her was like a madness.

In a series of smooth and swift movements, Hudson rolled her beneath him. She gasped as he yanked her T-shirt over her head, baring her entire body to him before taking her mouth with primal desperation.

"I want you." He hooked his ankles with hers and spread her

legs wide. With the nightmare still fresh in his mind, all he wanted was to be lost in the softness between her thighs, to feel her wrapped around him. For just one moment he wanted to be free of his past. To be free of his guilt.

"Wait, Hudson. Wait," she panted, and pushed against his chest. "We need to talk. You were screaming."

He pressed his lips to her throat, sucking gently. "I don't need to talk. I need you. I need this." She moaned, bowing into his hands as his cock stroked between the lips of her sex. Sealing his mouth over hers, his tongue dipped into her with deep, lush glides. He laced his fingers with hers and slipped her hand between them. "Feel me as I take you."

With a necessity fueling what was already an almost debilitating desire, he entered her on a solid stroke.

36

$\mathcal{A}$llie tapped her foot on the lobby floor, glancing up at the descending numbers above the elevator doors, willing them to move faster. She was late, seriously late, and she was never late to work. Ever.

"What is taking so long," she mumbled.

Wanting to check the time, she fished her phone out of her purse, only to realize she'd never turned it on. As soon as she did, it started to vibrate with missed calls and messages. The most recent was a text from Harper. Allie read it as she stepped into the elevator.

Meeting NOW. Where R U?

"Shit," she cursed under her breath while shoving the phone in the pocket of her jeans. Jeans, at work! Another thing she never did, but desperate times and all that. She'd overslept—item three on the morning's "never" list—and had barely had time to brush her teeth and throw her hair in a ponytail, let alone swing by her place for work clothes.

The elevator doors slid open. Allie bypassed her office and bolted straight for the conference room. Mr. Ellis never broke stride as she slipped into the room, continuing as if nothing was amiss while she quietly took her seat at the table. Allie ignored Harper's raised brow, dropping her purse on the floor and powering up her tablet. An incoming message filled a chat box in the corner of the screen before she'd even had time to pull up the agenda.

When did we start Casual Mondays?

Leave it to Harper to not let the jeans go unnoticed, let alone unmentioned. But either way, Allie did need more suitable clothes for the rest of the week. She made a mental note to swing by her apartment after work and grab a few things. Clothes, shoes, underwear. Come to think of it, she might need to run out at lunch and buy more underwear, given the rate Hudson tore through them. The thought of his fingers shredding through satin and lace made a warm blush spread over her cheeks.

Within seconds another message appeared.

OMG, you spent the weekend with HIM, didn't you?

Followed by another . . .

Don't bother denying it. I know the walk of shame when I see it.

And then another . . .

You can't avoid me forever.

No, but she could certainly try. Allie shot Harper an annoyed look, then turned her attention to the meeting's agenda. She scanned the bullet points, desperately trying to decipher which item they were currently discussing.

"Could you and Harper handle that, Alessandra?"

Allie's head snapped up at the sound of her boss's voice. *Handle what?* Jeez, she was a mess. And it was only Monday. "Sure thing," she said, wondering what in the hell she'd just agreed to. A message popped up from Harper, who had clearly read her mind. Or at least her panicked face.

Textbook budget.

Ah, okay. "Thank you," Allie mouthed across the table. A

yawn came out of nowhere and, embarrassed, she quickly covered her mouth with her hand. Harper's eyes grew wide and she immediately began typing. Allie frowned. *Great, what now?*

`Holy shit, you finally did it!`

Harper rolled her eyes at Allie's blank look. She tapped a few keys on her tablet and then stared pointedly at Allie's left hand.

`You finally kicked Lord Lame-Ass to the curb.`

Allie's eyes darted to her hand where she saw . . . nothing? She let out a small gasp. Julian's ring was gone. She'd no sooner had the thought when she remembered Hudson slipping it off her finger and placing it on one of the bookshelves. *Tonight you're mine.* Her toes curled at the thought of his unyielding power, his unwavering authority. He'd completely possessed her —mind, body, and soul.

`This calls for a celebration!`

`Dancing? Drinks first, of course.`

`We should totally hit . . .`

Harper's messages came in rapid succession, rambling on about all the ways in which they were going to celebrate, but Allie had stopped reading them. She couldn't take her eyes off her unadorned finger. She'd grown so used to the sight of Julian's ring that it seemed strange to look down and see nothing but her bare hand. Strange and wonderful. It was as though an enormous weight had been lifted from her. Some tether to a life she neither designed nor enjoyed. It felt . . . perfect.

In that moment Allie knew what she wanted. Deep down she'd known it all along. Julian might have been the right choice for Ingram Media, but he wasn't the right choice for her. She knew her parents would be livid, but somehow she'd have to make them understand. The past two weeks with Hudson had changed her, awakened a side of her that had been waiting to be set free. Life before him was neat, orderly, and boring as hell. She'd never felt more alive than she did when she was with him.

It was the same way she'd felt ten years ago, but the connection between them had grown stronger, more intense. Had she really thought she could give that up? Give him up? It broke her heart to walk away from him once. There was no way she was making that same mistake twice.

The meeting dragged on, as did the rest of the afternoon. All day her mind drifted to thoughts of Hudson. She was dying to call him, if for no other reason than to hear his voice, but fought the urge. She knew if she gave in she'd end up spilling her guts over the phone, and she wanted to look into his eyes when she told him she was ending things with Julian; that she was choosing a life with him.

When six o'clock finally rolled around, she sent him a quick text.

Stopping by my place for clothes. Meet you at PH. Late dinner?

There was no reply. Come to think of it, she hadn't heard from Hudson all day. She'd been so busy trying to keep her mind off calling him that she hadn't even realized he'd never tried to call her. Not once. At first she thought it was odd, but then she reminded herself he was probably busy handling all the calls he'd ignored over the weekend. Or maybe he was with Nick.

Sweet little Nicky. Her heart sank at the thought of all that had happened to him as a young boy. And now he was in even worse shape. Just picturing the way he looked when he stepped off the elevator last night, like a stray that had been beaten and starved, made her shudder. She sent up a silent prayer that he'd finally accepted the help his older brother was offering.

Hudson never did tell her what had happened after he dropped her off at the penthouse, but whatever it was had been bad. Really bad. And knowing how Hudson felt about his brother, the responsibility he bore, she knew it was tearing him up inside. Was that what brought on his nightmare? The haunting image of him writhing as he fisted the sheets filled her mind. Allie had never witnessed a nightmare like that firsthand. It had been excruciating to watch him in so much pain, his legs tangled in the bedding, his face contorted, his chest heaving.

He wouldn't talk about it in bed last night. No big surprise there. Hudson was always so guarded about his life, particularly his past, but Allie planned to bring it up the first chance she had. If they were going to build a life together, she wanted to be a part of all of it. The good and the bad. But more than that, she wanted to help him if she could. It was obvious from what she'd witnessed that he kept something buried deep inside, something that surfaced when he slept, gripping him when he was most vulnerable, when he had no control. She would do anything if it meant never seeing him in that kind of pain again. Anything.

At her apartment Allie quickly showered and changed into a chocolate-brown jersey dress, pairing it with the hoop earrings Hudson had once said caught the gold flecks in her hazel eyes. She left her hair in loose curls, just the way she knew he liked it, and at the last minute decided to leave her panties in the drawer. A shiver ran through her at the thought of his reaction when his questing fingers discovered her lack of lingerie.

Anxious to get to the penthouse, she grabbed a few outfits for work and threw them in a bag. She was halfway out the door when her phone rang. The screen read "private caller." *Hudson.* Her lips curved into a wide smile as she answered the call. "Missing me?" she purred.

There was silence on the line, then a heavy exhale. "Oui, of course."

"Julian?" She glanced at her watch, quickly adjusting for the time change. "What are you doing up so late? Isn't it almost two in Paris?"

"I'm in Chicago. Actually, I'm stuck on the fucking Kennedy."

"You're back?" Her voice sounded much louder than she'd intended.

"My business concluded sooner than expected so I—how do you say?—caught a flight."

Oh shit. She wasn't expecting to have this conversation until next weekend. She needed time to prepare, time to sort out what she wanted to say. Maybe she could stall, at least buy herself one night.

"You must be exhausted. Get some sleep and we can meet for drinks after work tomorrow. The Peninsula, say six o'clock?"

"Don't be ridiculous." There was a brief pause as he took a drag off his cigarette. "I told the driver to drop me at your apartment."

She glanced around her apartment, but for what she had no idea. "How far out are you?"

"Je ne sais pas—fifteen, maybe twenty minutes. Sooner if these fucking imbeciles would learn to drive."

What? The ride from O'Hare was always a nightmare. Just her luck tonight would be the exception.

"Great. I'll see you then." Allie tried to keep her voice light as she rushed him off the phone. She needed to collect herself. She needed to call Hudson. He was expecting her to meet him at his penthouse. *Crap.* This was not a conversation she wanted to have over the phone.

The call went to voice mail and Allie breathed a sigh of relief. She knew he would have pressed her for answers, and right now she just didn't have the time. Hudson's outgoing message was gruff, to the point, and for some bizarre reason, made her smile.

"Hi, it's me. Um . . . Julian just called. He's back in town and headed over here." She paused, debating how much more to say, and then simply added, "I need to talk to him. I'll call as soon as I can."

When Julian arrived, he went straight to the kitchen to fix

himself a drink. And if his bloodshot eyes were any indication, it wasn't his first of the night. Or second, for that matter. If Allie had to guess, he'd probably had more than a few on the transatlantic flight. Had he always drank so much?

Glass in hand, he leaned against the counter, casting a leering glance down her body.

She felt her palms grow damp. There was no easy way to do this; might as well get it over with. "Julian . . ."

"Wait." He strolled toward her, oozing arrogance. "Forgot one thing." He leaned closer and the sour stench of alcohol mixed with the sweet scent of his cologne. Allie's empty stomach churned. What had she ever seen in this man? Just as he was about to kiss her, she turned her head a fraction, offering him her cheek instead.

"We need to talk," she whispered.

Julian snorted and tossed back the rest of his vodka. "Talk? Tu te fous de moi? I've been traveling all day; the last thing I want to do is talk." He set his glass down on the end table and slid his hands around Allie's waist.

"I can't do this." She tried wriggling out of his arms, but his hold on her tightened as his lips found her neck.

"I've been gone almost two weeks, ma chérie." He was everywhere at once. His long hands roaming down her back; his wet lips moving across her skin; his hardening erection digging into her hip. She flattened her palms against his chest and pushed, but he didn't budge.

"I'm serious, Julian. Stop."

"Let me guess, you have a headache?" His hands slid to her backside, feeling his way over her body and holding her tight against him. "I thought those excuses started after the ceremony?" he said, letting his tongue dip into her ear.

"I can't marry you."

He lifted his head. She'd expected shock, even anger, but

Julian's eyes blazed with raw fury. "The hell you can't," he said through clenched teeth.

"I'm sorry, but I don't love you." Her voice was small but firm.

"Love?" He sneered at her. "This has nothing to do with love, Alessandra." Julian released her and she exhaled the breath she hadn't even realized she'd been holding. "It's an arrangement. Part of the deal."

Allie's wide eyes darted to his. She was part of a deal? What deal?

"Don't act so surprised." The smile he gave her sent a chill down her spine. "You're one hell of a trophy wife."

And there it was, the cold truth.

Julian picked up his drink and beelined for the bottle of Grey Goose he'd left on the kitchen counter. Allie watched as he poured a hefty shot over the ice, making himself at home in her apartment just as he had in the rest of her life. She felt like such a fool. None of it had been real. The whirlwind romance, the impulsive proposal, not even the tender words whispered across a pillow. Allie's eyes drifted shut as a wave of nausea rolled through her, and for a moment she thought she might be sick. Everything had been a means to an end, all part of his plan to worm his way into Ingram Media.

Ice cubes rattled against cut glass and she opened her eyes. Julian was staring at her, his lips curled into a smirk. "You haven't learned a damn thing from your mother, have you?"

"I'm nothing like her." Tears of anger and frustration threatened and she wiped them quickly with her hand.

Julian's eyes flared over the top of his glass. "Where's your ring?" he asked, leveling his stare on her left hand. Before she could answer he slammed the glass down on the counter and stalked toward her. Allie stepped back but he grabbed her with both hands, his fingers digging into her arms to the point of pain. "What the fuck have you been doing while I was gone?"

"You're hurting me."

He gave her a hard shake. "Answer me. Where the fuck is my ring, Alessandra?" His nostrils flared and his face twisted with rage. Allie had never seen him like this. Angry over a botched dinner reservation? Sure. Impatient with a valet? Absolutely. But the man standing in front of her was volatile and wild, totally out of control.

"You'll get it back." Her mouth was so dry she could barely get the words out. "Do you honestly think I'd try to keep it?"

"Peut-être," he snarled. "Considering the money I've promised your father, you're no better than the whores I pay."

She flinched at first, then lifted her chin. What Julian was saying was ridiculous. He was just lashing out, trying to hurt her, and she'd be damned if she'd let him hurt her anymore than he already had. "My father doesn't need your money." She tried her best to sound unaffected, but her voice trembled, betraying her.

"Your *father*," he said with utter disdain, "is losing his company one share at a time." He let out a harsh, condescending laugh. "You didn't think I was actually in a hurry to get married, did you?"

He paused, waiting for a reaction, but she refused to give him the satisfaction.

"Someone's making a play," he continued, "buying up stock left and right." It was obvious how much he enjoyed being the one to break the news. "He needs me, or at least my cash, to save it."

Still gripping her tight with one hand, he ran his index finger down her throat until he reached the low neckline of her dress. He hooked the material with his finger then let it dip between her breasts. Allie's heart rate spiked and her eyes darted toward the door. Four steps, maybe five. Thank God it was unlocked. He'd catch her if she had to struggle with the deadbolt. All she had to do was break free.

A dark glint flashed in Julian's eyes and he slowly licked his bottom lip. "I'd say you owe me."

Allie struggled but he tightened his grip. Fear lodged in her throat, choking her and causing her breath to come in shallow gasps. She could barely draw enough air to speak. "Let go of me, you sick bastard."

From out of nowhere the back of his hand struck her face. The force of the blow knocked her off- balance and she fell hard, her head smacking against the coffee table with a loud crack. White light flashed behind her eyes and her head exploded with pain. She felt a gush of warm liquid flow down the side of her cheek and instinctively her hand flew to her face. When she lowered it, her fingers were bright red.

Allie looked up, her vision blurred with tears and blood, to find him coming back for more. She tried to scramble away only to feel a sharp burn in her scalp as he grabbed a fistful of her hair. The room shifted as he hauled her to her feet, and for a second she thought she might faint.

Julian yanked her back against his chest. "You fucking bitch," he growled in her ear. "All you had to do was play the damn part, stand up and say I-fucking-do." With a hard shove he bent her over the back of the couch. The blow to her ribs knocked the breath from her lungs in a powerful gust.

"I held up my end. Right now my dick's hard, you're here, and I'm just drunk enough." He kicked her legs apart with his feet, one hand still in her hair, pushing her face into the cushions while the other unzipped his fly.

Panic gripped her. She tried to cry, to scream, but unable to catch her breath, managed nothing more than a silent plea.

No . . . please no. . . .

*H*udson heard the guttural snarls of a man's voice funneling down the broad stairwell as he entered the foyer of Allie's brownstone. Panic washed through him and turned his blood to ice.

Without breaking stride, he bolted up the stairs two at a time. His heart started beating hard and fast.

Oh God, please let her be okay.

He burst through the door and the scene in front of him was instantly burned into his retinas. Allie bent over the couch, her legs kicked wide and blood running down the side of her face. Julian postured behind her, holding her down with one hand and working his fly with the other.

And he lost it.

Hudson's body went on autopilot, all action and very little thought. He launched himself forward, grabbing Julian by the back of the neck and throwing him off Allie. Julian slammed into an end table, taking a lamp with him as he crash-landed onto the floor. The porcelain base shattered beneath him and the shards dispersed like marbles across the hardwood.

Staggering to his feet, Julian turned to face Hudson. His

hand was bleeding from a deep gash in his palm, and when he clenched his fist, blood oozed between his fingers. The guy was definitely juiced up on something that was interfering with his pain receptors.

A calm menace vibrated around Hudson while he waited for the French import to get upright. "You just going to stand there, or are we going to do this?" His glare narrowed. "I've wanted to sack the shit out of you since day one."

Julian fanned his arms out in a challenge, blood dripping off his hand. "Isn't this sweet, the knight riding in to save his whore," he taunted. "That's all she is, just someone to wet the tip of your dick."

The guy had a serious death wish.

In a blaze of white rage, Hudson charged at Julian and the two men collided, force against force and fist to fist.

Allie fell back out of their way. "NO! Hudson, please . . ." she sobbed, unable to do anything to stop the fury breaking loose in front of her.

Taking a double shot, a nice one-two to the ribs, Hudson sucked in a huge breath and shut out the pain. He methodically returned the favor and nailed Julian with a stunner of an upper-cut, his bare knuckles absorbing the blow. Bones cracked and blood gushed. Julian's head snapped back up and Hudson rebounded with a strong left, splitting his brow wide open.

The determined fucker wasn't going down easily.

Julian wiped the blood off his face with his forearm and came back at him in a wide swing. Hudson dodged to the side and Julian's fist plowed into his kidneys, throwing him off-balance. Pain exploded up his spine and down his legs. His face screwed tight and his teeth clenched. Goddamn, that hurt.

Hudson's rage jacked further. That's the thing about pain—it either knocks you down or fires you up. Right now it was one hell of a motivator.

Before Hudson was fully aware of what he was doing, he

surged forward, caught Julian by the throat, and flattened him out on the ground. Julian's eyes widened and his pupils dilated as Hudson's Ferragamo came down on his throat. Julain grabbed the shoe with both hands and tried to pry it off, but Hudson kept his foot pressed tightly to his neck.

"Did you know it only takes a small amount of pressure to crush your windpipe?"

Julian's face turned red and his hands shook as he tried to push Hudson off.

"Ever come near her again and I'll rip your fucking esophagus out and use it as a garden hose. Now nod."

Julian nodded, his hands still white-knuckling Hudson's loafer.

"Good boy." He removed his foot from Julian's neck and left him coughing on the floor.

Hudson turned toward Allie, and the blow of seeing the tears streaking down her bloodstained cheek was worse than any hit he'd taken from Julian. He took his jacket off and wrapped it around her shoulders. "Are you okay?"

She sagged against him, barely managing a nod.

"Let's go." He held her tight as he guided her out of the apartment, shielding her from the curious eyes of her neighbors.

38

a llie closed her eyes against the bright light and shivered.
"Are you cold?" Hudson knelt in front of her, gently wiping the blood off her face with a warm washcloth.

She shook her head and it made the room spin. "No, I just can't stop shaking."

He frowned and a deep furrow creased his brow. "It's the adrenaline. Let me get this bandaged and then I'll find you some warmer clothes." Lowering the cloth, he quickly folded it in half, but not before she saw the blood. *So much blood.*

"How bad is it?" She was half afraid to ask. Her perch on the side of the tub faced away from the mirror, a position she was beginning to think wasn't entirely coincidental.

"Looks like the bleeding finally stopped. But you're going to have one hell of a shiner." Hudson reached into the first-aid kit for a brown bottle. A moment later he held up a cotton ball soaked in antiseptic. "Close your eyes."

Gently, he dabbed the cold liquid on the gash above her eye. *Ouch!* The sharp sting made her wince, and she heard Hudson suck in a sharp, sympathetic breath.

289

"God, Allie, I wanted to kill him." His voice was menacingly calm.

Allie opened her eyes. Hudson was staring at her, his lips pressed together in a thin line as he cleaned her wounds. She held perfectly still, letting him tend to her, knowing he needed to do this for her as much as she needed it done. When he finished, he pitched the cotton in the trash and rummaged through the kit for a large bandage, which he coated with antibiotic ointment.

"I've never seen Julian like that," she whispered. "It was like he was possessed or something. He just snapped."

A muscle in Hudson's jaw twitched but he kept his eyes focused on the business at hand. He brushed her hair off her forehead, then lightly pressed the bandage into place. "What set him off?"

"I told him it was over."

He stilled. "You did?

Allie nodded. "What you said last night, about two weeks not being enough? I feel the same way." She paused, trying to gauge his reaction, but he gave nothing away. Her heart raced as a thought she hadn't considered rushed unbidden through her mind. What if he'd been pushed too far? A cold chill ran down her spine. There was nothing she could do but lay it all on the line and hope he still felt the same way. She drew a shaky breath and continued. "I can't walk away from us, Hudson. Not this time. I need you in my life."

His expression softened with an unexpected vulnerability and he gently cupped her face between his hands. "I need you, too," he murmured.

Allie curled her fingers over his, wanting to hold tight to not only the moment, but the man before her on his knees. He leaned closer and his lips pressed against hers in a warm, lingering kiss. Her entire body shuddered in a rush of pure joy that was quickly followed by a wave of physical pain. It was too much, the intensity of her feelings for him and the sobering reality of what had almost happened in her apartment. Overcome with emotion, she began to sob.

"Don't," he whispered. His thumbs swept over her cheeks, catching her tears. "It shreds me to see you cry."

"If you hadn't gotten there when you did . . ."

"Hush, I'm here." His strong arms wrapped around her and he carefully pulled her into his lap, cradling her as if she were the most delicate glass. "You're safe with me, Allie. Always will be." He held her close, soothing her with tender words and gentle touches, until her breath no longer came in trembling gasps. When she finally calmed, he lifted her to her feet. "Come, let me get you into bed."

Hudson undressed her with the utmost of care, slowly unwrapping her bloodstained dress. As he slid it off her shoulders, his eyes flared. Allie followed his gaze to her ribs, where dark bruises had already begun to form.

"It looks worse than it feels," she tried to reassure him.

He gave a tight nod and reached for a stack of neatly folded clothes that were piled on the end of the bed. "Can you raise your arms?" he asked. His tone was grim.

She complied and he slipped a T-shirt over her head, careful not to disrupt the bandage on her forehead. Allie inhaled deeply as the soft cotton brushed over her face. It smelled like fresh laundry and Hudson Chase. The combination made her feel warm and safe, and for the first time all night, her body began to relax.

"Lift your foot." He crouched down in front of her with a pair of his boxer briefs in his hands. The sight of him blurred the fine line that often existed between emotions, and in spite of everything a small laugh escaped her lips. He looked up at her, confused. "Something funny?"

Allie smiled and ran her fingers through his unruly hair. "You, offering me your underwear."

He smirked. "While I do prefer stripping them off, now is

hardly the time. You need to rest."

For once he'd get no argument. She did as he asked, placing her hand on his shoulder for balance as she stepped first with one foot and then the other.

"I have a pair of sweats here if you want them. We can roll the ends."

"I'm fine like this."

He pulled back the duvet and she climbed in. The cool, crisp sheets felt like heaven against her aching muscles. He arranged the blankets over her then bent and touched his lips to her forehead just above the bandage. When he turned to leave, she reached out and caught his hand.

"Aren't you coming to bed?" Even she could hear the panic in her voice.

Hudson gave her fingers a comforting squeeze. "I'm just getting you some Advil. I'll be right back."

He returned a few minutes later with two capsules and a tall glass of water.

"Thank you."

"You're welcome." He studied her face as she swallowed the medicine. "That should help with the pain."

"I'm feeling better already."

His answering smile didn't quite reach his eyes. She knew Hudson wasn't buying her act for a minute, but he let it go and made quick work of the buttons on his shirt instead. Allie leaned back against the pillows, drinking in every detail. The hard planes of his chest flexing as he peeled off his shirt and tossed it onto a nearby chair; the rippling muscles of his abs curling as he lowered his pants and boxers in one fell sweep; and the firm curves of his very fine ass clenching as he pulled his pajama pants up over his thighs. It was quite a show.

When he was ready for bed, he slid in beside her, tugging her carefully across his chest and kissing the top of her head. Allie sighed as she melted into the warmth of his body. She lay like that for long moments, her breaths in perfect harmony with the steady rise and fall of his chest, until something occurred to her.

"Why did you come to my apartment tonight?" she asked, tilting her face up to see his.

He stroked her cheek with his knuckles. "I wasn't going to let you go without a fight. I know I said I'd accept whatever you decided, but then I got your message that Julian was back in town . . ." Hudson flexed his arm over his head and ran a frustrated hand through his hair. "Goddamnit, Allie, you wouldn't answer your phone."

"I'm sorry you were worried," she said quietly.

His eyebrows shot up as he lifted his head to look at her. A fistful of hair was still clenched in his hand. "*Worried*? I was going fucking crazy just thinking about you in the same room with that asshole." His head fell back against the pillow and he made an exasperated sound. "Honestly, what did you ever see in him?"

"I was asking myself that same question earlier tonight." Allie tucked her head back down against Hudson's chest. In hindsight, she felt like a fool for ever getting involved with Julian in the first place. But hindsight is 20/20, and although Hudson's question was probably rhetorical, Allie still felt the need to somehow justify her decisions. "Julian can be very charming when he wants to be. In the beginning he was very attentive; thoughtful, even."

Hudson let out a short, harsh laugh.

"I know it's hard to picture, but he was. He'd surprise me with flowers for no reason, stop by for lunch just because he missed me, or even leave little notes on my pillow." The offhanded reference to sharing a bed with Julian slipped out without much thought and she instantly regretted it. Feeling the muscles in Hudson's arm tense against her back, she quickly steered the conversation in a different direction. "Of course now I know he had an agenda."

"What do you mean, agenda?"

"Julian was only marrying me so he could gain control of Ingram Media. He told me tonight that someone is buying up stocks and my dad is in serious danger of losing the company. All of it—the newspaper, the magazines, even the cable network. I guess Julian promised to give him the cash he needs to regain control." Allie sat up, wincing at the pain in her ribs. The sudden movement made her head swim, but it didn't stop the pieces of the puzzle from falling into place. "It all makes sense now."

Confusion creased Hudson's brow.

"What does?"

"My dad's plan for an early retirement. It was so sudden. One minute he's working eighty hours a week, and the next he's saying he wants to scale back, work on his golf game like the other board members. Whoever is behind this takeover must be getting close."

"What makes you say that?"

"This whole rush to the altar. My guess is Julian was holding onto the cash until after the wedding. Moving up the date didn't have anything to do with a cancelation at the Drake. It was all about saving the company. I didn't think anything of it at first since everything about our relationship had moved quickly. It was a whirlwind romance from the moment my dad introduced . . ."

"Oh my God . . ." Allie choked on a strangled sob. "It was a setup from the beginning. I was just another asset for them to leverage. A way to keep the company in the family." Shame burned in the pit of her stomach. "How could I have been so stupid? The three of them have been playing me like a fool this whole time."

Tears streamed down her face and Hudson reached for her, pulling her back into his arms. "Shh, I've got you."

Allie curled into him as the emotions of the day came crashing down around her. Hudson held her tight as she sobbed quietly against his chest. Sometime just before dawn, when there were no more tears to cry, she finally drifted to sleep in his arms.

39

$\mathcal{A}$llie's eyes fluttered open, one more than the other, and she winced. She didn't need a mirror to tell her how bad the swelling was. Her half-open eyelid told her all she needed to know. She blinked and the face across from hers came into focus. Hmm, talk about a sight for sore eyes. Literally. She could definitely get used to waking up to Hudson's beautiful face on the pillow next to her. Of course the mornings she woke to him between her thighs weren't too bad either.

"Good morning."

She gave him a sleepy smile. "Good morning. How long have you been awake?"

"Not long." Hudson scrubbed a hand over the rough stubble that grew in overnight. "How do you feel?"

Allie took stock of her injuries. Her eye was obviously more swollen but her head seemed to have improved. She touched the bandage covering the right side of her forehead. What had been a pounding throb was now a dull ache. She moved slowly, testing her limbs. Arms and legs seemed okay. "I still have a bit of a headache, but other than that I feel pretty good, considering." She rolled to her side and sucked in a sharp breath.

"Ribs?"

She nodded. "Just a little stiff." The pain subsided quickly and she gave him a reassuring smile. It wasn't merely for his benefit. Despite everything that had transpired, she felt oddly at peace after her night in Hudson's arms. "Thank you for taking such good care of me last night."

"My pleasure." He lifted his hand, brushing her cheek with his knuckles. "There's nothing I wouldn't do for you, Allie. Though I do wish you'd have let me take you to the hospital. You really should have an X-ray."

"Honestly, it feels much better today." Allie tried to remain impassive as his fingers touched her, probing gently.

"They could be cracked. Or broken."

"Or just bruised," she countered.

He scowled, clearly unconvinced.

"I promise, if it's still hurting tonight, I'll go to the ER." Allie shifted closer and Hudson wrapped an arm around her, his fingers brushing rhythmically down her back. She let out a small sigh. Nearly everything about her life had been turned upside down, but in that moment she was perfectly content to ignore the rest of the world and concentrate on the one thing that was absolutely perfect. Selfishly, she wondered how much time she had until the alarm clock would burst her happy bubble. "What time is it?"

Hudson glanced over his shoulder at the clock. "Eight."

"Oh, shit! I need to get ready for work." Allie bolted upright in bed. *Whoa!* Her brain lagged behind, slamming into the front of her skull upon arrival.

"Absolutely not." Hudson gripped Allie's shoulders, gently pulling her back down on the bed. "You're badly bruised and you need your rest."

It wasn't a request, and she could tell by the tone of his voice there was no sense in arguing. Badly bruised? Allie gingerly touched the tender skin around her eye. "How bad does it look?"

Hudson's brow creased.

"That bad, huh?" Her heart sank. After all these years she and Hudson were finally together and she looked like she'd gone eight rounds in a boxing ring.

His expression softened as he tucked a strand of hair behind her ear. "You look beautiful, Allie. I just thought you'd rather not have to explain."

"Mmm, good point." The last the last thing she wanted was to answer questions about the bruises on her face. The more people who knew about Julian's attack, the more likely it would make the news. Her father would undoubtedly block Ingram subsidiaries from covering the story, but his influence only extended so far. Plenty of rags and websites would be thrilled to run with the story of a battered heiress. Her privacy had to come first, which was why she'd opted not to file a police report. There was no doubt Julian deserved to go to jail, but calling the police would have alerted the media as well. And while the image of Julian in an orange jumpsuit bitching about the lack of caviar and French champagne was tempting, it wasn't worth being dragged through the tabloid mud.

She knew none of her coworkers would tip off the press. Most of them were her friends, and the rest were far too afraid of the wrath of Victoria Sinclair to risk it. But she also knew if she showed her face at the office, it would only be a matter of time before word of her condition reached her mother. She wasn't ready for that confrontation just yet. Eventually she would tell her parents what that monster had done to her. The monster they'd unleashed. But for now she had no desire to leave Hudson's arms, let alone his penthouse.

Allie's eyes drifted shut.

"Is the pain worse?" Hudson asked, his concern evident.

She opened her eyes to find him staring at her intently. "No." She placed her hand on the side of his face and smiled. "It's much better, actually."

For the first time in her life, Allie was exactly where she wanted to be.

"So a day in bed, huh? Is that your professional opinion, Dr. Chase?" Her fingers stroked across his bare shoulder and down his bicep.

"If you're head's still hurting, you probably have a concussion. So yes, your day will be spent in bed."

"Sounds perfect." Allie's fingers trailed down his stomach before disappearing under the sheet. "Perhaps you'd like to do a more thorough examination?"

Hudson caught her wrist. "Resting in bed, Alessandra."

Uh-oh, the full name. "Where are you going?" she asked as he slid out of bed.

He leaned down, dropping a quick kiss on her mouth. "To take a shower."

Allie felt a stab of disappointment. "You're going to the office?"

"No, I'm working from home today."

Not her first choice, but better than the alternative. She propped a pillow against the headboard and leaned back, crossing her arms over her chest. "Well, I still I need to call my office," she pouted.

"Already took care of it. I texted Harper last night, let her know you weren't feeling well."

Her mouth popped open. "How did you do that?

"With a phone. Now rest."

Allie wanted to ask him to elaborate, but Hudson disappeared into the bathroom before she could get the words out of her mouth. She shook her head. Under normal circumstances, such an intrusion would have annoyed her. But how could she be angry with him for going all alpha male when somehow he always seemed to know exactly what she needed?

The sound of running water came from the master bathroom. Hudson was in the shower. Naked. Her thoughts drifted to images of water cascading over his chest . . . his body pressing hers against the cool granite . . . his fingers gliding over her wet skin . . . his hand lifting her leg around his hips . . .

For a moment she considered joining him, but she knew Mr. Overprotective would flip even though she was pretty sure he'd climbed out of bed hard as a rock.

Honestly, what was all the fuss about? She felt fine. Actually, she felt great. Liberated, even. She was finally taking charge of her life. The first step had been ending things with Julian. Granted that hadn't gone very well, but the end result was the same. He was out of her life. As for her parents, she was done letting her sense of family obligation dictate her decisions, and she planned to confront them about their lies and manipulations as soon as the rest of her life was in order. At the top of her to-do list was reconsidering the job offer from the Harris Group. Just thinking about a new position based on her own merits, not her birth certificate, put a smile on her face.

A fresh start. That was exactly what she needed. And the sooner the better.

Her mind made up, Allie threw back the duvet, not wanting to wait another minute to start this new chapter of her life. She slipped out of bed and into the adjoining study to call Oliver Harris. Hudson would be thrilled when she told him the good news. A celebration would definitely be in order.

As the phone rang, she leaned back in Hudson's leather chair. The gentle rocking motion brought back memories of the call she'd interrupted. A lascivious smile spread across her face. On second thought, maybe she would join him in the shower after all. No need to wait until tonight to start celebrating.

A receptionist answered the phone, interrupting Allie's illicit thoughts. She was all business as she efficiently transferred the call to whom Allie assumed would be a personal assistant.

"Mr. Harris," she said, surprised to hear him answer the call directly. "This is Alessandra Sinclair. We spoke a few weeks ago?"

"Of course, Miss Sinclair, how could I forget? Not every day I ask someone to join my company."

"That's actually why I'm calling. I'd love to come to work for the Harris Group." A thought occurred to her, and she quickly added, "Assuming the job is still available."

"Absolutely. This is wonderful news, Alessandra. We've already discussed salary but I'm sure you have questions about our benefits package. My HR director can go over all that with you and start the necessary paperwork. Let me give you her name and number."

Allie swiveled Hudson's chair, searching the drawers for a paper and pen. When she opened the center drawer, a name on a document caught her eye. She scanned the paragraphs of legal jargon, barely listening as Oliver Harris provided the necessary information.

. . . extensive due diligence of significant assets . . .

"I have a very good feeling about this," he said. "And I'd like you to start as soon as possible."

. . . resistance to acquisition . . .

"I assume you'll need to give notice to your current employer?"

Allie answered without giving the question any thought. "Yes."

. . . through shell companies and charitable foundations . . .

"Would you be able to start in two weeks?"

. . . Chase Industries . . . sufficient shares . . .

Her throat burned and she swallowed hard. "That's fine," she mumbled.

"Great. I'll see you then."

. . . for controlling interest of Ingram Media.

Allie wasn't even sure she managed a good-bye before she hung up the phone and fell back against Hudson's chair.

40

*H*udson leaned against the wall of the shower, the hot water cascading down his chest and abs. As the soap ran down between his legs and dripped off the end of his still-erect cock, he tried not to think about the woman in the other room who he was dying to make love to. He'd managed to convince his brain not to go back into the bedroom, but his hard-on was still behind the curve.

God, did he really have it in him to go through with this, knowing the personal cost to her? The alternative was to tell her he was the one taking her father's company piece by piece in an intricate deal designed to force Richard Sinclair out of the trade.

Fuck. As if he had a choice.

"Allie," Hudson yelled as he turned off the water. Stepping out of the shower and into the hell of his own making, he snapped a towel off the rack and wrapped it around his hips. "Allie?"

He strode out of the bathroom and, seeing an empty bed, started toward the living room. He halted midstride outside his office door. "There you are. What are you doing out of bed?"

"I needed to use the phone. I wanted to accept the job at the

Harris Group, have a fresh start." The blood seemed to drain from her face as she finished the sentence.

Dozens of thoughts fired in Hudson's head. "You okay?"

Allie's eyes dropped to the document on the desk in front of her. "I was looking for a pen . . ."

Hudson moved farther into the room and stopped dead in his tracks at the sight of his company's letterhead. "I was going to tell you. I wanted you to hear it from me."

Her eyes shot up to his. "When, Hudson? When were you planning to tell me?"

"I was waiting for the right time."

"And how much longer were you going to fuck me before the time felt right?"

Hudson's jaw tightened and his shoulders straightened. "You were never just a fuck."

"Funny, since right now that's exactly how I feel." Allie's bitter exterior slipped and tears pooled in her eyes as she pushed up from the desk and stormed back into the bedroom.

Hudson followed after her, tightening the grip on his towel. "Damn it, Allie. Let me explain."

"I think it's pretty clear. What I don't understand is why?"

"It's simple. The company fits nicely into my portfolio. I saw an opportunity and I took it."

"And all the better since it's my family, right?" Allie's eyes darted toward the bathroom where her bloodstained dress hung over the side of the tub. She grabbed the sweatpants he'd offered her the night before and yanked them up her legs. "Was this all some plan to get back at me for hurting you ten years ago? Or was it just part of the thrill, taking the company while taking me to bed?"

"You were never a part of the plan, Alessandra. The wheels were in motion long before I saw you at the museum." Hudson blew out a harsh breath. "Christ, I didn't even know it was your family's company."

"You expect me to believe that?" Allie rolled her eyes at him while shoving her feet into her pumps.

"I knew you as Allie Sinclair. How the hell was I supposed to know you were a fucking Ingram?"

"I'm sure you came across the names of the board members during your research. The name Richard Sinclair didn't ring any bells?"

"I didn't know your father's name was Richard. If you recall, you weren't exactly bringing me home to meet your parents."

Allie pushed sideways past him and into the Great Room.

"Damn it. Goddamnit to fucking hell." Hudson was tight on her heels. "By the time I realized the connection, we were . . ."

Stopping short, Allie whirled around. Her stare was absolutely furious. "I get it. By the time you realized the connection you were already fucking me across the living room floor. No reason to mess up a good thing when you could keep stringing me along till the deal was done."

"I should have told you, but I wanted time to get to know you again. I was afraid you wouldn't give us a chance if you knew." The silence in the room became tangible and he waited for some sign, any sign, that she might forgive him.

"You could have stopped the deal." Her voice wavered to the point of cracking.

When he didn't answer, Allie grabbed her purse off the chair and headed toward the elevator.

Hudson followed. "It wouldn't have made a difference," he offered as some sort of consolation. "Your father's company is a sinking ship and he knows it. If it wasn't me moving in to salvage Ingram, it would have been someone else."

"But it wasn't someone else, Hudson. It was you. You were the one responsible for all of this."

The hell if he was taking the bullet for Julian and her father. "I wasn't the one bartering your affections." He knew damn well it was a cheap shot and he regretted the words the minute they left his mouth.

Fuck.

Allie flinched and tears sprang to her eyes as she turned to punch the call button. He wanted her to punch him instead. Use him to bear her pain. Let him feel her anger and disappointment in his skin. And when she was finished, let him hold her as she cried.

"I'm sorry," he said. "I shouldn't have . . ."

"Why not? It's true, isn't it? Last night, right before he attacked me, Julian told me I was no better than the whores he paid." Tears streamed down her cheeks. "I hated him for that, but he was right. My engagement was nothing more than my parents selling me to the highest bidder." She wiped her face with the back of her hand. "The worst part is, I didn't even care. All I kept thinking was how none of it mattered because after all these years we could finally be together."

Allie stepped into the waiting elevator and pressed the button. "You were the one person I thought I could count on."

Hudson raised his arm to stop the door from closing. "I'm sorry. I never meant to hurt you." His throat was raw and a blazing pain burned the center of his chest. As he looked at her, he could see the resolve in her eyes, along with the heart-wrenching betrayal that was going to haunt him for the rest of his life. He relinquished his hold on the elevator doors, letting them slide closed.

And just like that, she was gone.

FOUR DAYS LATER . . .

*A*llie slipped her sunglasses on and started the engine of
her silver BMW. She'd spent the past four days holed up
in her brownstone, letting her bruises heal while she tried to sort
out the mess that had become her life. It had taken countless
hours of soul searching and an obscene amount of Häagen-Dazs
Chocolate Chocolate Chip, but she was finally ready to confront
her parents.

Ready to start living life on her own terms.

And she had to do it *all* on her own. No Astor Place brownstone. No Barneys credit card. No trust fund disbursements.
Nothing. She would live within the means her new job allowed,
just like any other twenty-seven-year-old.

Nerves churned in Allie's stomach as she merged onto the
highway. She tried to distract herself by running through the rest
of the items on her list. The next step was finding a roommate.
Rent in Chicago was sky-high, and even though her job at the
Harris Group would pay more than her previous position, it was
hardly enough.

Allie hit the speed dial for Harper's cell and waited while the
phone rang over the car's Bluetooth system.

"Jeez, I thought he'd never let you up for air," Harper said without so much as a "hello."

"What?"

"Hudson."

Allie's heart lurched at the sound of his name. Of all the times for the queen of nicknames to change her ways. She could have handled any of the annoying terms of endearment Harper was so fond of using, but hearing Hudson's name echo through her car made a lump form in the back of Allie's throat.

"I mean I can only assume he's the one responsible for your terrible case of the *flu*," Harper said, stressing the last word sarcastically. "Seeing as how you haven't taken so much as one sick day in the past three years." Allie steered her car onto the exit ramp as her friend prattled on. "I also assume he's had you tied to his headboard this whole time, which would account for all the unanswered texts."

"Are you done?" Allie asked, trying to keep her voice steady. She could make all the lists in the world, but it wouldn't erase his image from her memory . . . or his touch.

"For now. What's up?"

"Any chance you're free for dinner?"

"Blue Agave do-over?"

Allie could almost hear Harper salivating over the phone. "Sure."

"Excellent. Let's make it early so I have an excuse to skip the gym."

In spite of everything, Allie smiled.

"Oh, and do you have a costume? A few bars are waving cover charge if you dress up."

Allie had completely forgotten it was Halloween. "Let me text you when I know what train I'm taking." She stopped at a red light and pulled the schedule out of her purse. Trains out of Lake Forest weren't as frequent in the afternoon, but there were a few options that would get her back into the city in time to meet

Harper for dinner. And with any luck, she'd have a new room-mate by the end of the night.

"Train?"

"Yeah, I'm headed to my parents' house now, but I'm taking the Metra back."

"Why the hell would you do that?"

Because I can't very well tell them to let me live my own life and then drive away in the car they bought me, now can I?

"I'll explain everything tonight." Revisiting the events of the last week wasn't something Allie wanted to do over the phone. In fact, she'd probably wait until she had at least one margarita in her system before laying it all out.

"You better. And I want the director's cut, not some PG-13 version."

"I promise I'll tell you the whole story," Allie said as she drove through the gates of Mayflower Place. She knew Harper would be disappointed when she realized there were no juicy details to share. But she also knew her friend would be livid when she heard what had happened. Julian and Hudson both better hope they didn't cross paths with Harper Hayes anytime soon.

Then again, maybe that's exactly what they deserved. And then some.

———

Four days.

Four days since Hudson last saw his brother. Four days since he'd resigned himself to the fact that Nick was so far down the pharmaceutical rabbit hole he wouldn't hit bottom until he was six feet under. With no words adequate to describe the terror of the what-if's, Hudson had found himself slammed facefirst at a crossroads that left him with only one choice: admit Nick to rehab.

Strict policies had prevented Hudson from seeing Nick

during the detox phase, but now that he was moving into the treatment wing he was allowed visitors. As Hudson approached the reception desk, he found himself not wanting to be alone in this. The impulse to reach out to the one person he knew would reassure him was overwhelming. Except when his fingers curled, all he got was a handful of air.

"May I help you?" a nurse asked.

"I'm here to see Nicholas Chase. He's being moved from the medical unit over to the rehab facility today."

"And you are?"

"His brother."

She arched a brow as she pulled a thick blue file from a slotted stand.

He exhaled an exhausted breath. "Hudson Chase."

The nurse scanned the file with efficiency before closing it and returning it to its place. "You'll have to wear this." She set a visitor's badge on the Formica counter. "It must be visible at all times."

Hudson picked up the badge, and clipped it to the V of his cashmere sweater.

"And I'll need your phone," she said, holding out her hand, all business as usual. "You'll get it back when you leave."

He hesitated a moment.

"Protocol." She wiggled her fingers, coaxing him to get the lead out. Reaching behind him, Hudson yanked his cell out of the ass pocket of his jeans and glanced briefly at the screen. He'd left numerous voice mails for Allie and all of them had gone unreturned. Her message was loud and clear, and waiting for the when-hell-freezes-over phone call was futile.

Feeling like he'd been popped in the chest, he shut the phone off and handed it to the nurse. A moment later a lock slid with a click. Hudson moved through the detox center not wanting to disturb the stillness. The atmosphere was just too calm and serene. And that wasn't the reality of his life.

He pushed open the door to the lounge. Like the rest of the joint, the room was stripped down to the basic, most functional components—hospital-grade couch, chair and table.

He shrugged out of his leather jacket and tossed it over the back of the couch, uncertain of what to expect when Nick finally showed. He thought back to the day he'd checked him in. There'd been no promises of joy or sustainable satisfaction on Hudson's face. Just a longing, a hope for happiness for his little brother. And the only information the doctors had given him was a fuck-ton of "he could be's" or "he might be's." Bottom line, they didn't have a clue how Nick would be once he emerged from his binge session.

The knob hitched, the heavy door opened, and Nick entered. "Hey."

Hudson turned around and assessed Nick from head to toe. His dark hair was loose and clean; his eyes exhausted after what had undoubtedly been a rough week of DTs.

Nick shuffled into the sparse room and parked his ass on the chair. Hudson followed his lead, sitting on the tweed couch opposite him.

"How are you feeling?"

Nick leaned forward, resting his elbows on his knees and rubbing his eyes before refocusing on Hudson. "Like I've woken up from the world's biggest fucking hangover."

"I bet."

The silence between them was hairsplitting. They'd always had something to bullshit about, tease each other with. Now? Not a damn thing was coming to his mind.

"Hudson." When Nick finally spoke, his voice was low. "I don't remember anything but some random shit. It's all a blur. Tell me I didn't do it."

There was a long pause before Hudson replied. "I can't tell you that."

"Oh God . . . Fuck." Nick cleared his throat as if he intended to continue, but nothing came out when he opened his mouth.

"You're not to worry about it, clear? I've handled it."

"What do you mean?"

"I said don't worry about it. Focus on getting yourself clean."

Nick dropped his head in his hands and his shoulders began to shake. Hudson shifted over and pulled Nick against him. The feel rather than the sound of his brother weeping busted through the first layer of the walls Hudson had built up. They both had endured a lot in their lives, and this was just one more tragedy stacked up against the others.

"Everything will be fine, Nicky. You just focus on getting yourself clean. I'll take care of the rest." The conviction in Hudson's words was absolute, but he felt as if his feet were planted on quicksand and he was slowly sinking.

No matter what the cost, he'd never lose his brother again.

Julian pulled a pack of cigarettes out of the breast pocket of his suit, not giving a rat's ass about the no smoking policy at the Peninsula Hotel. The Marlboros were still wrapped in cellophane and Julian slapped them on the heel of his hand. "Fils de pute!" He cursed when the last tap came in contact with the bandage on his palm. That whore had cost him twelve fucking stitches.

His mouth drew back in a sneer as he stared down at the nondescript manila envelope; a little gift from the private detective he'd hired. The guy charged a small fortune but had proved invaluable when it came to a few of his less savory business transactions, not to mention the more personal matters. Sources and silence were worth any price.

He slipped the cigarette between his lips, cupped his hand over the end, and lit it with a quick rasp of his lighter. He tossed the gold-plated torch onto the coffee table and ripped open the envelope. Inside was a complete dossier on Hudson Chase. He'd asked his guy to look into the mysterious Mr. Chase the night the SOB pledged a million dollars to dance with *his* fucking fiancée, but till now he hadn't had a reason to open the file.

He had one now.

Julian thumbed through the first set of documents. Lists of property, corporate holdings, a few charitable foundations. Nothing out of the ordinary. Then he reached the surveillance photos. A few of Chase leaving his penthouse, one of him ducking into a limo outside his office, and one of him with a man who bore a striking family resemblance. Julian flipped the last photo over and read the back. *Subject: Nicholas Chase. Age: 22.*

A detailed report followed. It showed a few odd jobs, but nothing that lasted longer than a month or two; and if his source was correct, which he always was, the younger Mr. Chase had more than his share of run-ins with the law when he was a teenager.

Three more pictures were included, all showing Hudson's brother exiting a dive called Anchors. A billionaire brother and that shithole is where he spends his time? Julian's eyes narrowed as he spread the documents out on the coffee table and took a long drag from his cigarette, the end glowing orange, the soft paper crackling as it burned. There was a kink in the perfectly polished armor and he knew exactly how to exploit it.

EXCERPT: RELEASE ME

Allie tried her best to ignore the blue flashing lights in her parents' driveway. But from her seat in the living room she had a clear view of the brick-paved courtyard just beyond the front door. And she knew that just beyond the courtyard's limestone fountain stood a row of uniformed officers forming a human barrier along yellow tape. And beyond that tape stood a crowd of reporters with cameras and microphones, all jockeying for a better position among the curious who had gathered at the gates.

Instead she focused her attention on the detective standing in front of her. The middle-aged woman wore clothes more suited for a man and her hair was pulled back in a tight bun. Yet despite her hard-as- nails appearance, there was an undeniable kindness in her eyes when she told Allie it was time to take her statement.

Allie nodded but didn't speak. She hadn't said more than a handful of words since placing the call to 911.

The detective stood and reached inside her jacket for a small notebook. Her movements revealed the badge she wore clipped to her waist and the gun she kept holstered at her side.

Allie's eyes drifted shut and her mind filled with images of gunshot wounds and blood.

So much blood . . .

"Alessandra."

She opened her eyes to find Benjamin Weiss, general counsel for Ingram Media, making his way through the foyer. As always, he was impeccably groomed in a dark suit and tie with a perfectly folded handkerchief peeking out of the breast pocket. Only this time his tie was askew and a thin sheen of sweat covered his forehead.

"My apologies," he said, out of breath. "I came as soon as I heard, but the roads are clogged with news vans."

As soon as he heard? Allie had no idea who had called Mr. Weiss, but she was glad to have him at her side. Benjamin Weiss was more than just the family's attorney; he had also been her father's best friend.

A few quiet words were spoken between Mr. Weiss and Detective Green, and then she was ready to begin. She sat on the coffee table across from Allie and uncapped her pen. "Walk me through what happened after you pulled into the driveway," she instructed. Her tone was all business; just another day at the office for a homicide detective.

Allie tried to speak but her words came out on a strangled sob.

Mr. Weiss placed his hand on her shoulder. "Would you like some water?" he asked, glancing toward the kitchen and paling as his gaze fell on the scene unfolding in the dining room.

Don't look.

Allie kept her stare trained on the detective's pen as she answered Mr. Weiss. "I'm fine." There wasn't a person in Chicago who would've believed that statement, but a bottle of water wasn't going to make things any better. And with the way her stomach felt, she doubted she'd be able to keep it down anyway.

"Just take it slow," Detective Green said.

Allie drew a shaky breath and began to retell the events of the past few hours. "I knew something wasn't right as soon as I opened the front door."

"How so?" the detective asked. "The alarm didn't make any noise."

"You mean it was unarmed?"

Allie shook her head. "No, I mean it wasn't working. Even if it's unarmed, the system still chimes to announce when a door or window has been opened."

Detective Green scribbled a few notes on the small pad of paper in her hand. "What happened after you came in the house?"

"I could see the light was on in my dad's study, so I headed that way first."

Tears clouded Allie's eyes as she looked across the expanse of the paneled living room to the hallway just to the right of the front door. Her throat tightened as she thought back to how confident she'd felt striding down that hall. For as long as Allie could remember, every aspect of her life had been dictated by what was best for the family legacy. But this time her parents had taken it too far. Going behind her back to arrange a marriage that was nothing more than a business transaction was the last straw. She was done playing the role of the dutiful daughter, and she'd planned to tell them so in no uncertain terms.

But when she'd reached the door . . .

"And that's when you discovered the body?"

"Yes," she whispered, recalling the image of her father's lifeless body slumped over his desk. Her gaze shifted to the Kleenex she held clutched in her hand. It had been twisted into something more closely resembling twine than tissue.

"Is your father normally home during the day?"

A few months ago she could have answered without a doubt. Her father would have never been home in the middle of the day. But lately he'd been scaling back, letting Julian lead some of the day-to- day meetings as he prepared to take the helm after their wedding.

Julian.

Just thinking about her former fiancé sent a chill down her spine. Her finger touched the remnants of the black eye he'd given her the week before. She'd done her best to cover the shadow of a bruise with concealer, but the makeup had surely been washed away with tears by now.

"Miss Sinclair?" Detective Green prodded.

"Oh, um, no. Usually it's just my mother and the housekeeper." Allie gasped.

"She's fine," Detective Green assured her. "She was out running errands until just a short while ago."

"I assume you're taking her statement as well?" Mr. Weiss asked.

The detective nodded. "We'll need confirmation from the medical examiner, but it looks like this all took place shortly after she left. If that's the case, the perpetrators may have waited for her to leave, assuming no one else was in the house."

A flash came from the dining room, and without thinking Allie turned toward it. *Flash.* A photographer stood with his back to her, his camera pointed at the mirrored wall. Allie watched his reflection as he focused his lens on the blood splattered across the wall right behind the spot where her mother had last stood. *Flash.* He stepped closer, his lens telescoping, and she knew he was capturing details of the images she'd seen when she'd first stumbled into the room; blood and gray matter mixed with shards of mirror and bone. *Flash.* A moment later he squatted beside the blood that had pooled on the Aubusson rug, photographing her mother's face, her eyes open and frozen in fear.

Allie tasted bile in the back of her throat and for a moment she thought she might throw up. This was not her life. This was some horrible dream, the result of watching one too many police procedural shows. It had to be.

"Why are they doing that?" she whispered, not really meaning to say the words out loud.

Detective Green looked up from her notebook. "Doing what?"

"Why are they bagging her hands?"

The detective's eyes darted to Mr. Weiss, then back to Allie. She hesitated for a moment, but when she answered her voice was level. "To preserve any physical evidence that may have resulted from a struggle."

A commotion by the front door drew Allie's attention. Two men in black jackets wheeled a gurney across the marble floor. "Coroner" was printed in white lettering across their backs, and when they turned toward the library, she could see a long black bag stretched the length of the bed.

Oh God . . .

An involuntary sob escaped her lips at the thought of her father being zipped into a vinyl bag.

Mr. Weiss offered her his handkerchief and she took it.

"If you don't mind, I'd like to get Miss Sinclair home," he said, his voice tight. "She's been through quite an ordeal."

Detective Green regarded Allie for a moment, then stood and smoothed the wrinkles from her wool pants. "I'll need to take a more detailed statement in the morning." She held out her business card. "But in the meantime, if you think of anything else."

Mr. Weiss took the card. "Thank you, Detective." Before she walked away he assured her his office would call to set up an appointment.

"I've arranged for a car to drive you home," he told Allie once they were alone. "And for private security to be stationed at your brownstone tonight."

Her eyes grew wide.

"Just as a precaution," he quickly added. "Right now the

police think this was nothing more than a home invasion gone wrong, but I'm not taking any chances with your safety."

Allie nodded.

"Is there someone I can call for you?"

Hudson.

His was the first name that came to mind, just as it had repeatedly for the past few hours. She needed him now more than ever. Needed the strength of his arms around her, holding her up when she felt too weak to stand.

But she wouldn't let herself call him. She couldn't. Not after the way he'd deceived her. She had to keep moving forward. No looking back.

Hudson Chase was out of her life. For good this time.

"I'll call my friend Harper," Allie said.

"She's not a redhead by any chance, is she?"

"Yes, why?"

"She saved you the trouble of a call." He smiled weakly. "She's been raising hell at the barricades for the past hour."

Yep, that would be Harper. "Would you mind bringing her around back to the garage and having the car meet us there? I really don't want to deal with the crowds out front."

"Of course. And I'll see that both your cars are returned to the city in the morning."

Allie stood. "Thank you for . . ." Her voice trailed off. She knew she'd never get through the rest of that sentence.

His eyes crinkled and he gave a quick nod. "There is one more item we need to discuss before you go."

"Can it wait until tomorrow?"

"I'm afraid not. Although I imagine some of the press corps will leave once they realize you're no longer in the house, a few will remain until a statement is released. I can have the PR department draft something from the company as a whole, or you can certainly write your own if you'd prefer. There's also the matter of an internal memo to your employees, but we can address that tomorrow."

"My employees?" *What in the world is he talking about?*

He met her confused expression with one of his own. After a moment the crease in his brow relaxed. "Forgive me, I thought you realized." His voice was soothing yet firm. "As you know, both your mother and father were both heavily invested in Ingram."

This wasn't news. In fact, for decades the company her maternal grandfather built from the ground up had been privately owned. It wasn't until a rough patch in the late seventies that her father had been forced to take the company public; but even then the family had retained controlling interest.

"As the sole heir to their estate, those shares are now yours. Alessandra, you are the new majority shareholder of Ingram Media."

Allie rubbed her forehead. She hadn't even considered the effect her parents' death would have on the family business, let alone what role she'd play. Hundreds of questions raced through her mind, but the pounding in her head was making it hard to focus.

"I'm sorry. I know you're tired. We can hold off on everything else until tomorrow and just release a statement from the company tonight. I'll have the PR team draft something, and if you prefer I can run it by Mr. Chase."

Allie's head snapped up. *Hudson? Why in the hell would he run it past him?* She realized the answer just as Mr. Weiss began to explain.

"Over the past few months there have been various investment groups quietly purchasing shares of Ingram. It wasn't until recently that we realized these purchases were on behalf of one individual.

"How this will impact day-to-day operations remains to be seen. A substantial percentage of shares are still held in smaller quantities by numerous individuals, but Mr. Chase's most recent acquisitions make him the second largest shareholder outside of the Sinclair/Ingram estate." He exhaled a heavy sigh. "We can discuss this more at length after we get through the next few days. I don't want to overwhelm you right now."

Too late. "Okay."

"I'll go find your friend." He gave her arm an awkward pat before turning toward the door. A question popped into her mind as she watched him walk away. It seemed ridiculous in light of what was happening all around her, but for some inexplicable reason, she needed to know.

"Mr. Weiss?" she called out before he reached the foyer.

He turned to face her. "Yes?"

Allie took a deep breath. Maybe it wouldn't be too bad. Maybe she could limit their interactions. "What's the margin?"

"Pardon me?"

"The difference in stock percentages, between me and . . ." Her voice caught on his name. She cleared her throat and tried again. "What's the difference in stock percentages between . . ."

Damn it. Why couldn't she get the words to come out of her mouth?

"Between you and Mr. Chase?"

She nodded.

"One percent."

The weight of the day crashed down around her and Allie sank to the couch. On top of everything else, it seemed Hudson Chase was her new business partner.

ACKNOWLEDGMENTS

Our first group hug is for our agent, Pamela Harty. You read our "super sexy romance" the day it arrived, loved it before you even finished it, and have championed it ever since. Your patience, professionalism, and unwavering support have meant the world to us. Without you, Pinocchio would still be a puppet and for that we will be eternally grateful.

A huge thank you to our editor, Leis Pederson. Despite the odds, and what is surely one of the most crowded mailboxes in the industry, our little love story made the cut. You saw something on the page that made you give us the chance of a lifetime, and we strive every day to write words that will make you proud. Thank you for believing in us.

To our publicist Nina Bocci, we loved you from hello. Granted, the conversation was about David Gandy, but it ended with knowing we wanted to work with you some day. Thank you for helping us spread the word. And to Craig Burke and Erin Galloway, thank you for making us feel like gladiators. Oh and Craig, we hope you're having red wine and popcorn while you read this!

A box of cupcakes for our pre-readers, the giant kind you

need a fork to eat. Bethany Myers, Melissa Marino, Sarah Gutchall, Graham Jaenicke, Ally Hayes, Karen Carroll and Margaret Fahey: your comments and enthusiasm made us believe our words might actually be read by people who didn't know us. And of course, Kiley Roache. No chapter was complete until we'd been "off to see the wizard."

To the authors who have offered their support and encouragement: Joelle Charbonneau, who literally changed the course of our careers and is always ready with advice or a sanity check. Cecy Robson, who is not only quick with an RT or a phone call, but is the best sprint write partner on the planet. To Christina Hobbs & Lauren Billings, clearly you gals never met a stranger and swapping stories over cocktails was what we needed to keep the faith. We've said it before and we'll say it again, we might be older than you but we totally want to be you when we grow up. And to Tara Sue Me, the kind of woman who will offer you chocolate in her blanket fort when deadlines are looming and agree to a cover quote without so much as a second thought.

Finally, to the fandoms that not only brought us together, but inspire us on a daily basis. From Fifty Shades to Crossfire to Gandy Girls, we have loved taking this journey with each of you and hope you'll welcome Hudson Chase into the ranks of your book boyfriends.

Lemon drop martinis for everyone!

ABOUT THE AUTHORS

Ann Marie Walker writes steamy books about sexy boys. She's a fan of fancy cocktails, anything chocolate, and 80s rom-coms and her super power is connecting any situation to an episode of *Friends.* If it's December she can be found watching *Love Actually* but the rest of the year you can find her at AnnMarie-Walker.com. Ann Marie attended the University of Notre Dame and currently lives in Chicago.

Amy K. Rogers writes contemporary romance about sexy, alpha men. She loves good wine, cheese of any variety and finding hidden speakeasies. On a rare quiet night she can be found watching old James Bond films. After living in San Francisco for 20 years followed by a short stint in Oregon, Amy recently relocated back to the beaches of Los Angeles.